HEART HALF BLACK

A BECKER GRAY NOVEL BY

CHRIS WENDEL

Holden Publishing, Inc.

BOOKS BY CHRIS WENDEL

BECKER GRAY SERIES
Human After All
Whispering of Echoes
The Walls

TONY MASON SERIES
The Fate of Leaves

BUSINESS
Converting Customers to Clients
On Strengthening Business Relationships

POETRY
Unfinished

PROLOGUE

Most days Saleena Salah longed to walk the beach of white sand, to let the turquoise waters rush across her feet, to breathe in the thick, salty air, but today was different. She wasn't lathered in sunscreen or taking her skimboard into the water. Today she was working. Instead of a swimsuit under a linen cover with a matching pair of flat sandals, she wore a business blouse, pair of slacks, her holstered gun and her detective shield. She corralled and fastened her thick hair into a bun, but still couldn't contain every one of the million loose springs.

"Good morning, Jared. Odd one, huh?" she asked the Manatee County sheriff's deputy who raised the yellow crime scene tape for her. She bent at the waist and slipped smoothly beneath.

"Bizarre is more like it." He pointed to his right, out toward the sea shore. "Lt. Davis is running point."

Salah saw her rotund supervisor, Lance Davis, standing with two other detectives. Between them, a square had been erected with four small posts and more crime scene tape. It looked like the protective structures built to defend sea turtle nests from humans' destructive feet. But turtle nests weren't typically that close to the water.

She looked beyond her peers. The beachline, usually bustling with activity and dotted with tents, umbrellas, towels, coolers, and the like, were all gone. She'd never seen the seaside so empty. All that remained —

for about a mile down the shoreline — were more of the same type of four-post structures.

"Lieutenant," she greeted her supervisor, interjecting herself into the group of three.

"Sal, you made it."

She detected a layer of displeasure. Davis hated when detectives were late to crime scenes. "I was in court." She ignored his tone. "What do we have?"

"Cord and Dallas will fill you in," Davis said, motioning to her detective peers, Cordrey Phelps and Alex Sanchez.

Everyone in Davis' unit had a nickname. That is, everyone except him. He was simply called *lieutenant*. Everyone called her Sal because her first and last names both began with the same three letters. Cord's name was self-explanatory, like Sal's, but Alex was called Dallas because that's where he grew up.

"Walk her down the beach and show her. It's way too hot in this goddamn sun, even for autumn," Davis said. "Wife would kill me, being out here without a hat or sunscreen. If they cut more skin cancer off my face, I'll need plastic surgery just to look normal."

"What makes you think you don't need it already?" Salah joked.

That was one of the good things about Davis. He was egotistical enough that you had to call him lieutenant, but he didn't mind someone taking a jab at him now and again. You just had to pick your timing.

Davis laughed, but didn't respond. He just turned, wiped the sweat from his forehead, and headed back toward the parking lot.

Dallas joked outside of Davis' earshot. "I'm not sure there's enough plastic surgeons in all of Florida to fix all that."

It was one thing to take a humorous swipe at the lieutenant while staring him in the face, but Salah wasn't going to do it behind his back, even though she knew Dallas was joking and meant no harm. As a female in the department, she had to religiously protect her reputation. She had fought extremely hard to prove herself and continued to do so every day. The last thing she needed was to be seen or heard talking behind someone's back and be marked a petty, gossipy female. If the lieutenant ever thought she was undermining him, then she'd never be promoted again.

"I heard they found a hand. Just a hand. What is all that up there?" Salah asked, pointing at all the four-post structures down the beach.

"There was just a hand. At first," Cord said. "Then a foot. Then another hand, a lower leg up there, and a couple more hands."

"Then another foot. A thigh," Dallas continued.

"Then yet another hand. There's two arms down the way too." Cord chuckled, not out of humor but out of the weirdness of the situation. "Damndest thing."

"Holy shit," Salah said. "What time is it?" She checked her watch. "We only have about two hours before high tide. Is CSU coming out?"

"Yeah, everyone is on the way. Holmes Beach PD is coming. Bradenton. All the neighbors."

They stopped at the next four-post. A water-bloated foot laid there. Covered in sand, damaged by the water, and nibbled by fish. Toes sticking straight up in the air. It looked almost like the rest of the person's body was buried in the sand, and only the foot stuck out.

Salah squatted down for a closer look.

"Ain't nothing to see, Sal," Dallas said.

"Just the bone," she said.

Cord snickered. This time, he found humor, not weirdness. Salah sensed the weirdness this time because she knew his sense of humor was juvenile.

"Whatcha mean?" Dallas asked.

"It was cut. Like, with a saw. Nice and clean."

She stood up and looked down the coast again, thinking about the count of what was found.

"There are five hands here, you said?" she asked.

Dallas lifted his notepad and pushed up his sunglasses to read his writing. "That's right," he confirmed.

"So, we're at least talking about three people here."

Cord did the math. "True."

She turned and looked out at the clear water, wondering when the sixth hand would wash up, when the other four arms would come ashore, if there were torsos bobbing around out beyond the waves, or heads even?

"We may want to get the Coast Guard out here," she said.

~ ~ ~ ~

The nights were tricky. Attacks of all kinds broke out. Scores settled. New alliances made. Old alliances broken. Nerves on edge. Sleep seldom restful. Careful eyes ignore what they see. The guards seemed to only be present if the warden felt something was brewing. Such was nighttime life in the general population, bootcamp style bunking house at the Florida State Prison. None of that mattered to Kenneth Lamont Duncan, who operated above all of that activity, who generally caused the majority of that activity. This prison belonged to him as much as it did to the Warden. In some ways, it belonged to him more.

The rigged tattoo gun aimed at him. The motor had been ripped from a CD player and attached to the empty barrel of an ink pen. The power for the gun came from a battery pack the artist had purchased in the commissary.

"You said you were ready," Duncan objected to the wait.

"I need fire for the needle."

"You need to hurry."

The part of the prison that belonged more to the Warden were the guards – *most of them* – and the rules. If they were caught in the act, the artist would get 90 days ripped off his good time served and Duncan would get solitary. Neither mattered to Duncan. He liked being alone, and the artist accepted the risk simply by being the in-house artist. However, getting caught would complicate his plan.

The artist used a spoon to pop the cover of the electrical socket. Nimbly, he jammed a pencil behind the outlet and exposed an electrical wire. He'd done this a hundred times. He used the metal eraser bracket to generate a spark. He pushed a sheet of toilet paper against the wire and threw another spark. The tissue lit up. He dropped it into an empty can of boot polish, where it combined with a small amount of cooking oil his contacts in the kitchen smuggled for him. He dropped a black checkers piece into the can then added more oil. While the plastic piece melted, the artist took the spring from a pen and unraveled it as best as he could. He then held it over the fire and used the heat to straighten the metal. Soon the spring popped, splitting it into two pieces. The artist took the sharper of the two spring pieces and sanded the edge, making it the ideal needle – *under the circumstances.* He inserted it into the tattoo gun. As he secured the needle, the fire began to die, leaving behind the soot of the checkers piece.

"Show me," the artist said, taking another tissue and another can of cooking oil to use as lighting for the job at hand.

Duncan ripped apart his jumpsuit, separating the Velcro holding the two sides together.

"The heart. Cover it."

"Are you shitting me?"

Duncan nodded.

"That took us for-fucking-ever."

Duncan didn't respond. He didn't have to. He said what he wanted. No objection would change his mind.

"I'll need more checkers pieces."

The artist clicked the power on the motor. The needle kicked into action. He dipped the ink and went to work. He traced a circled around the heart tattoo, dipping the needle when necessary. Then his agile hands began coloring in the circle, covering the heart tattoo.

"I was really proud of this work," he said.

Duncan remained silent. Grinded his teeth. Refused to acknowledge the pain.

An hour passed. Four additional checkers pieces were melted and used. The needle dulled, and the pain increased. And the work was only half finished.

"I need to change the needle."

He killed the power, which exposed the sound of nearing footsteps.

"Shit," the artist said, scooping up his equipment and blowing out the fire acting as their light.

"Shut up," Duncan demanded, grabbing the artist's arms.

They could hide in the darkness. There was a possibility that the guard wouldn't see them. It was a slim possibility, but it was real. With luck, the guard was a friendly guard – one that kept the peace but allowed the prisoners freedom. But that possibility was slim, too. The warden was weeding out those guards and replacing them with others who were more aligned with his regulations.

The cone of a flashlight came into view. *We're caught,* Duncan thought. Three more measured steps and the guard and his flashlight were right in front of Duncan. He raised the light.

"You're new here, aren't you?" Duncan asked.

"I've been here long enough to know who you are."

"So you're moving on and letting us alone?"

"Afraid not."

The guard reached for his radio.

"It's not done yet," Duncan said.

The guard stopped and asked, "What's not done?"

Duncan put his hand over his heart.

"I'm sure after your solitary stint, you'll figure out how to finish it."

The guard radioed for assistance.

No, Duncan thought, *this will have to work.*

CHAPTER 1

Detective Becker Gray kicked his car door open. The familiar squeak coming from the Accord's door hinge went unnoticed, as did the pain of climbing out of his car. His anxiousness held tight control of his hopefulness, which kept him focused on one thing: Tony Mason.

It had been shy of two weeks since Mason had shot Gray in Sumterville, Florida, and had then escaped. Gray's protective vest had thwarted the gunshots' impact, but the force had broken four ribs. Upon release from the hospital, he and his partner, Jeffrey Parker, were placed on desk duty until the Officer Involved Shooting team cleared them. However, the city management team formed an emergency citizen oversight committee, and it recommended a third-party investigative firm be hired to conduct a thorough investigation of the police corruption and mismanagement that came to light during the Mason case. The firm, TEAM Consulting, immediately ordered Gray and Parker put on paid suspension until their actions leading up to the events at Sumterville, as well as the breakdown of procedure while there, could be fully investigated.

Since the suspension began, Gray had heard nothing official about the search for Mason. The only new information he'd learned came from news outlets and his television reporter friend, Jordan Butler. She had told him about the Crestwood, Kentucky, home of Sophia Mason, Tony Mason's ex-wife, before the information made it on air. So, he did what any good detective who was being iced out of an investigation would do; he covertly followed the lead.

The Oldham County, Kentucky, patrol cruiser rolled to a stop alongside Gray.   Roy Axelrod, a veteran with the local sheriff's department, pulled himself from the cruiser. With a thick folder in hand, he gave Gray a short salute as he rounded the car.

"You found it all right?" Axelrod asked.

"Right where you said it would be."

A smile spread under Axelrod's imperial mustache. He looked more like a hipster barista than a cop.

Gray had driven to the city of Crestwood out of a sense of helplessness and frustration. Being denied access to the investigation was driving him mad. He was the investigator most familiar with Mason. How could he be sidelined by some pointless procedural investigation, he wondered? *Fucking politics.* And worse, from what he'd learned from Butler and news broadcasts, it sounded like the investigation was going in the wrong the direction.

At first, the reports indicated that the arson at Sophia Mason's home was a murder/suicide situation. They said Sophia Mason lit the house on fire and trapped her and her son inside to be burned to death. Then investigators discovered the family's ties to Tony Mason, and, thus, in the task force's eye, he became the monster who killed them and then burned down the house.

But Gray knew Mason hadn't killed Sophia and Ryker. The task force was simply making Mason appear to be more of a monster than he actually was. Either the task force was playing a guessing game, while accruing no new usable information, or they were just spinning a narrative to keep the story alive in the attention-deficit media. Either way, Gray feared Mason would never be brought to justice. And he wasn't going to let Morgan Beringer's killer escape again.

What Gray hadn't expected when he drove to Crestwood was the cooperation of the local police department. He had underestimated people's innate desire for inclusion. When he had introduced himself,

Axelrod invited him into the arson investigation without hesitation. Gray gave the media credit for that cooperation. For a few days, the news had blasted Gray's name across the nation. He was the man who had caught the Pen Pal two years before, who had uncovered police corruption in his own department, and who'd cornered and was subsequently shot by a deadly drug cartel assassin. His sudden notoriety had opened this door without a single question. What Axelrod and his team hadn't apparently heard was that Gray had been suspended from duty.

"I want to thank you again for helping out, Roy."

"Hell, it's my pleasure." Axelrod handed the file to Gray. "Everything's in there, far as I know."

Gray looked across Sophia Mason's property. "Not much left is there?"

The burned out 1920s bungalow-style house sat on a dirt road off the Veterans Memorial Highway. Gray studied the ruins. He saw where the steps had led to a porch that stretched along the front of the house. The wooden steps had burned to nearly nothing and then crumbled. Same with the porch and most of the house, too, including the chimney. Only the rear walls managed to stay upright. They were likely only salvaged by the fire department's arrival. He could see the remains of furniture and appliances in the ruins as well.

The breeze picked up and blew against Gray. The musty, charred scent from the debris hit his senses. The branches of the American tulip trees lining the property swayed in the wind. The rustling noise of the leaves caught Gray's attention, and he looked up at the branches. It was easy for him to imagine them providing shade on a sunny day. But now the leaves were retracted, singed by fire, and the branches were tattooed black with soot. When the wind gust died down, the low rumble of traffic coming from the Kentucky 329 reached out with a gentle grip from behind the tree line.

"I seen ya look up at the trees." Axelrod's voice jarred Gray from the sounds of the traffic. "Hard to imagine the flames reachin' that high, but they did. The fire department was worried that all the leaves and branches would light up."

"Valid concern." Gray looked up at the branches again.

"Sure was a sight, though."

"I bet."

Gray cracked the file Axelrod had provided him. He saw a photo of the house before the fire. He was right about how the stairs and porch burned. He read on. The fire had been fueled by an accelerant. The method of application ensured the house would burn beyond repair and would likely crumble to the ground. The arson report illustrated the origin of the fire in the yard, near the dirt driveway. Gray spied the burn trail, which ran through the grass straight for the home. There, it split into three directions. One path led up the stairs and through an open front door. Two paths circled the house. This resulted in a well-planned, flank attack on the home. Additional containers of accelerant were strategically placed inside, and the fire, as if it were a starved animal, consumed the structure gluttonously.

"You were curious 'bout the bodies, you said. You see that in the report yet?"

Gray flipped through the next few pages, until he reached the diagram of the house floorplan. On it, Axelrod had marked the location of Sophia and Ryker Mason's bodies. Below the diagram, he read that the human remains had been found in the master bedroom, in the bed, next to one another. Also noted was their positioning, which suggested they were dead before the fire. Usually people who perished in fires were found in a fetal position, but that wasn't the case for Sophia and Ryker. From a behavior standpoint of this positioning, it was accepted that victims would attempt to make themselves smaller and thus protecting them from the fire. From a scientific standpoint, muscle dehydration and shrinkage of body tissues caused by the extreme heat of the fire resulted in this positioning.

So where and how were they killed? Gray asked himself.

"What was he like?" Axelrod asked.

Gray pulled his eyes from the report. "What do you mean?"

"You was face to face with 'im, right?"

"You mean Mason?" Gray asked for confirmation.

"Rumors say he shot you."

Gray sighed in embarrassment. Having been shot by Tony Mason wasn't a badge of honor.

Axelrod picked up on Gray's shift in mood. "You seem all right though," he said in recovery.

Touching his ribs, Gray replied, "I'll live."

Gray indicated the conversation was over when he opened the file again. He found where he'd left off — the victim profiles. Tony and Sophia Mason had built the house in 2010. Since their divorce in 2012, she had no job to speak of, and her tax returns didn't indicate much income. However, the home's mortgage was paid off. She had one credit card with a $15,000 limit. It had only been used once in the last four months — for fuel — and the balance had been immediately paid off. She had a checking account for paying normal bills — electricity, cable, internet, and the like. Her financial review appeared as though she spent no other money. And, she had no savings account.

As for Ryker, the 6-year-old had little online presence. He had no social media accounts, but he did enjoy playing Minecraft. He didn't miss more days of school than the school district allowed, but his number of absences butted up against the high end of the school policy. Interestingly to Gray, the boy, generally speaking, never missed school in the middle of the week. His absences occurred on Monday and Tuesdays or Thursday and Fridays.

Based on this information, Axelrod's report drew no conclusions. Yet Gray surmised Sophia and Ryker were in regular contact with Tony Mason. He was providing them cash to pay their bills, which allowed them to live off the grid to a great degree. Continuing his conjecture, Gray guessed when Mason visited with Ryker he used the weekend as part of his visitation time. Gray further imagined there were tremendous rules Sophia and Ryker had to follow in order to stay in Mason's good graces. He wondered if those rules were followed with graciousness or if they were a point of contention between the divorced parents.

"What's the latest 'bout the place in Birmingham?"

Gray didn't know what Axelrod was talking about.

"You have anything about it in here?" Gray asked, motioning to the report.

"Nah. News only broke yesterday."

Gray closed the file and tucked it under his arm. Butler had called him the night before, but he hadn't called her back because he didn't hear the voicemail until late. Now he wished he had called her. She was probably going to give him the latest updates.

He had met Butler in the course of the Mason investigation. She quickly had attached herself to him and had ultimately become an important piece of that investigation. She had also quickly become an important person to him.

"I can't really say," Gray said.

He toed the line of misrepresentation with that response. When Gray had arrived in Crestwood and Axelrod had assumed Gray was part of the Mason investigative team, he hadn't refuted that belief. So his statement could be implied as being unable to comment on the ongoing investigation. However, it also gave Gray deniability because he never said he was representing the team. Thus, he couldn't say anything about the place in Birmingham because he didn't actually know anything about it.

"What have you heard?" Gray asked.

Axelrod swiped his index finger along the base of his mustache. "The loft was traced to Mason through one of his aliases. Three blood stains were identified. DNA matched the bodies discovered here. The third remains unknown yet."

Axelrod hooked his thumbs over his belt. He let his hands and arms hang there.

"That what you heard?" he asked Gray.

As Axelrod waited for a response, Gray tried to quickly process that information. After reading about Sophia and Ryker's body positioning when he'd first opened Axelrod's file, he had wondered where they'd been killed. Now he knew.

"Word is getting around, I guess." Yet another statement with multiple interpretations.

"Yep. Killed down there and brought up here." Axelrod shook his head in disbelief. "That's a long damned road trip to be driving 'round with two dead bodies in your car."

Gray nodded and then returned his attention to the file. He hesitated and looked at Axelrod, as something occurred to him. "Something you just said there ... "

"Whatcha got?"

"Driving around with *two* dead bodies."

"What 'bout it?"

"You said there were *three* blood stains at the loft. What makes you think Mason wasn't driving around with three dead bodies?"

"Well, primarily, there ain't three bodies here. Seems to me he'd dump all three. Maybe not. What do I know?"

Gray grunted, thinking about Axelrod's assumption.

"Maybe he's gonna burn up 'nother body somewhere else," Axelrod offered another scenario.

Gray shrugged his shoulders. "I don't know what to think anymore."

"What else would he do with that third body?"

"Good question," Gray said, contemplating that idea.

The subject changed without notice. Axelrod asked, "You came up here on 75, right?"

"I did. Why?" Gray asked.

"You said you stayed in Atlanta overnight?"

"Right."

"Hmmm." Axelrod nodded then changed subjects again. "Well, that third body ain't been found yet, no matter." Then he changed subjects once more. "I'm a tad surprised that you comin' here didn't set off no flags."

"What do you mean?" Gray responded naively, but then he felt stupid when he realized what Axelrod had meant. And he cursed himself for not paying more attention to Axelrod's comments. Gray was playing a game here, and he was getting close to being caught.

"Well, you drove on up here, so your department had, what, thirteen or fourteen hours drivetime to notify us you was coming."

Usually there would've been an official notification that Gray would be visiting the area on business. But this wasn't an official visit, which meant there was no notification.

"I can't even tell you the mess my department's in right now."

"I bet." Axelrod ran his finger across his mustache again. He seemed to accept Gray's response. "TV news made it look like a war zone down there."

Gray nodded. He decided to say as little as possible for the remainder of the conversation.

Lakeland's mayor had been killed. A firefighter, too. Eight members of a local gang. A police officer. The daughter of the chief of police had been kidnapped. And another police officer had been exposed as a cartel mole. All that culminated for Gray in a shootout with Tony Mason in a campground in Sumterville, Florida, where Mason had killed a member of the Santa Lucia Four drug cartel.

"Still, it seems funny that no one would've called 'bout ya showin' up here."

"Is the autopsy report in here?" The question would hopefully change the subject and tell Gray how the Masons died.

"Surely is."

While Gray thumbed through the report, Axelrod sauntered over to his vehicle and leaned against it. He eyed Gray's Accord.

Gray found the autopsy reports and learned the bodies had been too badly damaged for the majority of the typical tests. What mattered most to Gray was that both victims had been killed by a single gunshot wound to the head. The boy's wound was in the back of the head, at the foramen magnum, the base of the skull. The woman's kill shot entered her skull at the supraorbital magnum, at her eyebrow just over her right eye. Both victims had exit wounds.

He considered this, which called to mind the news reports that had prompted him to visit Crestwood in the first place. The Mason task force and the news outlets were demonizing Mason for killing his family and setting their bodies on fire. While the man was indeed a demon, Gray knew it wasn't for that reason. He recollected what he'd seen and heard before the face-to-face encounter with Mason in Sumterville that left him shot. Marcos Cervantes, the SL-4 leader who Mason ultimately killed that day, had tried to leverage Mason's family for his own escape. However, Cervantes had already killed them.

He hoped the narrative — and the direction of the task force's investigation — would change once additional information surrounding Mason's residence in Birmingham was released.

"This here ain't your police car, is it?" Axelrod asked, pointing at the Accord.

Shit. He needed to get out of there. Gray hurried over to his colleague.

"Listen, thank you so much for bringing me out here. You were a great help. I'm just ... trying to put all this behind me and fit the last pieces together, you know what I mean?"

"I reckon."

Gray shook Axelrod's hand.

"I'll let you know if I have any more questions. Thanks again."

Gray pulled the door to his Accord open. A grinding sound came from the hinge again. A streak of pain came from his ribs.

"Hang on there, fella."

Gray froze with one leg inside the car, thinking Axelrod was about to announce he'd figure out Gray's deception.

"I'll take that folder back."

Gray acted like he'd forgotten about the folder. "Oh, right. Sure." He handed it back to Axelrod.

"I can send you an electronic copy, if ya want."

"That'd be great."

Gray pushed out his business card. Though, if Axelrod did send the file, Gray knew he wouldn't see it any time soon. Even the email on his phone had been disconnected by the department.

"You betcha, my friend."

They shook hands one more time before Gray drove off.

CHAPTER 2

The elevator doors parted, revealing a dimly lit hallway shooting left and right. Cool air from the hall invaded the small elevator compartment, and Gray felt the clean air push against his face. It refreshed him, even woke him. The drive from Kentucky, to Birmingham, Alabama, had exhausted him. At this point, his body's engine ran mainly on caffeine and the idea of hunting down Tony Mason.

Mason's loft building sat in the heart of Birmingham's trendy and revitalized Five Points South district. With all of the fine dining options, boutique stores, designer-chic bars in the area, it must have been expensive to live there, and it made Gray wonder how much money Mason had earned from killing people.

Off the elevator, Gray looked on the exposed-brick wall for a sign that might indicate the direction to Mason's loft number. There was no sign, but to his right he saw the door at the end of the hallway with crime scene tape. He headed toward it, checking over his shoulder for other people in the hall. He'd figured the folks who lived in the building were professionals and would all be gone during business hours. The last thing he needed was someone catching him breaking the crime scene seal and entering Mason's loft.

Gray checked the door handle, hoping that it had accidentally been left unlocked, but it hadn't been. He pulled from his pocket a set of lock picks he'd brought. Before working the door's lock, he checked over his shoulder again. No one was there, so he got to it. He was out of practice, having first learned the process as a patrolman. It was a skill his first patrol partner and mentor had advised him to learn, just in case he ever needed it. As the task took longer than expected, he wondered if he'd ever been good at it.

Crouched at the door, a wave of sweat traversed his body. Tense with worry at how long he was taking, he kept checking over his shoulder, which only made the process take longer. Nearing a state of panic, he took a deep breath and exhaled slowly, concentrating on the tools in his fingers and on feeling the clicks inside the lock. Finally, it worked. He let out a quick, relieved breath, and looked over his shoulder one last time. He was still alone in the hall. More relief spread, and his sweat seemed to dry instantly. He pushed the loft door ajar, did a limbo move under the crime scene tape, and closed the door behind his entry.

Of all Gray's senses, his hearing was the first to register. As he closed the door gently, he encountered an eerie, mute stillness he'd only discovered at murder scenes. The vacuum of life.

The entryway led to an open living area. No dining room to speak of. A brick fireplace in the center. And a wall of floor-to-ceiling windows. To his right was the kitchen, only separated from the open area by an island counter and barstools. The hallway to his left likely led to bedrooms. He stepped further inside and saw another door at the right corner of the living room. Master bedroom, Gray supposed. The loft was nicely fashioned. The furniture looked contemporary and stereotypically bachelor. There was no warmth, just style and utility.

Two more steps inside the loft, Gray found the first two signs of the trouble that had occurred at the loft. The first being the remnants of the dusting the crime scene unit had performed looking for prints. The residue was prolifically spread throughout the home. That stood as a reminder to him to be careful. Gray pulled two rubber gloves from his back pocket. He noted to himself the need to wipe clean of prints the exterior and interior handle of the front door. He fought the gloves onto his hands. Then he squatted to get a better look at the second sign of trouble — a blood stain in the shape of a large kidney bean. A small chunk of the carpet had been cut and removed for forensic purposes. He scanned the room, seeing no blood spatter, and he surmised the person killed here was flat on the ground when shot. Maybe a pillow had been placed over the head or body to eliminate spatter.

Standing, he wondered what the official write-up of the scene had been. He considered going to the local police and pulling the same stunt he had in Crestwood, but he quickly discarded the idea of pretending he was a visiting detective. That would push his luck too far.

He headed down the hall to his left. He found a small bathroom, a child's bedroom, and then what looked like an office. Gray ducked into each one, looking for something that would help him find Mason. He knew if something of value had already been discovered, the item or information would already be in evidence, but he couldn't help himself. Periodically, there was information missed at crime scenes. He hoped this was one of those times.

The bathroom held nothing but the usual items a child would need for hygiene. The bedroom followed the same pattern, respective to dressing, sleeping, and playing. In the office, however, Mason stopped in front of a large credenza used for the storage of rifles. There were either none there when the police entered the loft, or they'd been confiscated by local law enforcement. He opened the closet door. It had been cleared out, too.

He saw that planks of wood had been removed, leaving exposed a small hidden compartment in the floor. He noticed the removed planks had a coloration that didn't exactly match the rest of the wood flooring. Gray squatted and looked at the empty compartment in the floor and the surrounding wood planks. Because of the differences of color, Gray guessed the hiding place had been installed after Mason moved in. He wondered when the planks had been ripped up? Had Mason done it, or had the police found it and tore it open? What had it held for Mason? Passports? Maybe money. Something sentimental?

Gray knew he'd probably never get the answers to those questions. He stood up and went on his tiptoes to see above the top shelf. It appeared empty, like the rest of the room. He swiped his hand across it to be sure. There was nothing there.

Same with the desk. The drawers had all been cleared. He hung his head, thinking of what to do next. Trying to find Mason was a herculean effort without being able to use his badge. His eyes rested on the flooring, and he noticed the color again. Something about the wood's tint made him curious. He looked at the planks that had been ripped up over Mason's hiding place. Then, though subtle, he saw a rectangle of slightly discolored wood surrounding the desk. *And what does that mean or matter,* he asked himself? He didn't know. *I'm grasping at straws.*

Gray hammered his fist against the desktop in disappointment. Ultimately, he knew he wasn't going to find any clue that would unlock the Mason case. That's not why he was disappointed. He had hoped to, at least, learn something about the man. Something — anything — that might be useful to him.

He left the office behind and made his way to the door in the right-hand corner of the living room. Behind it, the master bedroom opened before him. He noticed again the amount of forensic dust present in the room. It looked like the crime scene team had come in with a gas-powered sprayer and blasted the room. Then he saw the bloody mattress. The sheets were gone. Parts of the mattress where blood had set had been cut out and taken away, like a biopsy. Sprinkles of now-brownish blood remained on the bedroom wall at the head of the bed. The spatter displayed like a macabre art piece signifying greed, power, family, and vengeance.

His cell phone rang and vibrated in his pocket. The sudden burst of noise in an environment devoid of sound sent a tremor of shock through his body. His movements became clumsy with the explosion of adrenaline. He fumbled getting the phone from his pocket.

"Gray," he answered the phone with a shaky voice.

"Detective Becker Gray with the Lakeland Police Department, badge number 0529."

Gray didn't like where this was going. He immediately thought of Axelrod in Crestwood. Had Gray's visit there been discovered so quickly?

"Sure," Gray replied. "Who's this?"

"This is Julian Weech with TEAM Consulting. I'm calling — "

Gray's heartbeat reached its normal rhythm. "I'm not interested." And he ended the call.

He opened the top drawer of Mason's dresser. All the clothes were gone. He opened another — gone — then another — gone — then all the drawers. Each was empty. Either Mason had no clothes, or the task force took everything the man owned. Unsatisfied, he removed the top drawer, sliding it out from its railing. He turned it upside down. He'd seen before envelopes taped to the bottom of dresser drawers. Mason was too smart for that or the task force found what was there and took it. *This is a waste of time,* he told himself.

His phone rang again. He startled, but only barely this time. The screen showed that the same number was calling again.

"Gray."

"Detective, don't hang up. It's very important we speak."

"Who are you again?" Gray asked, while resetting the drawer in the cabinet.

"Julian Weech with TEAM Consulting."

"What the hell is that?"

"Sorry, what is what?"

"TEAM Consulting." His tone, admittedly, was condescending.

"We were hired by the City of Lakeland's mayoral office to do a third-party audit of events surrounding the Anthony Mason investigation, which resulted in the death of Lt. Maxine West, and the arrest of Lt. Lexie Cannon."

"Okay."

"I can tell by your tone you're unimpressed."

"Quite."

Gray knew what was coming, but he wasn't going to make it easier on the man. Meanwhile he continued on to Mason's bathroom.

"We have a 9 a.m. conversation scheduled tomorrow morning. I wanted to make sure you'd be there."

Gray opened and closed the drawers of Mason's bathroom cabinet. "No one told me I had to be there tomorrow to *converse* with you." All the items in Mason's bathroom drawers had been taken too.

"It's an open investigation. We interview as information comes up. All department personnel are to be readily available to us when requested."

"Well," Gray said, opening the doors beneath Mason's sink and peering into the dark, empty space. "Then I'll see you at nine."

"Perfect. Thanks for your cooperation."

"Anytime, Justin. See you tomorrow."

"It's Julian."

Gray ended the call, purposely having called the man the wrong name. And, he knew he wouldn't make it to Lakeland by nine the next morning. He felt exhausted. He was going to drive from Birmingham to Pensacola where he'd spend the night. That was at least an eight-hour drive. *What could Justin really do about it?* he asked himself.

He clicked his phone to silent and returned it to his front pocket. The bareness of Mason's loft unsettled him. Disappointment overcame him again, coupled with tiredness. *What the hell am I doing here?* Mason was too smart to hide something here. Gray knew that, yet he was there anyway. Was this really, subconsciously just about being in the same space Mason had been in? To try to know him? Feel him? Get inside his head?

As Gray's ribs began to ache signaling the ibuprofen was wearing off, he left the bedroom and closed the door the way he'd found it. At the loft's front door, he paused, disheartened, then turned again to the blood stain on the living room carpet. He studied it like he expected it to reveal something to him. But, it didn't reveal anything. It just made him think through the murders that occurred here. He recalled that Axelrod told him only two bodies had been found. Yet, there had been three people's blood found in the loft. Where was the other body?

He sighed again. *More questions without answers.* More discouraging feelings set in.

Gray turned away from the stain and wiped the handle with his glove, smearing any prints he'd left when he'd entered.

Wait!

He thought he had something, but it wasn't fully formulated yet.

He left the door again and started walking through the living room, circling the kidney-shaped blood stain, concentrating on the most important question he could think of — *Where is the other body?* His eyes jumped around the apartment as he recalled everything Axelrod had told him, all he knew about Mason, the events at Sumterville, and everything he'd seen inside the loft.

Like a slap across the face, he got it. *Yes!*

Gray hurried down the hall to the office, using the door frame to help navigate his entry. His eyes zeroed in on the flooring around the desk. He remembered the differences in coloration on the floor from his walk through. This time, though, he studied the floor carefully and with purpose and meaning. The discoloration stretched around the room in a rectangle, like the shape of a large area rug. It was only slightly different, but Gray saw the meaning this time.

Gray returned excitedly to the living room and stared again at the stain, imagining the scene that played out here at Mason's loft. Mason's family had been killed in the bedroom. A third person killed here. Mason returned after Sumterville and found them all. Then he kicked into survival mode, and he cleaned up. He took time and care with his family.

What did he do with the third body? There had been no time, no care with that body. *None indeed,* he told himself, as the scene rolled through his imagination. Mason had sent the third body to the landfill. He had taken the area rug from his office and drug it to the living room. He rolled the third body inside and then dropped it down the garbage chute, which buildings like this were known to maintain. *But why? And who?*

Gray's exhilaration almost sent him into the hall to locate the chute opening, to check it for blood residue or carpet fibers or to confirm it was big enough to jam a body through, but he again stopped himself. The hopeful eagerness drained as quickly as it had filled his veins. Surely the task force had to have figured that out, too. *Right? Of course they had.* They'd probably already processed the chute and checked the dumpster downstairs. They probably already knew the identity of the third body. They probably knew everything, and Gray was wasting his time and energy double-checking them, doubting them, and fooling himself about his ability to find Mason on his own.

Probably.

CHAPTER 3

After sleeping in, Gray awoke to a sunny day in Pensacola. Although unimpressed with the historic sites, the local naval base, and the beautiful beaches, he did take a moment for himself before his day kicked into gear.

He swiped the curtains back and stepped onto his hotel room balcony, closing the sliding door behind him. The unfamiliar surroundings attacked his senses. The heat of the morning hit him full blast. A combination of the waves crashing and the traffic from the nearby street collided in his ears. A breeze carried the briny scent of the waters toward him, and he could almost taste the gulf's saltiness when he inhaled through his mouth. He squinted his eyes, shielding them from the sunshine reflecting off the blanket of water stretching to the horizon.

Leaning against the rail and allowing the moment to overtake him, he realized that for the first time since Sumterville his ribs hadn't ached when he'd pulled himself from bed. The revelation delivered a smile to his face and a sense of appreciation to his mind. And that combination opened his mind to what laid out before him. He noticed the beauty of the white sands and blue Gulf of Mexico water. The groupings of people enjoying their day at the beach actually pleased him rather than generating some sense of heavy annoyance. Most importantly, he realized that being far away from the source of his stresses allowed him a sense of harmony. He was, for that unexpected moment, at peace. And he needed it. It had been a long time since he'd experienced it.

As if the universe had sensed Gray's peace, his cell phone came to life, ruining his tranquility. Like one of Pavlov's dogs, he hurried to check the caller ID. He pulled the door open, and — again, coincidentally perhaps — his ribs immediately began aching.

The caller had an 863 number, but the digits weren't ones he recognized, so he let it go to voicemail. The caller log showed the same number had called five additional times while Gray had slept. He must've been exhausted to have slept through the ringing. The call log showed the attempts to contact him began at 8:15 a.m., which — because of the time zone difference in Pensacola — was really 9:15 a.m. Eastern time. That meant the calls were likely related to the meeting with the third-party investigators he was missing.

He pushed aside the thoughts and hastily turned back toward the balcony, searching to recapture the peace he'd discovered. Yanking on the sliding door, Gray's ribs sent another unwelcomed message to his brain, stealing with it a bit of his breath. He halted at the threshold and cast his eyes to the sky. To the east, a large rain cloud was now blowing into view. The sun was being overtaken by clouds. The wind shifted, taking with it the briny scent and salty breeze. He looked down at the beach. The people who were having fun in the sun were now packing their belongings. Gray sighed, sending the last particles of serenity out of his body.

Gray sucked in thick, humid air, which seemed to weigh him down. He thought of Tony Mason, of how little he could do to help catch him, of the possible consequences of the third-party investigation, of his partner, Jeffrey Parker, not having returned any of his phone messages in a week, and of the nine-hour drive home.

Conceding to the universe's negativity, Gray closed the sliding door.

As he headed for the shower, Gray's posture slumped, and his face locked in a scowl. *Back to normal,* he told himself.

~ ~ ~ ~

Darkness had fully eclipsed Lakeland by 9:52 p.m. as Gray steered his Honda Accord into the parking spot outside the steps that led to his third-floor, two-bedroom apartment. At the beginning of the drive to Crestwood, Gray worried the car may not successfully make the trip. It had over 200,000 miles on it and was nearing 20 years old, and he'd never driven it that far in one jaunt. As the car rattled to a halt, he rubbed the dash, thanking the car for completing the voyage.

Pushing the car door open, he ignored the hinge squeak, instead aiming his attention on a slow approaching vehicle. The headlights blinded him. Gray pulled himself from the car and closed the car door, worried about his safety. In recent months, a trend of targeted attacks on police officers had arisen across the United States. Many of them ambush style, which is what this felt like to Gray. He moved his right hand toward his holstered weapon just in case he needed it, but then remembered he'd been suspended. His shield and gun were at the police department. To see better, he adjusted his positioning, sliding to his left, moving out of the direct beam of headlights. From his new position, he could make out a light rack across the top of the vehicle, which meant to him the vehicle was likely the apartment security guard making the rounds. That eased his concern, yet his state of caution remained elevated. As the car moved even closer, Gray saw the car wasn't just security, it was a Lakeland Police Department patrol car. The tension faded away fully. Fatigue and rib pain returned.

"Detective." The voice came from the dark cabin of the patrol car.

He walked toward the car, which pulled alongside. It wasn't a good sign that the patrolman was addressing Gray directly.

Gray looked through the open window, trying to determine who was inside. "Bonnin, right?" They'd met five months ago when Gray and his partner, Jeffrey Parker, investigated a home invasion in West Lakeland.

Officer AJ Bonnin was the first on scene that day. "What are you doing here?"

Bonnin pushed the gear into park. "Looking for you."

"What did I do now?"

Bonnin smiled. "Are you in trouble that often?"

"More often than not," Gray replied. "Are you watching my place?"

The mixture of displeasure and shame on Bonnin's face served as his response.

Gray leaned on the car. "What's going on?"

Bonnin shook his head. This wasn't an assignment a cop wanted, staking out a colleague and having to bring him in. It was a loathsome task. Yet, Bonnin knew Gray had made his own bed by missing the meeting that morning with the third-party investigators.

"You missed your appointment with TEAM this morning."

Gray nodded, understanding the situation now. "And you're here to make sure I show up tomorrow?" He pushed off the car.

"Pretty much." Bonnin hooked his left arm out the window. "I don't want to be here, detective."

"I know. It's all right."

Gray pulled a duffle bag from his back seat.

"Look, Bonnin ... I've been out of town, trying to get away from all the bullshit going on here. That's all. I'll go upstairs and get a good night's sleep and be at the department by eight. No worries. All right?" Gray stepped toward the stairs.

"Wait." Bonnin threw off his seat belt and climbed out of his cruiser. "That won't work," he said. "I have orders to bring you in and park you at HQ."

"Are you shitting me?"

"No, I am not."

"Christ almighty."

Gray's temperament twisted and aimed at Bonnin. He knew the patrolman wasn't to blame for this, but Gray wasn't going to the department tonight. Bonnin needed to realize that quickly.

"My ribs hurt from being shot. I need a shower. I'm tired. Come on, Bonnin. I'll be there first thing in the morning."

"I don't want to get in trouble," Bonnin said.

"You're not going to get in trouble, man."

Bonnin sighed, conflicted over the situation. And Gray knew it. He needed to push a little harder.

"This is a bullshit assignment you were sent on over a bullshit investigation. You know it, and so do I."

"They're serious about this mess, man."

"What difference does it make if I show up there tonight or tomorrow morning? This is a waste of everyone's time and the city's resources. You have better things to be doing, and I need to get some rest. Come on, man. Help me out. I'll be there first thing tomorrow morning. Promise. I won't let this come back on you."

Gray saw he had Bonnin on the ropes.

"Why don't we do this?" Gray opened the back door of his car again and tossed the bag inside. "Let's pretend you didn't see me. I'll grab a hotel room and just show up at the department tomorrow morning. It'll be like I was never here. No harm, no foul."

"I don't know, man."

"You're killing me, Bonnin. I'll owe you one."

Bonnin checked his watch. There was no reason he did it. It was just habit, just a gesture to buy him a moment to think about Gray's proposition.

"You'll be there by seven?" he finally asked.

"Sure, seven. I swear." He held up his right hand to go along with his statement.

"I get off shift at seven, so I'll be there, too. I want to see you before I leave."

"I'll bring you a coffee and a pastry."

Bonnin sighed again, knowing he was about to agree to do something he shouldn't. "All right." He jutted his head left, telling Gray to get out of there.

"Thanks, Bonnin."

Gray slid behind the wheel of his old car and fired up the engine. He wasn't going to wait around for Bonnin to change his mind.

CHAPTER 4

The next morning came fast, but mornings usually did for Gray. Nights hardly ever seemed long enough, and at the same time most of them were too long. Troubled in the past by a proclivity for neurotic overthinking, Gray used to have chronic sleeping problems. He had usually slept in his car. He simply had refused to toss and turn in bed as his mind raged forward. To the point he'd practically avoid his bed at all costs. Instead he'd drive his car at night all over central Florida until he grew tired. Wherever he was when exhaustion took hold, he'd pull the car over and sleep. But lately he'd found more success in sleeping at home than ever before, given that the recurring nightmarish thoughts of his toddler daughter's death in a car wreck had abated. He'd found the closure he needed. Only he didn't know how successful he'd been in sleeping at home until he stayed in a hotel the last couple nights. The hotel beds were bouncy and poor quality, while the pillows pressed flat, and the covers too thin. He had grown used to his bed, and now no other bed would do.

Gray yawned, sending only slight discomfort from his ribs. He carried a coffee in one hand and a pastry inside a paper bag in his other. He was making good on his promise to Bonnin from the night before — something he'd learned from his partner. He swiped his department ID badge over the magnet lock, expecting the light to turn green and allow him entrance. But the light flashed red. Irritated, he swiped again. The red light activated once more. Then he knew what was going on. Like his email account, his access had been turned off because of his suspension.

"Dammit."

He huffed out a quick breath and began the trip around the building. Even though it was autumn and early in the morning, the temperature was on the underside of 85 degrees and the humidity was high. Combining those two environmental factors with Bonnin's hot coffee in Gray's hand, his body's cooling mechanism kicked in full power. He needed a towel by the time he opened the front doors to the department's lobby.

The high ceiling and tile floor acted as the perfect echo chamber for his footsteps. Echoes of the conversation taking place at the reception area bounced about. The concession machine dispensed a soda to a uniformed officer. The elevator arrived on the ground floor with a loud ding. Conversation and laughter spilled out of it along with the five riders. The collective noise led the receptionist, working behind a thick bulletproof window, to say, "I can't hear you." Then the people at the desk groaned and started their story over, only recounting it at a higher volume than previously.

Gray hurried to the officer with the soda.

"Will you swipe me through? I have a meeting upstairs."

The male officer, who Gray had seen around but didn't recall his name, surveyed Gray up and down, like he didn't belong there.

"Sure." He finally acquiesced.

"You seen Bonnin around?"

The officer, an oversized muscle from neck to calves, scanned his card, and pushed the door open for Gray. "His shift's over. He left fifteen minutes ago."

"What?" Gray checked his watch. He had arrived just a little late. "Shit."

"Why?" the meat head asked.

"No reason." Gray dropped the coffee and pastry bag into the garbage can at the next desk he passed.

"Have you seen Jeff Parker lately?"

"Nope."

CHAPTER 5

There were four people in the conference room waiting for Gray's arrival. His police representative Horace Ambrose, who was a lieutenant in the department and managed the motor pool with an iron fist, rose from his chair to greet Gray. He'd been in the department for more years than anyone else, and often acted like the department historian. He would soon retire, and out the door with him would go the key to the department's past. Its *real* past, not the one documented for public consumption, but the *internal* past that only cops knew.

Ambrose met Gray at the door. They shook hands.

"Glad you could finally make it," Ambrose said in a low voice so only Gray could hear him. The sarcasm dripped from his statement like water off a saturated sponge.

"I guess I misunderstood the arrangements."

Ambrose didn't bother responding, knowing Gray was lying. He'd known Gray since he was an infant of a police officer. He'd watched Gray grow throughout his career and become a headline in the national news twice. Gray had been lucky to survive the scrutiny the first time. Ambrose figured Gray wasn't going to survive this go around, not without some scarring, at least.

"I'd like a moment in private please," Ambrose ordered.

"I'd like to introduce myself, lieutenant."

A slender man in a sporty, navy suit stood at the head of the table. His dress, demeanor, and tone of voice exhibited his power. This was his investigation, and he was in charge.

"After. We need a minute." Ambrose spoke with no fluff in his message nor bend in his tone.

The slender man opened his mouth to object, but Ambrose shut him down showing him who was really in charge.

"I have not had a chance to consult with Detective Gray, and he will utter no word, even of greetings, until I do. Is that understood?"

Gray turned away from the man in charge, who indignantly collected the folder in front of him. Gray took a position in the corner of the room. The spot was far away from the three people exiting, making it difficult for them to ignore Ambrose's order to not talk to him. He watched as Ambrose ushered the team out of the room then closed and locked the door behind them.

"Check the camera." Ambrose pointed to the recording device set up at the end of the table, near where Gray stood. "Make sure it's powered off."

It was the first time Gray had noticed the camera. Or the room. One of the three people had a stenotype device prepped and ready to go. The other two had pads of paper and a stack of pens in front of their seats at the table. A microphone pointed at what had to be Gray's seat. Two legal boxes were staged on the table. The lids were off both and had been stacked neatly in the corner of the room, revealing a full complement of papers and folders and giving the impression the investigation had amassed a mountain of evidence. The equipment and legal boxes were supposed to intimidate Gray, but they didn't. He often did the same thing when interrogating suspects. It was a classic tactic, and one to which his anxiety wouldn't fall prey. A tray holding three carafes of water, clean glasses, and a small assortment of bagels and pastries acted as the centerpiece of the meeting. It was present solely in an attempt to counterbalance the feeble attempt at intimidation. The two affects put together were meant to impact Gray's inner balance. He wouldn't fall for that either.

Gray confirmed the camera's record feature was turned off. "All good," he said.

Ambrose checked the areas where the three people from TEAM had been sitting. He'd seen cell phones left behind with the voice recorder program in action, and he didn't want anything he and Gray said to be recorded without their knowledge.

"Check the mic," Ambrose ordered.

Gray clicked the switch to the off position. "Got it."

"All right."

Ambrose had found no additional recording devices.

At capacity, the conference table could hold twelve people, but it had been set up today for eight, which made the room and table appear, respectively, larger and longer than usual. Opposite Gray and the recording camera at the end of the table, behind where the man in charge had been sitting when Gray had entered, was a credenza underneath a wall-mounted television. Ambrose pushed a decorative fake plant aside and sat on top of the credenza.

"This is how today is going to go, far as I understand it. We're scheduled for a break at eleven, reconvene at one, and then we'll wrap up the day at four."

"Good God."

Ambrose nodded in agreement. "Long day. And I suspect they'll drag your session into another day or two."

"I don't have that much to say, quite frankly."

"Maybe you don't think so, but they believe you do. Most of the conversations so far have begun with the Beringer and Wentworth murders, and they move on to and past the attempted arrest of Anthony Mason in Sumterville, while stopping for an extended period on Lt. West's murder. And, Becker, your hands are all over every bit of those topics."

Ambrose was right, of course. Gray sat down in the closest chair, feeling the weight of the day immediately.

"Listen," Ambrose kicked off the credenza and stood at the head of the table, "that shit you pulled yesterday, missing this meeting … wasn't smart. Don't take this lightly."

"I understand."

"I don't think you do, son. They're gunning for anyone who had even the slightest culpability in any wrongdoing associated with the corruption, mismanagement, and case procedure."

"I get it." Gray's defensiveness surprised even himself.

"That tone of voice tells me you don't get it. The mayor pro tem and city manager are using this investigation in the pro tem's bid for a new mayoral election, and he's going to run for election on a platform of cleaning up the police department. And that means every one of us here is in danger. You remember five, six years ago when they overhauled the department and Boudreaux was promoted to chief?"

Gray nodded.

"Well, this time we may not be so lucky to have a chief promoted from the inside. And you and I may not be so lucky to have jobs either once this thing wraps up."

"They're blaming Boudreaux for the corruption?"

"Of course, the chief is always to blame, Gray. You've been around long enough to know that."

Gray had been there long enough to have seen multiple chiefs of police removed for one political reason or another.

"I'm assuming you're not ready to retire or be retired?"

"No, I'm not," Gray said.

The idea hadn't occurred to him. Gray may have self-centered tendencies, but self-preservation often fell by the wayside.

"How should I play it?"

"Now you're talking." Ambrose sat in the seat at the head of the table. "You need to be honest but only answer the questions they ask. Don't offer up anything over and above what they're asking. And, if you think you may be getting jammed into a corner, stop the meeting and sidebar with me. And, trust me, you've been a cop a long time and asked suspects a lot of questions, but it's different when you're on the receiving end."

"All right."

"Becker, it's different, and you have a shitty attitude sometimes, so don't let it get the best of you. It won't help."

Gray locked his jaw, irritated at Ambrose's candidness.

"Exactly," Ambrose said, noticing Gray's irritation. "Now take a minute to yourself. Collect your thoughts. I'll let them in soon."

Ambrose stopped talking and closed his own eyes, taking his own time to meditate and cool down.

Gray wanted to take his moment and clear his head, but he couldn't. He'd never thought about not being a police officer. He'd never thought about Boudreaux losing his job, as Ambrose implied. And he'd never thought his actions would hurt his friend's career.

"Has Parker been in yet?"

"You need to worry about you," Ambrose fired back, keeping his eyes closed, trying to stay in his own clear moment.

"I know, Top. I just want to know."

Ambrose opened his eyes. "Will that impact how you answer questions?"

"Of course not."

"You can't talk to him about what you two say in these interviews."

"I'm not concerned about that. I just want to know."

Ambrose nodded. "He comes in tomorrow."

"What time?"

"What's the issue, Gray?"

"If they were trying to hang this on me, wouldn't they have interviewed him first? That's what I would've done. Gathered as much information as possible so the person of interest could be caught in lies."

"He had to reschedule."

So that was their plan, Gray noted.

"Then why was my absence so bad?"

Ambrose shook his head, frustrated at Gray's questions. He rose from the chair and walked to the door of the conference room.

"It just was, Becker."

He wrapped his fingers around the cold brass knob.

"You ready now?"

CHAPTER 6

The squad of three from TEAM reentered the conference room. Ambrose shot them a pleasant but insincere smile, welcoming them. Gray did the same and shook each of their hands as they entered. The slender man in the sporty suit and dress sneakers entered last. He ignored Ambrose and went straight to Gray. He held Gray's handshake longer than the social norm.

"Detective Gray, it's nice to finally meet you. I'm Peter McKee."

The M in TEAM – Tullis, Elliot, and McKee.

What a typical consulting firm name, Gray thought. There was nothing about teamwork in this whole process.

"We should get started," Gray responded, nearly tearing his hand from McKee's grip.

McKee moved toward his chair at the head of the table. "I trust the two of you were able to confer on all pertinent topics?"

"We're ready," Ambrose responded, sitting in his seat.

Gray stepped to his seat, pleased Ambrose had taken the one between him and McKee. He sat, and as he did, he noticed McKee stayed standing. There was some power trip in being the last to sit. The action annoyed Gray. If he was wondering at all if he'd like McKee, the answer clearly now was that he would not.

"Gentlemen, to my right are two of my associates. Kristie Keegan is our stenographer. While we do video record our interviews, Kristie's here to speed up the transcription process." McKee finally sat down. "You may or may not know, but the city has asked us to complete our inquiry as quickly as possible. Hence, Kristie's presence. Between Kristie and myself sits Julian Weech. I believe, detective, you and Julian have already spoken."

Gray smiled politely to Keegan, and he nodded a greeting to Weech.

McKee nodded toward Weech, who reached across the table and turned on the microphone. Everyone waited as Weech then stood and made his way to the video camera. He pressed the record button and confirmed the frame of the shot. He gave a thumbs up. The equipment was ready.

McKee spoke as Weech returned to his seat. After he read off the date and time, named the people present, and stated the reason for the meeting, he opened the folder in front of him and read from it. Keegan's fingers worked smoothly and agilely with only the slightest of clickety-clack.

"All parties stipulate that this is an administrative investigation with the intent to improve the management of the department and to implement new policies and procedures as identified through the testimony provided. All parties also stipulate that this is not a criminal investigation. However, all records, transcripts, conclusions, and departmental actions taken as a result of this inquiry will be made available to the district attorney's office, if so requested." McKee looked up from the pre-written statement and looked directly at Gray. "Detective Gray stipulates that, while not under oath, his responses will be the whole truth and nothing other than the truth."

Gray nodded, but didn't like any of the stipulations. To him they signified this was a criminal investigation, even if preliminarily; this was a witch hunt designed to replace management and other personnel as desired; and Gray was the only one in the room expected to tell the truth.

"Please respond verbally, detective."

"I heard the stipulations."

That response told McKee this interview would ultimately turn combative.

"Good. We'll accept your further cooperation as agreement to and understanding of the stipulations."

McKee reached across the table and retrieved a glass and a carafe of water. He poured himself a glass and then offered the carafe to others at the table. No one accepted the offer, and he returned it to the tray. He sipped from the glass and set it on a coaster, covering up the Lakeland Police Department shield logo.

Gray sighed audibly at McKee's stalling and continued power plays. McKee grinned slightly, pleased at Gray's frustration.

"Detective, you were lead on the Douglas and Morgan Beringer homicide investigations, is that correct?"

"It is."

"Who assigned you to the case?"

"No one. My partner and I were next in rotation."

"Your assignment wasn't a direct appointment from Chief Boudreaux?"

"I already answered your question."

"Who is your partner?"

"You're asking about things that are already universally known."

McKee smiled, knowing Gray was the one who'd appear unreasonable in these conversations. It would make him look guilty, if this was, in fact, a criminal investigation.

"We're just painting a picture, detective."

"A picture of what?"

Ambrose cracked his knuckles, sending Gray a signal to calm down.

McKee said, "Please just answer the questions, detective."

"You know who my partner is."

Weech pulled a folder from one of the legal boxes. "It is on record in the official murder book that Detective Gray was partnered with Detective Jeffrey Parker."

"Thank you, Julian," McKee said, as if to say, "See, detective, that was easy."

"You had on occasion been known to socialize with both Douglas *and* Morgan Beringer, yes?"

"Define 'socialize'."

"You had attended at least one social gathering at their home, yes?"

"That's true."

"What was the occasion?"

"A holiday gathering."

"How did you come to be invited?"

"The mayor invited me."

"Had you been to a gathering of his prior to this?"

"No."

"You knew Douglas Beringer from his days on the police force?"

"Not really."

"Define 'not really'." McKee mimicked Gray's previous clarifying question.

"We weren't friends, but I knew who he was."

"Were you acquainted with him after he left the police force?"

"No."

"Then why were you invited to the holiday party?"

"You'd have to ask Douglas Beringer."

Gray hoped that would suck the air from the conversation, but McKee fired another question at him. He felt he had momentum and didn't want to lose it.

"Did you know his wife prior to the holiday party?"

"No."

"You never had the occasion to meet her or talk to her prior to that night?"

"No."

"How did you meet then?"

"At the party. She was the hostess, and she welcomed me."

"And what did you two discuss at the party?"

Gray pulled up in his seat and leaned on the table. His hands interlocked in front of him "What are you doing?"

Gray's response jerked Ambrose to attention.

"What do you mean, detective? We've already discussed this. How many times are you going to stop the proceedings? It's just as easy to answer the questions."

Gray felt Ambrose's tension beside him, though he refused to acknowledge it. He gritted his teeth and said, "We discussed the hors d'oeuvres. What importance does that have on this inquiry?"

McKee leveled with him. "We'd like you to detail your personal relationship with Morgan Beringer."

Gray sat back in his chair before he realized his body language probably told them what they'd hoped it would.

"Define 'personal relationship'," he requested.

"I was hoping, detective, that's what you would do."

"No. You tell me what you think you know or what you suspect, and I'll tell you if it's true."

McKee's smile looked sinister to Gray.

"How long have you been partnered with Detective Parker?"

"Why are you changing subjects?"

"We'll revisit the Beringer homicide investigation later."

"What you were asking had nothing to do with the investigation," Gray protested with force.

Ambrose scribbled on a pad of paper and held it up for only Gray to see: EASY DOES IT.

"May we move on, gentlemen?" McKee asked.

"Go ahead, Mr. McKee," Ambrose said, tearing off the piece of paper and crumbling it.

"My last question had to do with your partner. How long have the two of you been paired?"

Gray didn't want to answer. The questions were not what he'd thought they'd be. He wondered if he should stop the interview and confer with Ambrose again.

"Detective?" McKee asked, regaining Gray's attention.

"Five years, maybe."

"Would you say the two of you are close?"

"I would."

"Friends?"

"Yes."

"Best friends?"

"Likely."

"If you were to bend the rules, would he go along with it?"

"You'd have to ask him what he'd do."

McKee smiled, knowing they were sparring over wording. It was going to make his job harder, more interesting, and more fun.

"Do you think he'd go along with it, if you were to operate outside the policies of the department?"

"It's not anything I've ever thought about."

"Has he ever broken procedure and you've allowed it?"

"I don't recall."

"You don't recall?"

"That's what I said."

"Interesting."

"Is it?" Gray asked with a mouth full of sarcasm and scorn.

McKee continued without acknowledging Gray's tone.

"You were particularly determined to solve the Beringer homicide case, yes?"

"I'm determined to solve all my cases."

"Yes, I'm sure, but I said 'particularly determined' and I'd like you to speak to that determination."

Gray shrugged his shoulders. "Define 'particularly determined'."

McKee sighed, feigning annoyance for the camera. "Detective, please stop playing this game of semantics."

Gray shot back. "Please ask better worded questions."

Ambrose stepped in. "Mr. McKee, why don't you get to the point of your questioning. The picture you said you're painting is coming across as an impressionist piece, and it needs to be clearer."

McKee nodded, accepting Ambrose's statement.

"Detective, did you know Detective Parker has had to reschedule his interview?"

"I did. Lt. Ambrose informed me of that during our conference."

"What do you make of that?"

"Nothing."

"Did you know his wife is pregnant?"

The questions launched numbers through Gray. Personally, he and Parker were on bad terms, but pregnancy was something Gray wouldn't imagine ever that Parker would keep from him. Parker and his wife had experienced multiple miscarriages. He'd always shared the news with Gray. But, if what McKee had asked was true, then Gray figured the possibility of losing Parker as a friend was real. Professionally, the news meant something altogether different. Worse, whatever McKee's plan, the slender man knew it was working. There was no way to hide Gray's emotions. His face gave McKee the answer he was looking for.

"You didn't know, did you? But, you two were close, you said. Likely best friends."

Gray tried to reel himself in before losing his temper. "We were advised to maintain radio silence during your little inquiry."

"His wife was taken to the hospital for dehydration. I guess the morning sickness was getting the best of her."

"Okay." Gray chose to accept that as information and refuse to react to the statement.

"Did Detective Parker know about your personal relationship with Morgan Beringer?"

Even though his thoughts were clouded, Gray was beginning to clue in to McKee's objective. *Instability.* Just like the differences between the staged boxes and welcoming drinks and pastries. The whole approach from room preparation and staging to this method of jumping from topic to topic resulted in instability.

"I informed Jeff that I had attended the holiday party after being invited by Douglas Beringer, yes. As for what you keep calling a 'personal relationship', I'm going to need you to be more specific."

"Tell me why you and Detective Parker left Lakeland and traveled to Sumterville in the pursuit of Anthony Mason alone."

"It's in our reports. I'm sure you have them in your boxes."

"We do, but I'd like to hear it from you."

McKee was presenting the situation as if Gray and Morgan Beringer had an intimate, personal relationship that pushed Gray to break procedure, and thus forcing Parker to go along with Gray's rogue pursuit of Mason. McKee was pushing Gray into a corner. He'd need to fall on the sword, or McKee would take down Parker in the midst of his wife's troubled pregnancy.

"No," Gray said. "You start asking me specific questions, preferably with yes or no answers, or I'm walking out of here."

"Hold on," Ambrose said.

"No, lieutenant. I'm serious. This is playing out like a game, and I'm tired of it." He turned to McKee. "Get to your point, McGoo, or I'm leaving."

"We should take a break," Ambrose said, grabbing the crumpled piece of paper and standing to leave.

"Detective," McKee said, "I have been empowered by the City of Lakeland leadership team to conduct this inquiry in the best, most comprehensive way possible. I've been performing inquiries like this for fifteen years. They trust my methods, which are proven to unearth the truth in these types of situations."

"I don't care. You must be forgetting I do just about the same thing for a living as you. I know the games and the tricks, and I'm advising you to ask me specific questions or I'm walking."

"We're taking a break," Ambrose said. He looked at Gray, "You ... outside now."

Ambrose rose from his seat and stepped quickly to the conference room door. He opened it and waited impatiently for Gray to rise from his chair, but Gray remained seated, glaring at McKee. He wanted to tell him off, but the fast fingers of Keegan never left his peripheral vision. He knew whatever he said would be recorded, and for once he was holding back. He finally stood, brooding but not leaving.

"Come on, detective," Ambrose prompted.

McKee stood, crisp and calm. "It looks like Detective Gray is considering staying and complying with the investigation."

Ambrose spoke before Gray could. "You be quiet. I told you we're taking a break."

Ambrose left the door and moved to Gray. He grabbed the detective's arm.

"Let's go."

As soon as the conference room door was closed behind them, Ambrose snapped at Gray.

"I told you it was different on the receiving end, didn't I?"

"He's already made up his mind."

"What the hell is wrong with you? Turn it around, Becker. You'd do the same thing. Have you thought that maybe he started down his line of questioning because you were being obstinate? Or maybe someone told him you'd be a pain the ass to deal with? Maybe this is what you get for skipping yesterday's appointment."

"No, he's got it out for me. Some sort of pre-existing bias."

"Jesus," Ambrose shook his head at Gray, "you can't see past yourself for anything, can you? Everything is some sort of an affront to you. You've always been like that, far back as I can recall. You need to get over it and see the writing on the wall, man. Cooperate, or they'll jam you up and take down Parker, too."

"I don't need you to analyze me, lieutenant."

Gray stormed down the hallway.

"Where are you going?"

Gray turned. "For a walk. Maybe figure out how to see past myself."

Descending the staircase to the department lobby, Gray brushed past the people gathered at the bottom. He threw open the glass doors as hard as he could, hoping to empty his body of frustration. But that didn't work. Every step outside in the Florida heat seemed only to stoke his rage over the investigation, about what Ambrose said to him, and about how he'd put Parker's career — and ultimately their friendship — in jeopardy by his own narrowminded focus on Tony Mason. He wanted to scream; McKee and Ambrose were both right about him. That's what infuriated him the most.

Gray's walk was short. He climbed into his Honda Accord and sped out of the parking lot without regard for others.

CHAPTER 7

Lakeland was founded on the phosphate and citrus industries, beginning in the late 1800s. The most vital element of that growth was the railway system, brought into Lakeland by Henry B. Plant and supervised by Herbert J. Drane, while Abraham Munn built the first train station giving Lakeland a stop on the South Florida Railway line. By 1920 and west of downtown Lakeland near Lake Bonnet, a railyard was established where the train cars were stored and dispatched. The railyard was complete with a man-powered turntable, coal chute, water tower, railroad offices, and repair shops. More than two dozen tracks sent railcars all over the state — Tampa, Orlando, and Fort Myers. Parker and his wife lived on Lake Bonnet. If they'd lived there during the 1920s, they'd have been able to see the railyard across the lake. Today, they would see a housing development and fire station, as well as a cell phone tower stretched high toward the clouds.

Gray steered his car down Parker's long driveway. There was no gate across the driveway, but to the left and right of it, a two-rail estate fence ran along the property line. Gray recalled hearing Parker talk about installing the fence. It had been such hard work that he was jokingly afraid of having a heart attack during the process. The house was a ranch-style design with a two-car carport, red-brick with white trim and shudders. The hunter green front door was decorated by a colorful autumn wreath. Both of the family's cars were in the carport.

Bringing the car to a stop at the edge of the sidewalk that led to the front door, Gray realized this was only the third time he had been to the house. That fact accompanied with the feeling he was losing Parker as a friend troubled him and made him feel empty.

Gray held down the power button on his cell phone, turning it off. By now Ambrose and McKee had grasped that Gray wouldn't be returning from his "walk," and they'd be calling him any second. Once out of the car, he slipped the phone into his front pocket before heading to the front door to ring the bell. But before Gray reached his destination, the house door opened and Parker emerged. He was wearing shorts, a t-shirt, a flipflop on his left foot, and a medical boot on his right. While Gray had suffered four broken ribs during the Sumterville confrontation with Tony Mason, Parker had fared worse, suffering a concussion and a torn ligament in his right ankle. His hands were tucked in his pockets. His posture looked rigid, and he sported an uncharacteristically blank expression on his face. Usually Parker donned a smile a mile wide when he saw Gray. The boot and the lack of a welcoming smile were visual representations of the status of their friendship, and they made Gray halt his advance and think that he'd made a mistake in coming by.

They stood 10 feet apart. Both were shielded from the sun by the enormous oak tree in the front yard and its vast collection of moss hanging down. Parker held position on the front step towering over Gray, who remained motionless on the sidewalk.

"How's Karen?" Gray asked.

"She's doing all right, thanks."

"And your ankle."

"Healing. Shouldn't you be busy right now?" Parker checked his watch to be sure of his statement.

"I left when I heard Karen had been taken to the hospital."

"That was probably ill-advised."

"I didn't ask permission."

"Never occurred to me that you did."

They let silence fill in the space between them. Normally Gray wouldn't think anything of the last remark from Parker, but based on their falling out, he knew it was an acerbic shot aimed right at Gray's self-centered behavior.

Parker finally asked, "What are you doing here?"

"You haven't returned my calls."

"I didn't have anything to say to you."

This time Parker's response stung, which immediately deployed Gray's guard.

"Maybe I had a few things to say to you. Ever think of that?" Gray fired back at him.

"I thought I'd been clear with you. It doesn't matter anymore what you have to say."

Parker's words were beginning to leave wounds.

"You were clear, but I have a right to be heard."

"Just like I had the right to decide if I wanted to run off with you to confront Mason in Sumterville."

The wounds were deepening.

Parker immediately wanted to throw a rope around the comment and pull it back into his mouth. It wasn't like him to lash out at people, to take his frustration out on others. And that's what he was doing, taking things out on Gray. He knew there was more at play than just Gray's actions in Sumterville. He wasn't only mad at Gray. He was mad at his wife, too. At the time of the Mason case, she hadn't yet told him about the pregnancy. As long as they'd been trying to conceive and as disappointing of a journey it had been for both of them, she didn't want to tell him about the baby before she knew how sustainable this attempt would be.

Further, he was mad at himself. Even if he'd known about the baby and if Gray had told him about Mason, he knew he still would've gone with Gray. They were partners. Friends. They backed each other even when they should choose family over partnership.

"It would've been one thing if you'd been honest with me about why Morgan Beringer mattered so much, but you weren't."

Gray's temperament had entirely soured. He only came to apologize to his friend in an attempt at correcting what he'd done wrong, to check on Karen, and maybe figure out how to protect his friend from the investigation. Naively, he hadn't figured on Parker's continued animosity.

"Because I didn't really know. I still don't. She was a friend. She was a victim. She was nice to me. I don't know." Gray was nearly yelling now. "Whatever it was, she meant something. And that's all I do know."

"You may want to figure it out because, whatever it was, it killed our partnership." Then Parker said, as if under his breath but completely audible, "Not that it was all that great in the first place."

"Well, you were the fucking best," he shouted, trying to speak more openly and honestly than he ever had. Then he said at a calmer, normal level, "And I'm sorry for what I did."

Parker, surprised by Gray's weakly attempted apology, stared at him blankly, waiting to see if there was a catch.

"I keep hearing what a selfish ass I am — it's apparently a common theme these days — and I'm figuring out people may be right." It felt weird to say this out loud. It made him feel vulnerable. "I don't want to be like that anymore."

Parker nodded, accepting what Gray was saying. But Gray doubted whether Parker accepted the apology.

"I'm trying not to be," Gray concluded his mea culpa.

"Good," Parker said.

Gray noticed that Parker's wife, Karen, had emerged from the house. She stood in the doorway behind Parker. The baby bump wasn't yet noticeable, but the bandages from her IVs were. The shouting likely drew her outside. Gray waved hesitantly to her and gave her a half smile, neither of which she returned. Parker turned abruptly, startled at her presence as well. She walked toward her husband, who welcomed her to his side.

The sight of Karen Parker sparked a memory for Gray. He recalled the months before his daughter, Gracie, was born. He and his ex-wife worried about how they'd afford all they needed. Maintaining insurance coverage for the family was one of the biggest concerns. He remembered how important his job at the department was for their family. At the time, his ex-wife wasn't working, and finances were tight. The baby was going to restrict their finances to levels they'd never experienced.

"Congratulations," Gray said. "I'm happy for both of you."

CHAPTER 8

When it had first opened, the outdoor bar and grill had tables situated across a patio the size of a residential lot. Palm trees acted as corner flags for the patio. Potted shrubs, hibiscus, ferns, and an assortment of other perennial plants edged the rest of the property line. Bleached riverbed rocks had been spread across the lot and acted as the walking surface, but they had been removed because women couldn't walk in heels across them. Now the ground was covered with pine straw, and plastic walkways had been laid between the tables and the entrance. The tables were no longer under the stars. A tent had been erected to protect the guests from the fast-changing Florida weather. Without the tent, one minute the guests could be enjoying their wine and listening to an acoustic rendition of James Taylor's *Carolina on my Mind*, and in the next minute they could be running from a pop-up thunderstorm in search of shelter. Now there was little need to run for cover.

While the food was delicious at the establishment, it was better known as a good place to grab an alcoholic drink. Jordan Butler walked through the entryway, worried at what she'd find. Since Gray had told her he didn't drink and was a recovering alcoholic, this was an unlikely place for him to ask her to meet after her 11 p.m. newscast. Even more worrisome to her was that he'd called her at 8 p.m., and it was now after 1 a.m.

The lighting was dim and came from the stringed lights running the perimeter of the tent. There was no live musician, but *Bright Lights* by

Gary Clark, Jr. played from a speaker hidden somewhere. She recognized the song from a movie, but she couldn't recall which.

Butler glanced through the thin crowd of 15 to 20 people and found Gray quickly. He was the only person sitting alone at a table. The other parties ranged in groups of two to six people. Laughter and conversation came from the larger groups. Butler worried what would come from Gray's table when she made her way to him. The remains of a meal were spread across his table. Her eyes zeroed in on an empty tumbler in front of him.

It was only when she approached the table that Gray realized Butler had arrived.

"Hi. Welcome."

He pushed his chair back and stood. The pain in his ribs only scarcely present.

"Thank you," she said, relieved that Gray didn't appear intoxicated.

A quick, gentle hug served as their greeting. He pulled out her chair and allowed her to sit. Gray waved over the waitress before returning to his seat. They were warned that the kitchen was closed, so only limited food items were available, and they were informed that last call was in 30 minutes. Butler ordered a chardonnay and a cheese platter.

"Just bring me another thing of water." Gray held his tumbler in the air.

Before the waitress left, she cleared the table of the remains of Gray's meal. Gray and Butler waited to speak until she hurried off.

"Today was your meeting with the inquiry team, right? How'd it go?"

Gray leaned on the table and fingered his tumbler, thinking of how best to summarize his day. After he left Parker's house, he had driven to Cocoa Beach in an attempt to find the peace he'd discovered in Pensacola. He'd found a restaurant on the beach where he had eaten a late lunch. Thin clouds stretched across the blue sky. Quirky palm trees twisted and turned before they sprouted at the top. Lush beach shrubs hid the white sand which stretched to the crashing ocean. But instead of peace, he had found only worry.

Despite his own advice recommending against it, he had finally turned on his cell phone. Text messages and voicemail alerts rattled like a machine gun's volley before falling silent. The text messages began as inquiries — *Detective, are you coming back to finish the interview?* — and ended as threats — *If you don't get your ass back in this seat, you'll find you have no ass to sit on.* He didn't respond to Ambrose, McKee, or even Chief Boudreaux, preferring to stay focused on fixing the situation and his friendship with Parker.

"Today was shitty."

Gray finally looked at her and smiled. It seemed odd that he was there with her. Odd that they'd found friendship. Odd that he wanted her there, that he couldn't think of anyone else he'd rather talk to.

"Tell me about your day first," he insisted.

She, in an instant, appeared tired. She'd arrived in flat shoes, jeans, and a blouse she'd worn on the nightly news cast, and her hair and makeup were perfect. She had originally looked vibrant, alive, and happy to be there. Now Gray noticed she looked ready to sleep. He suddenly felt bad for keeping her out so late.

"I spent the last few days on assignment in Anna Maria Island. Did you hear about the hands and legs washing up on shore?"

"What? No!"

"Yeah. Most of them hit Anna Maria, Holmes, and Bradenton beaches. There were a few limbs fished out of the ocean, and a couple more parts washed up in Fort Myers and Naples."

"I hadn't heard about any of it."

"Then you obviously haven't been watching my news reports at all this week."

"I haven't. Sorry."

"I love what I do, but the hotel I stayed in down there had the loudest A/C units," she said. "I slept terribly. Today was my first day back in town, and I had to co-anchor tonight to cover Anna Lee's vacation."

"Anna Lee?"

"Anna Lee Costas. She's the lead female anchor."

"Right. Of course." He wanted to kick himself for not having watched her on the news and not knowing more about her professional life.

"I'm just looking forward to sleeping in my own bed."

"I understand that."

She sat up straight and pretended to be vibrant again. "Enough deflecting," she said. "What's going on, Becker?"

The waitress returned and delivered the order. She set down the check, too. Gray paid it. Butler thanked him for buying her appetizer and drink.

"You're welcome. Thank you for coming."

She smiled, appreciative of his gratefulness, but she waited on him to speak while also digging in to the cheese platter.

He took a moment to build courage because he hated sharing with people, but Parker had taught him — just that morning — that to connect with people Gray had to share himself with them. Then he said, "It didn't go well, Jordan."

"What happened?"

"I'm handing in my badge tomorrow."

Butler shot up in her seat. "Wait! What? Why?" She swallowed the food in her mouth. "What happened?"

"They're looking for a scapegoat. It's pretty clear I'm in their crosshairs. And you know what? They're right to be questioning me. I didn't follow procedure. I put myself and my partner at risk. Shit, I told a high-ranking officer to eat her gun."

"That's intense when you put it like that, Becker."

"Intense and probably career-ending," he said morosely. "Especially framed within the police corruption that was exposed. Max's murder. Like, they're gunning hard for people to blame."

"Don't give up. Fight them. I can help. Let me talk to my news director and see how close we can get to the people spearheading this thing. Boudreaux owes me a favor."

It was a gracious offer. Gray said, "Thanks, Jordan, but no. It's all right. I'm not giving up. I'm not skipping out on the fight. I'm just going to save everyone the trouble and make it easy on the department and the other police officers."

"You got Cannon to turn herself in for Max's murder. You chased down Tony Mason. That has to count for something."

He thought about Mason with the mention of his name. He wondered how he'd keep tabs on the investigation if he wasn't a police officer.

"None of that matters now. Not with the politics behind the investigation. It's a done deal."

"Wow," Butler said, stunned. "I was not expecting this."

He chuckled. "It's not what I had planned for the day either."

"Are you really okay with this?"

"I think so. I've never really thought about not being a cop, but it beats the alternative."

"Which is?" she asked.

He hesitated. "I don't know. I haven't really consulted anyone. I just … I felt like I needed to tell someone, and I could only think of you."

"I'm flattered." She meant it, but she was still in shock. "You didn't tell Jeff?"

"He doesn't know."

"Oh," she said. She wondered if that meant Gray really hadn't decided? Had he invited her here to listen to him or to help him figure out what he wanted to do? "Are you going to tell him?"

"No, I don't think so. Not yet anyway."

Two of the larger parties stirred at their tables. They got up, said their good byes, and then left through the tent's narrow entryway. It started the domino effect. Within a few minutes, Gray and Butler were the only remaining customers. The staff members, in a passive aggressive approach to kicking Gray and Butler out, began stacking chairs and cleaning off the other tables.

During that time, Butler thought she had figured out why Gray hadn't or wasn't planning on telling Parker. "This is all about Parker, isn't it? Are you taking the blame, so he won't be punished?"

Gray didn't want to respond. Here he thought he was doing the right thing by protecting his partner, whom he put in danger in the first place. But, the way she asked the question, it seemed like maybe it was the wrong thing.

"Aren't you?" she pressed further.

"His wife's pregnant. He needs to keep his job."

"So you're sacrificing yourself and your career?"

Gray shrugged his shoulders. "Yes," he said as if it was the only option. "You don't think I should?"

She leaned against the chair. "I don't know. I'm just in shock. Honestly, this may sound harsh, I know, but I haven't known you long enough to have any say in this at all."

"That's not harsh."

She studied his face for a speck of doubt. When she didn't see any, she said, "There's got to be another way."

"There isn't, Jordan."

"You're a good friend. I don't know many people who'd do something like this."

Gray shook it off. It had been a long time since he'd felt like a good friend.

"I don't know if that's it or not. I fucked up out there. And all he did was cover my back. He shouldn't pay the price for my mistakes."

"Okay. I can respect that," she said. "Are you sure they wouldn't just slap you on the wrist? I mean, giving up your career is a big deal. Shouldn't you make sure they're really going to come after you?"

He shook his head. "They're coming."

"Let me put it another way. Will handing in your badge really protect Jeff? Or, will they accept your badge and resignation, and then go after him anyway?"

"I'd make it part of my agreement that Parker be left alone."

She thought about that. "You really think they'd go for it?"

"I do."

"Why would they? You make it sound like they have you cornered anyway. What is so special about your resignation that they'd agree to your terms?"

"They want someone to fall on the sword. I'm willing to do that. This isn't an investigation about what's right or wrong. The goal they have is to clean up the image. It's the city protecting itself."

She thought a moment before speaking. She analyzed his facial expression, still trying to assess the situation and provide reasonable input. And in doing so, she realized Gray hadn't asked her opinion, although she was giving it in her responses. She wasn't playing devil's advocate here. She truly disagreed with Gray's decision.

"Are you just doing this to make yourself feel better?"

"I don't think that's it."

The waitress and the bartender finally approached the table and shooed Gray and Butler from the premises. Gray asked her where she'd parked. She pointed to a lot across the street, behind a law firm's large building. Gray walked her to her car.

"We aired a story about the inquiry at LPD tonight. There'll be more follow-up tomorrow. You'll be on TV."

"It won't be the first time," Gray said.

"I guess I was just letting you know that they won't get any information from me. Unless you give me permission and an angle."

"Thanks," Gray said. This was the single best attribute of their young friendship that Gray had discovered. He respected her ability to keep their jobs separate from their relationship.

They arrived at her car. She unlocked it with the key fob, opened the door, and set her purse on the floorboard.

"I want to ask you one more thing."

She closed the door and leaned against the car.

Gray tucked his hands in his pockets and waited for the question.

"Why did you want to become a detective?"

His eyebrows rose in surprise. He thought her question was going to be, "What will you do if you're not a cop?" To which he'd answer honestly that he had no idea.

Embarrassed at misreading her, he said, "I haven't thought about that in years."

While taking a long time to answer the question, she maintained her smile and expectant eyes. She crossed her arms across her chest, proud that she was making him think. And showing him that she'd stubbornly wait all night for a response was just a bonus. Then his face changed. She guessed he'd found the answer. He frowned, or he crunched his face in what she thought was a frown. She wondered if he didn't like the answer he'd discovered.

Now he crossed his own arms. "I think that's a good question, Jordan. I'll put some thought into it before I do anything tomorrow. I promise."

Her arms fell to her sides, disappointed.

"That's it?"

She waited again for a response. All she got was a shrug of his shoulders.

He nodded. "I'll let you know," he said. "Thanks again for coming."

He gave her a quick, half-hug and turned to leave.

She sighed, still wanting desperately to understand his change of mood, his decision, his thought process. Butler decided she wasn't letting the moment go by. She hurried after him and tugged on his arm to turn him around.

"Becker, wait. What the hell just happened?"

Their eyes met, which sent an unsettling pulse blasting through Gray's body.

"I don't know," he said.

"Yes, you do."

She always did this — chased guys who were emotionally difficult and pushed them too hard, too soon. This time, as opposed to other times, her forwardness was about him, not her. She held firm. He was going to answer her.

He noticed she still had hold of his arm. He trusted her, but he didn't understand why he was having such a hard time answering her question? Was it her hand on his arm? Was it what that may represent? What did it represent? Was he afraid if he shared himself with her that she'd pull her hand away? Worse, pull away altogether? Or, was the reason simply too hard for him to say? It didn't matter, he decided, looking down at her hand. He needed to just say it. Butler was sincerely attempting to help him. She was the only one sincerely attempting to help him. He needed that person in his life.

"I had a daughter who died in a car accident."

"Oh my God." Butler retracted her hand and put it over her mouth. She instantly felt like she'd trampled all over his privacy. "I'm so sorry. You don't have to say anything else."

He smiled, appreciating her back peddling. "You opened the floodgates, girl. You're getting it." As best as he could, he delivered the statement in a jovial tone to make her feel more at ease, putting her feelings ahead of his own overwhelming discomfort.

She laughed awkwardly but didn't respond. She felt he needed to speak at his own rate, and she'd once and for all learned her lesson on pushing men to open up to her.

"She was ejected from the car." He eventually forced the words out of his mouth, but they felt like they had come from deeper inside. "Her mother was fine, minus a baseball-sized bump on her head. I was fine, I think."

Butler's fingers stayed over her gaping mouth.

"I got out of the car to look for her when I realized she wasn't in the back seat."

Tears built in Butler's eyes. The horror of the situation was too much for her. And, as for him, she could see it in his face; the pain was as raw now as it had been then.

Gray finally looked at Butler. Seeing her tears, he teared, too. He swallowed hard as if consuming his own pain, fighting to keep his tears under control.

"I remember the helplessness I felt when I was looking for her. It was ... " He searched for the words, but he quickly surrendered the effort and cleared his throat, pushing aside the raw memory. "I became a detective because I understood the helplessness people experience in these kinds of terrible situations. And I think people deserve hope in helpless times. Without it, what do people have?" He heard the words for the first time ever, and he understood the irony of why he became a detective and how he had treated himself since Gracie's death.

"Sorry." Butler apologized for her emotions, wiping away her tears.

He'd never felt so self-conscious. He wiped his face dry.

"What hope," she asked, "did you hang on to during that period of your life?"

"None." He thought about all the times he drank the sorrow away. "I had none." The vulnerability got the best of him. "It was stupid."

"It's not." She grabbed both his arms, looked into his eyes. "It's not."

"Okay," he said, not believing her.

"What was your daughter's name?" Butler asked, letting go of Gray.

"Grace."

Butterflies flapped in Gray's stomach. Saying her name aloud was surreal.

"Beautiful name," she said.

"Yeah."

That moment hung in the air between them, hopeful from Butler's perspective and uncomfortable for Gray.

"Maybe you should think about that before you hand in your badge." She stepped toward him, pushed herself onto her toes, and kissed Gray's cheek. "Thank you for telling me," she whispered in his ear.

Her warm breath against his skin sent goosebumps down his spine.

"It's late," she said, pulling away from him.

Gray agreed.

"Are you okay?" she asked.

"Fine. You?"

She smiled. She was.

"You'll let me know what you decide?" she asked.

"I'll call you tomorrow," he said.

Butler left Gray there in the parking lot, his mind spinning like an out of control carousel. His badge. Gracie. The memories. Butler. The touch on his arm. The kiss. The long, likely sleepless, night ahead. Round and round.

CHAPTER 9

Since waking early after a near sleepless night, Gray had phoned Parker eight times with no response. Nor had his old friend responded to the multiple text messages Gray had sent. Parker was still giving Gray the cold shoulder, which Gray understood but thought was growing stale. Gray, half dressed, checked his watch — there was still an hour and a half before Parker was to report for his interview with TEAM. Gray had to stop him.

From Gray's apartment, the drive to Parker's house usually took 20 minutes with traffic. Plenty of time to catch Parker before he'd leave for the interview. Gray finished dressing while hurrying down the stairs to his car. As he kicked the car's engine into action, his cell vibrated. Thinking — hoping — it was Parker, he pulled the phone from his trousers' pocket. Instead of a response from Parker, the vibration had been an arriving text from Jordan Butler.

Good luck today. Thinking of you. Hope it goes well.

Frustrated at Parker's nonresponse, he jerked the gear into reverse and pulled quickly out of the parking space. At a red light on Harden Boulevard, Gray texted her back.

Thanks. Will call you later.

The rest of the drive to Parker's house was stop and go. Red light after red light. It was as if he hit every possible delay along the way. On top of the red lights, morning traffic congested the winding route that stretched from south Lakeland and continued north past downtown where it had its first of two name changes within the city limits. He cut left on Hartsell and rounded Lake Beulah before reaching George Jenkins Boulevard where he steered along sideroads circling Lake Bonnet. Yet one more delay, a school bus ceased his progress right before the turn onto Candyce Avenue, where Parker lived. Gray checked his watch impatiently, as neighborhood children loaded onto the bus. His whole body quivered with nerves. Finally, the bus pulled away, freeing Gray's path down Candyce.

He soon yanked the wheel, taking the car into Parker's long drive way. He stopped short. Parker's car was gone.

He checked his watch again. It was only eight a.m.

Where is he?

Did he go get breakfast before going in? Did he go in early? Why would he go in early?

He went to get coffee.

Parker grabbed coffee at a shop in downtown Lakeland almost every morning. And Parker, he knew, was a creature of habit.

The drive to Munn Park didn't take long. Traffic along West Main Street was practically non-existent. It made Gray wonder why so many of the city's residents stayed on the busy roads during rush hour instead of hitting the side streets. Stress levels would be lower. There'd be fewer accidents. Plus, they'd find out-of-the-way retailers, like the coffee roasters and local gym hiding along this less-traveled road.

Gray double-parked on Tennessee and hurried toward the coffee shop. The line extended out the front door. Gray pushed his way past the line and into the seating area. Most people in the long line worked downtown. It was common for them to stop by the shop where the baristas knew their names, grab their morning java, and head to work, which left the seating area often quite empty. Parker wasn't there.

Shit.

Back inside his Accord, he ignored a horn blaring a protest of Gray's illegal parking job. The car rolled by, curving into the oncoming lane. Gray had to figure out what to do next. He was down to almost 30 minutes before Parker's interview was scheduled to begin.

He could only think of one thing to do. He grabbed his phone and searched back through the call log. He found the number he wanted and pressed the Call button.

"Hello?" Julian Weech answered his phone.

"Justin, it's Detective Gray."

"It's Julian."

Gray was not concerned that he got the name wrong again.

"What can I do for you, detective? We missed you yesterday. Lost a whole day of the investigation when you didn't return. Can't say the city management was happy about that." Weech's annoyance at Gray was evident.

Gray didn't care. "I'm ready to come in. I want to meet with McGoo."

"You mean, McKee. Peter McKee," Weech said, putting extra annunciation on the "K."

"Exactly."

"He's meeting with another detective this morning."

"Yeah, I know, But I need to speak with McGoo first."

"McKee."

"I'm on my way to the department. I want to meet with him as soon as I get there."

"Detective, I'm uncertain how you think you can dictate how all this works."

"Listen, kid. Cancel the meeting McGoo has with Detective Parker and have him meet with me instead. I'm ready."

"What does that mean?"

"Just tell him."

Weech sighed into the phone. It sounded like a tropical storm gust of wind into the receiver. Gray pulled his head away to protect his hearing.

"Fine," Weech finally said. "When will you be here?"

Gray threw the car into drive and coaxed the car quickly south on Tennessee toward Lemon, where he'd circle back to Massachusetts and the police department.

"Eight minutes. Tops."

"Fine. Meet in the conference room where we were yesterday."

Gray disconnected the call and pushed the speed to a limit unsafe on these short, downtown streets.

Caught by more red lights, he didn't get to the department for eleven minutes. He parked in the guest parking area and rushed through the glass, double doors at the front of the building. He bounded up the stairs. Sweat gathered on his brow and body.

He burst into the conference room. His breath caught, though, when he saw McKee wasn't there. Only Weech.

"Where's McGoo?"

Weech stood from behind the table.

"Are you doing that on purpose?"

"Where is he?"

"He elected not to attend your meeting. Much as you elected not to attend his yesterday. So, I'm here."

"He's meeting with Parker?"

Weech didn't answer the question.

"Where?" Gray moved to rush out of the room.

"Gray! He's not here. They're meeting off site."

"Don't make me ask you again."

"I'm not going to tell you."

Gray stepped further into the room. His gaze threatened Weech.

"You're going to tell me, and you're going to tell me now."

A voice came from behind, interrupting Gray's threat. "Gray." It reverberated through the conference room. The strength of the voice was undeniable.

Gray turned after a final glare at Weech.

"Chief."

Boudreaux nodded at him, knowing he was de-escalating a situation yet choosing not to address it.

"I have someone here who wants to meet you."

Detective Saleena Salah stepped from behind the chief of Lakeland police.

"We need to talk in my office now," Boudreaux said.

CHAPTER 10

After a transitory introduction outside the conference room, the party moved to Boudreaux's office. Weech was asked to tag along, which irritated Gray. Why Boudreaux wanted him to do so was beyond Gray's imagination. Inside Boudreaux's office were more people. Two of whom Gray wasn't happy to see, and the other was a stranger, like Salah.

Boudreaux played host.

"Have a seat where you can," he said, rounding his desk.

John Collanger had one of two guest seats parked in front of Boudreaux's desk. He ignored Gray when he entered. Collanger was the mayor pro tem and had been one of the two driving forces behind the TEAM inquiry, as well as the politicking surrounding the police department. He was running for mayor in the upcoming special election.

Joined at the hip since the mayor's untimely murder, Mike Walters, the city manager, was in the room as well. He was the other driving force behind the inquiry. Walters took his space along the lengthy, interior wall, leaning against the shelves of books and department memorabilia. Gray wondered why Walters was so closely involved in all this. The city manager wasn't a political appointment. He had a job, no matter who was mayor. He didn't need to follow Collanger around like a shadow.

Weech grabbed the first seat he could find. He pressed his hind side to the couch cushion in the back of the chief's office, closest to the door. He leaned his elbows on his knees, fidgeted with his phone.

Gray and Salah remained standing. Salah's supervisor, Lt. Lance Davis, held his position in the second of two guest chairs, next to Collanger.

Davis struggled against his rotund stomach to get to his feet. Once he did so, he moved toward Gray, and they shook hands.

"Lt. Lance Davis. Nice to meet you, detective."

"Likewise," Gray said.

Walters nodded to Gray, so he responded in kind.

"Introductions have all been made, minus Mr. Weech in the back. He's with TEAM Consulting, who is heading up the inquiry we've all briefly discussed prior to bringing Detective Gray into the room." Boudreaux announced, "Now we can get started."

Boudreaux waited for Weech to wave a greeting and for Davis to sit down again before he continued.

"Lt. Davis and Detective Salah are here from the Manatee Sheriff's Office. They have a case they'd like to discuss with Detective Gray."

Gray shot Salah a look, wondering what case. She nodded, telling him it was worth the wait but it wasn't time yet to talk about the case.

Boudreaux saw the objections coming from Collanger and Weech, but he headed them off. "In the spirit of interagency cooperation, I, of course, agreed to allow them access to Detective Gray," the chief said. "However, because of the tentative nature of the department inquiry initiated by Mr. Walters and the city, I brought you all here together, so we can discuss this cordially."

Collanger was the first to raise objection and it coincided with his standing. "Chief, this is unacceptable. Detective Gray is being investigated for a multitude of departmental policy and procedural errors. Not just errors, but grievous impropriety in the way he conducts his duties."

Gray started to speak, but Boudreaux glared at him, telling him to keep silent.

Boudreaux then said, "Interesting word choices, Mr. Collanger. It's my understanding that this is an inquiry and not an investigation. Furthermore, from the scope of work defined by the city, TEAM's focus is to determine 'improvements in departmental policies and procedures,' as well as to offer recommendations on 'potential structural and administrative changes' in an effort to increase 'synergy between interdepartmental teams.' Not solely to focus on one man." Boudreaux glared at Collanger. "Isn't that right, Mr. Weech?"

"That is, in fact, accurate, chief," Weech said from the back of the room.

Gray smiled. That was why Boudreaux allowed Weech to tag along. He was Boudreaux's tool.

Boudreaux continued, "Are you openly suggesting, Mr. Collanger, that there are other, undocumented agendas attached to this inquiry?"

Collanger was quick to backpedal. "I'm suggesting that Detective Gray is an integral component to the inquiries' completeness. Without him, the inquiry cannot be wrapped up in a timely manner, as the city has requested and the public deserves. For the record, he missed his first scheduled meeting with TEAM on Wednesday and he only interacted with the investigators yesterday for approximately one hour before skipping out on the rest of the eight-hour session."

"Stomach virus," Gray said.

As Boudreaux shot Gray a stern look, Salah smiled slyly, knowing a lie when she heard it. No law enforcement officers appreciated these types of inquiries, so she appreciated Gray's desire to make the process as difficult as possible.

"Detective Salah," Boudreaux said, "didn't we just pull Detective Gray from the conference room, where it appeared he wanted to finish out his questioning?"

She startled, surprised to hear herself being addressed, and wished to not be brought into this conversation. This wasn't her fight. However, she'd been asked a question. "We did pull him from the conference room while he was talking to Mr. Weech, yes."

"You're protecting him like you always have, chief, and this is part of the reason for the inquiry." Collanger felt his power being undermined by Boudreaux's manipulation of the situation.

"All right, enough," Walters finally said something. "The inquiry can continue without Gray for now, but he is a key member of the staff who needs to be questioned, chief."

"No one here has suggested otherwise," Boudreaux said.

Collanger sulked.

"How long will he be needed, lieutenant?" Walters asked Davis.

Davis pushed himself up straight in his chair, feeling much the same way as Salah about being included in the conversation. "If all goes well, just a day. Sal, do you agree?"

"If all goes well, yes, sir," she said.

"Hang on," Gray said, pumping the brakes on the conversation. "Does anyone care if I want to be involved in this? I mean, I don't have my badge or my gun right now, and I have no intention of being brought into a case and not seeing it through. I already have one of those on the table."

Boudreaux knew Gray was referring to the Tony Mason case.

"You'll be reinstated for the duration of your involvement."

Walters said, "That's a bit of a concern, chief."

"Not for me, it isn't," Boudreaux retorted quickly, caring little about the public perception of Gray's reinstatement. That was Walters and Collanger's issue, not his.

"I'd like to complete the inquiry first," Gray stated, thinking of protecting Parker.

"I think that's a good idea," Collanger said.

Salah stepped up. "We have a small window on this case, detective. Kind of need you now. Today, in fact."

"Why today? What case is this? And how am I connected?"

Davis suggested, "Chief, maybe we should discuss the specifics of the case?"

"Not in front of everyone. To be clear, gentlemen, I'm still the chief of police and this is still my department. Manatee County has asked for our help, and we're going to give it to them. This is happening. You can beat me up all you want after this meeting, in the press, or during your election. Right now, I don't care. I only invited each of you and included you in this conversation as a selfish gesture. I didn't want to have to inform each of you individually, thus repeating myself."

Walters sighed, disappointed at Boudreaux's line in the sand. Collanger sneered at him. They both stood. Behind them, Weech stood as well. Weech was typing on his phone, surely texting McKee about the change of plans.

Davis stood. "Nice to meet you all." He stuck out his hand for a cordial handshake, but Collanger stormed out of the office. Walters shook his hand and offered good luck on the case.

"Chief, we'll talk this afternoon," Walters said.

Boudreaux nodded and watched as all three exited, leaving just the law enforcement officers behind.

"I'm sorry about that, everyone. Kind of airing our laundry a bit," Boudreaux said.

"Ain't a problem," Davis said. "We all have laundry, chief."

Davis moved to where Collanger had been sitting. Gray ushered Salah to the chair freed by Davis's shifting of places. Gray remained standing.

"Grab a chair from the waiting area, Becker. Talk to Mary while you're out there. She should already have your badge and weapon."

Gray hurried out of the room to Mary Tillman's desk — Boudreaux's administrative assistant — and returned with a chair. His badge and weapon already hooked onto his belt.

"All right, folks. Please, detective, go ahead," Boudreaux said.

CHAPTER 11

Saleena Salah turned in her chair to face Gray. His chair blocked the walkway around Boudreaux's desk, to Salah's left. As she looked directly at him. Her dark eyes and dark hair were stunning, but what was most prominent was her confident demeanor.

"Does the name Kenneth Lamont Duncan mean anything to you?" she asked.

The name sent a rush of excitement, curiosity, and intrigue through Gray's body. He immediately pictured Duncan, baby-faced with piercings in his ears, eyebrows, nose, cheeks, and lips. While the quantity of piercings seemed many when listed out, they weren't when you looked at him. They weren't showpieces. They somehow accentuated his face instead of overpowering it. The hair on the sides of his skull were cropped short. The hair on top of his head was long, permed, and dyed purple and yellow. His complexion was smooth and tanned. He carried a healthy frame but wore it well.

"It does."

"What do you recall?"

Gray shifted in his seat and leaned toward her.

"My involvement was limited with him. A local family — the Chrittons — reported their twenty-year-old son missing. Duncan eventually was brought in somewhere in north Florida related to a string of disappearances. Up in Dixie County, I think. Maybe Leon, I can't recall exactly. During the questioning performed by the local PD, he confessed to multiple killings. One of them was Noah Chritton, which sent those investigators to me since I had his case here. I went to Tallahassee — it was Leon County — and interviewed him. The information he gave me seemed to check out. That was about it. Noah's body was never recovered, but Duncan led law enforcement to two other victims' bodies. He was convicted and sentenced to life. That's all I recall."

"Are the Chrittons still here in town?" she asked.

"Far as I know."

Davis spoke up. "Have you seen on the news anything about the body parts washing ashore down in Manatee County and further down along the gulf coast?"

This was the story Jordan Butler had mentioned the previous night. "I haven't heard specifics."

Salah said, "Back during your investigation, do you remember Noah's parents submitting their DNA for familial genetic matching in case a body was ever found?"

The reason for Duncan's sudden importance clicked. "Hold on. Are you saying some of those body parts are Noah's?"

"A hand and calf were a match to the familial DNA submitted by Charles and Claudia Chritton," Salah said.

"Holy shit," Gray whispered to himself, but everyone heard him. Then his detective mind flipped a switch. Ideas, scenarios, and information zipped through his mind like confetti being launched by a jet engine. "How can that be?" he finally said, again in a whisper.

"Exactly my question," Salah replied, believing he had come to the same initial conclusion she had. "If Duncan is locked up, then how did these body parts end up in the Gulf of Mexico and on our shores?"

"Right," Gray said. He considered her question. "Is the wrong guy in jail?" Gray asked, looking to Davis and Boudreaux for acknowledgement.

Salah smiled. He had thought of the same question.

"Funny you should ask," Davis spoke up.

"We went to up to Florida State Prison in Raiford to have a chat with him," Salah added, "but he wouldn't talk to us."

"He has no reason to cooperate now," Gray said.

"He doesn't, but that wasn't his issue. He told us he'd only talk to you."

"What?" Gray stood, confused. He paced and thought about that, about Duncan, about their history. "Why?" He stopped marching and looked at the Manatee County staff. "My interaction with him was ... momentary in the grand scheme. I think I asked him maybe twenty-five questions, and we were done."

"You can't think of any reason he'd feel connected to you?" she asked.

"No. Nothing."

Boudreaux leaned forward in his chair and cleared his throat so everyone knew it was his turn to talk. "Becker, you're going with Detective Salah to Raiford to talk to Duncan."

"Okay, sure. Yes. Of course." The rush of intrigue had shifted to confusion.

"But I need to speak with you before you go," Boudreaux said.

Davis and Salah rose and thanked the chief. Davis was heading back to his headquarters in Manatee County and Salah would meet Gray in the lobby in 30 minutes. They closed the door behind them. Becker still stood, the rush in full control. That rush ... that's what he'd miss the most about his job. Piecing the puzzle together. The chase.

"Sit down, Becker."

"This Duncan thing is odd." Gray sat in the closest guest chair.

"You'll get to the bottom of it." Boudreaux leaned back in his chair, like he hadn't the strength to hold his body upright. "I was hoping you'd take this inquiry seriously, Becker."

Gray tried to push aside the buzz brought on by Duncan's name, so he could focus on Boudreaux. As he did so, he noticed the air of power and command of the room Boudreaux had exuded during the meeting with Manatee County and the city management was gone. It had been replaced by weariness, stress, and exhaustion. A new curiosity overtook his concentration.

"I am," Gray said in a defensive tone.

"You are?"

"Now I am."

"As of today?" Boudreaux rested his case when Gray didn't respond. "I asked Ambrose to be your rep because I thought he'd be able to corral you and keep you focused, but I guess no one can do that." Then he said as an afterthought, "I sure as shit couldn't."

Gray raised his voice and spoke emphatically. "We both know Collanger and Walters told TEAM what result they wanted from the inquiry, and McKee's job is to find the pieces of information that support that. I didn't particularly want to participate in that bullshit, Reggie."

"You do now though. Today. Why?"

Gray scratched his head, stalling his response. He thought saying his reasoning out loud would sound stupid. He felt vulnerable, so he offered as little of a response as possible.

"Parker."

Boudreaux understood that Gray wanted to protect his partner. He respected that. But it wasn't Gray's place to protect other people. They were on their own in this.

"You have to worry about you. Parker can handle himself."

Gray grunted and shrugged a shoulder. He didn't agree, and Boudreaux read him.

"We've been on the force together for a long time. I like to think we both respect the other one for the results we get. I just don't think we agree with how we go about achieving those results."

Gray nodded. "Same objectives, different styles."

"Same goes with this inquiry, we have the same objectives, just different styles. You understand?"

"Sure." *No.* And he didn't want to.

Gray was still going to protect Parker. Nothing anyone else said mattered. That was his objective, and he didn't care about anything else.

"Good."

"I want Parker on this Duncan thing with me," Gray said.

"No. Work with Salah. Parker hasn't cleared concussion protocol, and he's wrapped up in the inquiry."

"Get him unwrapped. I need him."

"Becker, leave it."

"Then I want to go back and finish up with Weech before I leave with Salah."

"I'll handle him. Go with her."

"Everyone's been telling me to deal with the inquiry. I'm trying to and now no one is letting me. What the hell?"

"This is bigger than what you want. Stop being so selfish." The boom in Boudreaux's voice returned.

Gray fired back with his own strength and anger. "I need to talk to them *before* they get to Jeff."

"Then you should've shown up for your appointments over the last couple of days." Boudreaux stared at Gray until the point sunk in. Then he said, "Why did you miss them anyway?"

He didn't want to tell Boudreaux he'd been chasing Mason. "I just wasn't ready yet."

"The world doesn't wait on you to be ready, Becker."

"I got it." Gray wanted to shut down the conversation, not needing to be analyzed or parented by yet another person. "But Jeff didn't do anything wrong."

"I know," Boudreaux said with no hesitation. Then he changed the subject. "You really don't know why Duncan asked for you?"

"No idea."

Boudreaux grunted a response. His eyes lowered, and he lost himself in thought for a minute. While thinking, his strength visibly depleted again. He propped his elbows on the arms of his chair and made a tent with his fingers.

"You all right, chief?"

He spoke softly. "I thought I had it all figured out. When I got promoted to chief, I was sure I knew what the department needed, and I knew how to get it. I knew which programs and divisions were important and which ones weren't. I knew how to bridge the gap between the cops and the most criminally at risk in the community. I knew what the guys on the street needed to be better, more efficient, and to be safer. I was supposed to keep the department clean and whole. I knew how to do all of it, how to deal with the external stress, the media, my family, the city politicians, and, shit, even the state politicians. And my plans worked. We had the highest rankings in every measurable category. I had all the answers. I thought I did anyway."

Gray stayed quiet, wondering if this was part of Boudreaux's analysis of Gray or if it was something altogether different. *I thought I had it all figured out.* It sounded like something he could — and probably will at some point — say.

"You're the best person for this job, Reggie. Always have been."

"So, what happened? What did I lose sight of? How did this cyclone of bullshit land in my lap?" Boudreaux asked, bringing the tent down onto his lap.

There were no answers to those questions.

Gray asked, "Have you been interviewed by this McKee asshole?"

Boudreaux smiled, agreeing with Gray's assessment of the lead investigator for TEAM Consulting. "No." Then the smile withered. "I'm not even on the interview list, last I saw."

"How?"

"Because they don't care what I have to say. They're going to pin everything on me and then fire me."

"Do you have a rep?" Gray asked.

Boudreaux shook his head. "A lawyer."

Gray liked that Boudreaux was ready to defend himself.

"Look, Becker … The department will survive. It's just it won't be like it was before. Maybe that's a good thing, and it'll breathe life back into it."

"You don't believe that."

"I believe the spirit of negativity, not just surrounding this inquiry but engulfing the whole country, doesn't bode well for anything coming in our futures. But, as far as the department is specifically concerned, it *has* to be a good thing. I just … I just wasn't ready to give up my shield. It's who I am."

Boudreaux was coming to terms with the same thing Gray had the night before.

"It's not who you are. I've seen you with your kids, Reggie. You have more in your life than this job."

"Maybe."

"No, it's true."

Boudreaux nodded his head, realizing he was feeling sorry for himself. "Thanks." Then he turned the conversation back to Gray. "You … While I'm getting the blame for everything, there's a fair share aimed right at you. Collanger wants your ass, and McKee's coming for it. They've got plenty to hang you with."

Gray nodded. "I know." No regret, remorse, sadness, or emotion in his response.

"Doesn't seem like you care."

"That's not it. I just understand the situation. This thing with Duncan, it'll be my last official police work, I'm sure of it."

"Good," Boudreaux said. "I was worried about you."

"I know what mistakes I made. They're mine. But, Jeff needs — "

"Don't worry about Parker."

The chief leaned forward and grabbed a pen and pad of paper. He scribbled a name on it, then tore the page from the pad and handed it to Gray.

"This is the name of the man leading the task force to find Tony Mason."

Gray took the paper. Read it. ALTON CAMPBELL, FBI.

"It's my parting gift to you. When we're both in the unemployment line, call him. Tell him I think you should be a special consultant to that team. With luck, he'll bring you in or at least keep you informed of the progress they're making."

"Thanks, Reggie."

The chief stood and stretched out his hand. Gray did the same, pushing the paper into his pocket. They shook hands, putting behind them the hundreds of disagreements they'd had about the course investigations should take, the way they both reacted to the media, and years of tension and resentment. They were both in the same boat now. Targets. Losers in this inquiry.

CHAPTER 12

Despite Saleena Salah's insistence on taking State Road 471 through the Green Swamp to Interstate 75, Gray looked forward to the time in the car. If this was indeed going to be his last involvement in a case, he was going to soak it all in. He was going to be prepared. He was going to succeed. And he was going to enjoy the rush. He had a folder full of information on Kenneth Lamont Duncan. With that, Salah also provided him her folder detailing everything about the body parts that had been carried to shore by the gulf's strong currents and lapping waves.

"That's the place, isn't it?" she asked, steering the car past the sign for the Richloam Wildlife Management.

Gray looked up from the folder and out the car window. Not that he needed to. She hadn't said a word since he had cracked the file. It wasn't a coincidence that she'd break her silence now.

"You can't see it from here, but, yeah."

"Would it bother you to talk about it?"

Gray closed the file in his lap.

"I know there's a curiosity about it. About him. But I'd prefer not to talk about it."

She nodded and said, "I was just going to say I'm sorry about your friend."

She meant Morgan Beringer, the mayor's wife. When Tony Mason completed the hit on the mayor, he killed her, too. Gray and Beringer were rumored to have had a relationship that extended beyond friendship.

"Thanks."

He wasn't clear if he was appreciative of the gesture of sympathy or that she'd respect his wish to not discuss it further.

He changed the subject. "This is a thorough profile on Duncan. I hoped I'd have time before we left to go through my archive and find my notes on him, but I don't think I need them. Good job."

"It wasn't just me working it up, but thanks."

"It's helping me remember a lot of information."

"Like what?" she asked.

Gray figured the quiet ride had ended.

"Like him being born in Hemingford, Nebraska. Being raised on a farm until his father was killed in a tractor accident. Duncan was seven.

"His mother couldn't wait to get out of Hemingford. She wanted to go back to Lincoln, where she was from, if I recall correctly. She leased the farmland and took off.

"All of that I remember. This is new, though. I didn't realize he had a hard time in school in Lincoln."

Salah spoke up. "Yeah, according to his mother, the school system in Hemingford was good, but it moved slower than the one in Lincoln. The teachers had a vastly dissimilar teaching style. So, he struggled there, but eventually caught up academically. The kids, though, were the hardest part of the move. His mother hadn't considered that the kids wouldn't accept him."

"It seems like the first thing a parent should worry about with a move like that, no?"

Salah shrugged. "I don't have any kids. I don't know."

"Common sense, though?"

"Right," she agreed. "Did you ever meet his mother?"

Gray shook his head no. "I talked to her once on the phone, but it didn't amount to anything."

"She seems like what we call now a helicopter mom. Too doting."

"Too enabling, you mean?"

"Something like that."

Salah slowed the car's speed to 35 MPH as they entered the city limits of Webster, Florida, a small town known mainly for its large flea market.

"I think she really tried with Kenneth. It had to be hard after her husband died."

"All right."

It was Gray's turn to shrug. He didn't care if she tried. The result wasn't good.

"She did," Salah tried to convince him. "She redirected him and helped him find a new interest."

"Killing people?"

Salah sighed. "You blame his mom?"

"I blame him."

"She did the best she could, I think."

"Did you meet the mom?"

"No," Salah said. "Just talked to her on the phone."

"You seem to be on her side."

"She's a victim here, too. Duncan may have killed those other families' sons, but he killed her version of her son, too."

Gray grunted. He wasn't so sure Duncan's mother was a victim.

Salah blurted out, "You're hard to talk to."

That gave Gray a chuckle. "I've heard that before," he said.

And that lightened the mood.

"What was this new interest his mother helped him find?" Gray asked, giving Salah a break.

"Comic books. He fell in love with them. At one point, she said, he was reading dozens a day."

Gray skimmed the report and found that section. He read it out loud: "He pretended to live in the colorful comic world, where these humanized heroes ranged from social outcasts to physical weaklings to billionaires and everything in between. These heroes had the same 'real-life' struggles as non-heroes — friendship troubles, love life woes, death of a parent or guardian, various other social acceptance issues, and professional stressors — and they somehow always found a way to overcome those struggles as well as the danger brought on by their powerful villain adversaries. There was inspiration on every page with every character." Gray stopped, then looked at her. "Did you write that?"

"No."

"Good. I hate it."

She laughed, leaving Webster city limits and picking up speed. Cordrey "Cord" Phelps had written that. His reports were always like that. Wordy. Slightly psychological. He liked to explain the people he was investigating. Lieutenant and Alex "Dallas" Sanchez always poked fun at Cord's reports.

He read to himself this time: *By the time he turned twelve, his attention for reading comic books waned, and he began treating movies like he'd previously treated comics. Movies like the Star Wars franchise, Blade, Matrix, X-Men, The Lord of the Rings, and the Harry Potter films grabbed his attention the most. He spent most of his free time during the next few years at the theater. So much so, when it was time to get a job, the movie theater manager knew him and hired him on the spot.*

As Duncan delved deeper into the world of movies, he took his fascination with them to a new level. He began constructing costumes of his favorite characters, initially wearing them privately in his bedroom. As he perfected character mannerisms, he wore the costumes to the movie theater when blockbuster movies were released. At first, his attire wasn't welcomed by management, but the children flocked to him, wanting to take photographs with him. And if the kids liked it, then the parents liked it. Happy customers meant repeat customers. He was good for business. Duncan became an attraction in his costumes. It only took a couple months before the movie theater manager began paying Duncan extra for his efforts on release night.

"His mom thinks something happened to him."

"What do you mean?" Gray asked.

"She told me that while the children and the parents at the movie theater loved him in character, the costumes made him a target to meanspirited teens."

"No surprise."

"She assumed there had been some sort of an attack on him. He never told her what happened. Whatever happened, it caused an abrupt end to that part of his life. He stopped dressing in costume. He quit his job at the theater. He stopped watching movies. In fact, she said he threw out all of his DVDs and comic books. All of his costumes, too.

"That somehow turned into him doing drugs and drinking."

That's a bit of a leap there, isn't it?" Gray asked. "You get bullied and then slide directly into drugs and drinking?"

"We've seen crazier shit than that, haven't we?"

"I guess so."

"Of course, we have," she spoke for him.

"Like forcing your kid to join the army. No way he'll be bullied there?"

His cynicism forced a smile across her face. She'd been expecting that response.

"I think it was a last-ditch effort, Becker."

"She's always there to save him. Or, she thinks she is."

She smiled again. Less entertained now by his schtick.

"You're unrelenting."

"Devil's advocate."

Gray attempted to shrug off the notion he was difficult to deal with. He liked Salah. She had a good energy and gave off a positive vibe. He didn't want her to dislike him. Yet he could tell that she doubted the veracity of his response, but he could also tell that she wasn't holding it against him.

"Duncan was a mess when he turned eighteen. Uncontrollable. Depressed. It sounded to me like she didn't know what else to do with him."

"I don't know how many other mothers would drag their son to the U.S. Army recruiters' office and sign him up for service."

"Last-ditch effort."

"I guess."

"You don't have any kids either, do you?" Salah asked.

The question always hurt, but he didn't allow it to weigh him down any longer. "No."

She nodded.

"Can you tell? Is it that obvious?"

Salah responded by smiling at him. A jovial thought flashed in her eyes.

Gray let her enjoy her thought, and he flipped through the report, finding where their conversation had left off.

He read to himself again: *Duncan returned from his tour sober. His mother thought her plan had been successful. She was further pleased when Duncan rekindled his love affair with movies and character costumes. That was short lived, however. Just as his mother couldn't have been any happier — she'd gotten her happy, healthy, normal son back — he left home and never returned.*

"When I interviewed Duncan all those years ago," Gray said, "he told me he never spoke to his mother. She had no idea he'd been working the comic convention circuit as a cosplay actor. Or that that's where he was finding his victims."

"What was he like back then?" Salah asked.

He hadn't thought much of his time with Duncan yet. As she asked the question, the interview replayed in his head at a quick pace and he felt a level of agitation rise. The memories bugged him. There were so many questions he hadn't asked back then. He would have especially zeroed in on the event that Duncan's mother thought changed everything for her son. He scolded himself, making excuses for his lack of follow-through. The questioning came early in his detective career, he told himself, and he had missed the realization of how impactful that connection could've been. Instead, he had moved on with his prepared list of questions — something else he wouldn't do now either. When, really, the issue was that they had Duncan dead to rights, and there was no real reason for Gray to dive any deeper than he had.

Gray pushed aside the self-loathing about questions unasked, and he struggled to remember the questions he had asked. Maybe there was a clue in them that would explain why Duncan had asked for him. He had asked about Noah Chritton. What he was like. What he looked like. How and where they met. How Duncan had selected Chritton? How and where Chritton was killed. The location of the body? About trophies?

Ultimately, Gray found no reason in the questions for Duncan, seven years later, to ask for him.

Duncan's admission of guilt by itself wouldn't have been enough to convict him for Noah Chritton's murder. However, Duncan detailed the murders of a total of fourteen men. Then he led police to two of the men's bodies. The injuries of each body matched the manner and method of murder detailed by Duncan. So, if a district attorney combined all the murders into one case, it would be a strong case. The murders, though, were spread across nine jurisdictions. Collectively the law enforcement agencies decided the jurisdiction with the strongest case should be the one to proceed against Duncan. And that case was the one in Leon County, Florida. Duncan was convicted quickly and without much fanfare for the death of one man. He received a life sentence with no chance for parole. The rest of the cases would go untried and were closed by the respective local DA offices citing the admissions by Duncan.

The Chritton case was Gray's second as a detective and his first homicide solved. He and the local DA were pleased with the outcome. Yet, now, he realized he and the DA had been sloppy, lazy even, in their work surrounding Duncan. They should've pressed harder to obtain the whereabout of Chritton's body.

"What was he like?" Gray repeated her question. "He was … boyish. He seemed shy. Forthcoming, in his own way." Gray really thought through his response. "Not anything like the evil he perpetrated."

She uttered a surprised snicker.

"The evil caught up to him," she said.

"What do you mean?"

"Keep flipping," she said. "You'll see it."

Gray did as she said. He wondered what she was talking about, but when he saw Duncan's updated mug shot, he knew that's what she was talking about.

"Oh my God," Gray exclaimed.

"Right?"

The shock of the sight settled in Gray's stomach.

"Is this the right Kenneth Duncan?" Gray still couldn't believe his eyes.

"That's him."

"Holy shit."

When Gray had first met Duncan, the suspected killer was average looking with a full head of hair. His body wasn't stellar, but it was one that could acceptably pass for most costumed super heroes or movie characters. His face was that of a character actor in the sense that you could see him in a hundred films and still not know his name. Those physical characteristics served him well at the comic conventions. Now, though, those days of average appearance were gone. First, his body had grown emaciated and haggard. His head of hair had been either shaved or had fallen away. And, finally, his face was no longer memorably forgettable. The self-harming was all too evident. From cheek to cheek across Duncan's mouth, there were fine-lined, scarred-over lacerations in the shape of human teeth like those seen on a dentist's X-ray, complete with the extended roots. Tattoos covered most of the rest of his face and fully illustrated a skull motif. The tip of his nose had been blackened. Same with the delicate skin surrounding his eyes and on the sides of his face where the tattooed jaw bone connected to the skull. All three areas represented the caverns left by decomposed tissue and cartilage of an aged skull. A crown of thorns circled his head. Above the drawn crown, as if the frontal, parietal, and occipital bones had been sawed and removed like a cap, there were more scarred cuts depicting exposed brain tissue.

"This is jarring," Gay said, unable to look away from the destruction of Duncan's face.

"I bet."

"This guy," Gray poked the photograph, "I've never met. This isn't the Duncan I knew. I don't know why he'd ask for me, and I sure as shit don't know why this version of Duncan would. What did he say when you went to see him?" Gray asked.

"Not much. Just that he would only talk to you."

"Walk me through it. Please."

"Sure." She merged onto Interstate 75. "I went there with Lt. Davis and another detective on my team. Detective Cordrey Phelps. We call him Cord. Everyone has a nickname. Mine's Sal. My first and last name both start with S-A-L, so by default ... That's what they call me. Do you have one?"

"Sal." He tried to connect with her. "Please ... " Before he pushed her forward.

She understood. The photograph had terminated his general interest in Duncan and replaced it with confusion and the need to understand.

"Cord and I talked to Duncan. We explained why we were there. It didn't seem to faze him at all. We explained how the body parts were found, the connection back to him. He didn't say anything in response."

"What was his demeanor?"

"He seemed ... calm. Unsurprised. But he never acknowledged it. It's just, that's how he was."

"What happened next?"

"We started asking him questions. He didn't answer any of them. After about the fifth one, he started asking us questions instead."

"Like what?"

"He asked how many people's parts were found."

"Did you tell him?"

"We did."

"Did you give him the names?"

"That was his next question, and, yeah, we told him the names."

Gray thought that was a mistake on her and Cord's part — they could've used the information as leverage to get Duncan talking — but he wasn't going to say so.

"What happened next?" he asked.

"That's when he asked for you."

Gray nodded, expecting that answer. "With the names then, he knew he could loop me in."

"Why would he want to do that? You've already said you had little interaction."

"I still don't know, but when you gave him the names, he knew he could. Maybe he's just stalling. How'd the rest of the interview go."

"After that there was a minute or so of quiet. I finally started asking questions again, but he didn't answer. After a handful more of them, he just said he wanted to talk to you."

"Tell me exactly what he said."

"If I remember right, he said, 'Detective Becker Gray. You know who he is. I know what he's looking for.' And he said it just like that. 'You know who he is.' It wasn't a question. Just a statement. He remembered you somehow."

She latched on to the wrong part of Duncan's statement. *I know what he's looking for.* Gray was finally going to get the location of Noah's body. But why? And why now?

"Do you think he's looking for media attention, and he thinks your involvement will help with that?" she asked.

"Maybe, but to what end?"

"I don't know. It's just unreal the way these guys think." She changed lanes and pressed the gas, edging by a slow car in the left lane. "We can ask the warden when we get there, though."

"Yeah," Gray said even though his thought process had moved on. "How was his mental state?"

She gruntled a laugh. "Other than the cutting and self-mutilation? There wasn't enough interaction to tell his state of mind. We asked him how he knew you, why he wanted to talk to you, and that kind of thing. He wouldn't respond. We went at him again, even threatened him with not bringing you, but he didn't budge. Wouldn't say anything else. I guess he knew you'd come."

I know what he's looking for.

How could I not come? Gray wondered.

CHAPTER 13

Florida State Prison didn't have the storied past that Rikers or Folsom prisons, but it was the prison most feared in Florida. This prison housed Florida's death chamber, where either lethal injection or electrocution ended the lives of its death row inmates. Almost 100 executions had been completed since 1979, but the two most famous executions in recent history included Ted Bundy and Aileen Wuornos. With those two serving as an example, it was safe to believe the worst of Florida resided there. And after interviewing Kenneth Lamont Duncan, Gray thought the man fit right in.

Far and away from the prison, an outline of trees made the Raiford city water tower appear to hover in the sky. Palm trees lined the walkway from the parking lot to the institution's front door. Two walls of chain link fence enclosed the property. Shimmering webs of electrified razor wire topped each of the two fences, and it covered the ground between. An adult would realize the hell a human body would experience making it over one fence and hurrying toward the next. To a child, it would appear as though a crop of wire was growing between to the fences. At every corner of the property stood a manned watchtower.

Gray and Salah were processed — weapons and other personal belongings were confiscated, but they were permitted to keep their phones and paperwork — and escorted by armed guard through the entry to the warden's office. Gray noticed the surroundings as he walked. Grey and cold. The block walls, the barred empty cells, the vault-like steel doors — everything was cold, and everything was designed for utilitarian purposes. He stepped over the drains cut into the concrete flooring. There was one every 30 feet or so along the walkways. While the drains made it easy to clean, drinking up the mop water and cleaning solutions, they also swallowed any blood drawn when inmates attacked each other, which occurred regularly here. *See? Useful in every way,* Gray told himself.

The warden's office was different than the rest of what Gray had seen of the prison. The office had color. Mostly a dark wood color — the wall paneling and furniture matched — yet there were splashes of reds, greens, yellows, blues and more throughout. The upholstery on the guest chairs maintained a red dye. Paintings on the walls were abstract in nature and tied in the rest of the colors. Three plastic, potted plants had been situated throughout the room, giving off an imagined warmth despite the depressing drabness of the institution outside the office.

Warden Misner "Buffalo" Garrity got to his feet with the assistance of a cane. It helped prop up his right side. Garrity explained he'd just had a knee replaced. It had given out slowly under the weight of his massive frame.

"You can call me Buffalo. That's just fine." He spoke with what sounded like a South Georgia accent.

Garrity moved the cane from his right hand to his left and pumped his hand out in greeting. Gray couldn't get his fingers around Buffalo's hand.

"I'll stick with warden or Garrity, if that's all right with you."

Garrity shrugged it off.

"Nice to see you again, Detective Salah," he said as they shook hands. "I see your lieutenant didn't make the trip again. And instead of Detective Phelps you have brought the notorious Detective Becker Gray."

His tone didn't hit Gray's ears in a flattering way. He looked at Salah to see if she thought the same thing. Instead of acknowledging Garrity's tone, she was massaging her hand, like it had been crushed. Gray hadn't noticed the man's vicelike grip. Maybe Buffalo didn't like women and squeezed her hand to show her who's really in charge.

"Come in. Sit down." He gestured to his guest chairs and shooed off his assistant, Hargrove Munro, who had escorted Gray and Salah to the office. "We'll be fine, Munro. Just make sure everything is set up."

Once the door closed behind Munro, Garrity continued speaking, rounding his desk.

"Round two with Mr. Duncan, I see."

He positioned the desk chair behind him and went quickly from standing to sitting — no inbetween — with a leap of faith style plop. Gray wondered if the chair would break under Garrity's weight. Buffalo read Gray's eyes.

"Haven't quite got the knee to where I can gently transition to the chair."

Salah ignored Garrity's statement about his knee. "Detective Gray was gracious enough to accompany me at Mr. Duncan's behest, so we can get to the bottom of this situation."

"Must say, I'm not surprised you're back, detective."

"I know," Salah kowtowed. "You warned me that Mr. Duncan wouldn't cooperate and that he'd make us jump through hoops. With this case, we're willing to jump through a couple hoops, if it gets us closer to bringing it to an end."

"I understand," Garrity said. "But I warned you. Give him an inch, and he'll take a mile."

Gray spoke up, sensing he should stick up for Salah. "I suspect Detective Salah will shut him down if he gets to be too much."

"You would think that'd be so, Detective Gray," Garrity said, "but Mr. Duncan is a most manipulative human being. You remember back in 2015 when that fella down in Dade County caused a raucous with the newspaper there and exposed violence perpetrated by the correctional officers against the prisoners? Caused near 'bouts a complete restructuring of the systems and high-ranking personnel?"

Gray nodded to be polite, but he didn't recall the specifics. Salah remembered, though. A lifer named Harold Hempstead told the *Miami Herald* he'd seen officers torturing mentally ill inmates. One of them ended up dead. An investigation ensued, and secretaries, wardens, and officers were fired. It also led to prison reforms and the installation of new surveillance systems.

"It is said that the fella who exposed that was trying to do the right thing. I don't know if that's true or not. I do know, however, that before anyone believed him, someone had to die. If Mr. Duncan were to try the same thing — whether he be telling the truth or not — he'd need no evidence. He is wholly believable. That's the type of presence this man has. He manipulates for the sheer enjoyment of the challenge, and you cannot trust a single utterance emanating from his mouth. That you can be sure of."

Gray didn't know what to do with that information. It seemed preemptive, like perhaps Garrity expected Duncan to raise issues about the prison administration. So, Gray said nothing.

Salah remained silent, too.

"I just want you to know before you go in there."

Gray nodded. "Thank you, warden. Do you have any ongoing problems with him?"

Garrity leaned forward. "Nothing we can't handle, I'll tell you that much. While he follows the rules generally speaking, he's also the inmate who has clocked the most hours in solitary confinement over the last five years."

"Why's that?" Gray asked, wondering why this information wasn't in Salah's profile of Kenneth Duncan.

"Two main reasons. One: If there is a skirmish among the inmates or some sort of bogus protest against the administration, you better believe Mr. Duncan is somehow leading the charge. Most the time, he's the instigator. And that'll get him a day or two. And, two: He's a self-harmer. Whenever he cuts or defiles his appearance, we punish him for that as well."

Gray nodded. Salah had mentioned that Duncan was a cutter. The other fact would be hard for her to have known.

Garrity sighed, "I'll rejoice the day he's out of here."

"He's got a life sentence. Where would he go?" Gray asked, wondering about a transfer for Duncan.

"To hell, I presume." Garrity carried on without giving the detectives a chance to respond. "We try our hardest to keep him away from anything that he could use to harm himself. We had to retrain the guards to watch for that sort of thing. Had to put special processes in place, too. Yet, he still finds a way to slash his skin."

"Psych evals?"

"Repeatedly. The doctors get nothing useful from him. Probably because he manipulates them to do his bidding, like how he had Detective Salah bring you here for, likely, no reason."

Salah almost protested that she wasn't manipulated, but Gray continued before she could say anything.

"Do you have a theory on why he asked for me, warden?" Gray asked.

"I do not. I expected you would know"

Gray shook his head. "I don't."

"I'd say that proves my point about Mr. Duncan."

Gray doubted it, but there had to be some truth in Garrity's assessment of Duncan. *Right?*

"May we see him, warden?" Salah asked.

Garrity rested his thick arms on the desk and hoisted his shoulders upward. "I'd just like you to finish up your conversations with him today. As I mentioned before, he has the ability somehow to unsettle this place, if he so chooses. I'd like to keep the peace. Our motto is 'Custody, Care, and Control.' With Mr. Duncan, control is what's most important for the careful custody of the rest of the population."

"We'll see what we can do," Salah said.

"See to it."

Buffalo pressed a button on his desk. A moment later Munro came through the door ready to lead them to Duncan.

CHAPTER 14

Hargrove Munro and two other correctional officers — each built like college linebackers — led Gray and Salah through the depths of the prison, far from the inmates' cells, the chow halls, the showers, and just about every other inhabited portion of the facility. The atmosphere contrasted, Gray knew, where the prisoners lived. Here it was quiet with a sense of calmness, where there with the prisoners it would be loud with a raucous energy. The stench there would be a barely breathable combination of humid body odor, urine, feces, and bleach, while here the air smelled of nothingness.

The room, secured on one side by cinder block exterior walls and tempered steel bars on the other, was larger than the office of the Major Crimes office at the Lakeland police headquarters. In fact, Gray figured the room was almost twice as large. A row of thin windows stretched across the length of the room, up near the ceiling. They were thin and were protected by steel bars. Streams of natural light shined in.

"Sorry it took so long to get you down here," Munro finally said. His elocution was as slow as his gait. "The warden asked us to fasten a chair and table to the floor."

One of the guards stepped ahead of the detectives and used a key to open the barred door.

Gray leaned toward Salah. "Is this where you met with him before?"

"No."

"Then why are we here this time?"

Garrity's helper cleared his throat. "He's inside and waiting for you."

"Thanks." Gray ushered Salah ahead.

Duncan sat at the table. He wore a modified jumpsuit. Velcro instead of scrubs. Shoes were the same. Nothing metal anywhere on his person. Duncan's ankles were chained to the chair's front two legs. His waist was secured to the chair by a belly chain. As Gray and Salah walked further into the room, they saw that Duncan's wrists were cuffed and connected to a chain threaded through a bolt at the center of the table.

Gray stopped and conferred with Salah again.

"Is this different than before, too?" he asked, referring to the shackles.

She whispered, "His hands were chained and bolted. But his legs and waist were free.

"What's going on?"

"I don't know."

"Listen," Gray said, "I have a tendency to kind of take over situations like this. When we sit down, I'd like you to take the lead since this is your case."

"I appreciate you saying that. He asked for you to come here, though, so I imagine he'll mostly want to talk to you."

"Let's not give him that satisfaction. Not at first. We'll see where it goes."

They started toward Duncan and the table.

The cell door rattled closed. Gray turned and watched the guards lock the door. They stayed close to it on the outside. Available, if needed.

Salah led Gray to the table and sat in one of the two chairs supplied for the detectives. She sat to Duncan's left. Gray rounded the table and grabbed the back of his chair, moving it slightly to give him a diagonal sightline. As he sat down, Gray glanced up and set his gaze upon the prisoner's face, which halted him momentarily in a shocked pause. He was prepared for Duncan's face, but it still stunned him.

He winced at the thought of Duncan carving into his skin the design of both the brain's spongy tissue and the medial longitudinal fissure that separates the two hemispheres of the human brain. The pain. The blood. The insanity. He'd dressed in his final costume.

The carvings looked like a horrific maze. One that if Gray and Salah traced their path correctly, they'd find a way into Duncan's thought processes.

Gray scooted his seat forward, taking the time to regain his composure.

"Hello again, Mr. Duncan," Salah greeted the prisoner, setting her phone on the table and pressing record. "I have your permission this time to record the conversation, right?"

Duncan opened his eyes at her greeting. He ignored her and her phone. He looked to Gray instead.

"I remember you."

Salah having the lead didn't last long.

"Yeah? What do you remember?"

Duncan licked his thin, chapped lips to wet them. He lifted his chained wrists and pointed with his fingers, so thin that they appeared arthritic. The bulbous joints looked painful to maneuver. It was hard to believe that his scrawny arms were strong enough to lift the weight of the chains, yet his arms rose, and his fingers aimed at Salah.

He leaned toward Gray and whispered, "I only want to talk to you."

"Detective Salah and I are working as a team today, Kenneth."

Duncan sighed, and it seemed to weaken him further. "Only you," he whispered, lowering his chin to his chest. His spine bent, and he hunched over. The chains rattled again.

"That's not happening."

Duncan dramatically sucked in air, straightening his spine and tossing back his head. The chains scraped, matching his movement. He pushed the air from his lungs, out toward the ceiling.

"Saleena. Salah. Unbending." His head stayed bent backwards, face to the ceiling.

"Noah Chritton," Salah announced.

"What about him?" Disinterest mixed with annoyance.

"Tell me about him."

"Twenty-year-old. Gorgeous. Well-built. Gay, but hadn't acknowledged it yet. Insecure, yet funny."

"So, you remember him?" Salah asked.

"I remember all of them."

His fingers began moving, like he was counting his victims one by one. Right index finger to pinky, next came his thumb. Then with his left hand, he started with the thumb and progressed to pinky.

"Parts of his body washed up on the beach four days ago," Salah said.

"I know. You already came here and told me."

"How did that happen?"

Duncan craned his neck toward Gray.

That's the line then, Gray concluded. He wouldn't tell them much with Salah here.

"Why are you chained today?" Gray asked.

Duncan considered his response before speaking. "Punishment."

"For what?"

"My shirt." Duncan lifted his weak arms again, indicating the answer was behind his jumpsuit, that he'd show Gray but couldn't because of the restraints.

A blanket of apprehension settled upon Gray and Salah.

Duncan, though, seemed to revel in their trepidation. "You asked," Duncan coaxed Gray.

Hesitantly, Gray pushed his chair back and stood, stealing an uneasy glance at the recording cameras. The red lights were still there. Then he looked to the entrance. Munro and the other two guards watched attentively. The one with the key to the door had it near the lock, in case they needed to enter quickly.

Making his way toward Duncan, Gray measured the situation. Duncan was indeed already manipulating the meeting because he had the power: information. And Gray and Salah wanted it. That left Duncan in charge. And he liked it. On his walk around the table, Gray considered why Duncan wouldn't just answer his question. *Why and what did he need to show me? Was it a ploy to just draw me closer? Why?* Even as weak as Duncan appeared, this could be an attempt to attack Gray. There were no weapons except Duncan's mouth and head. A strike from Duncan's head could knock Gray off his feet, but he'd ultimately be fine. However, a bite could really injure Gray. Just from the potential infection alone.

"Turn your head to the right and keep it there," Gray commanded.

After Duncan did as instructed, Gray reached out and pulled apart the Velcro keeping the jumpsuit closed.

"All the way," Duncan said when Gray stopped halfway down his chest. The enjoyment in his voice disgusted Gray. He knew Duncan was elated by Gray touching him. Of his control over Gray.

Gray yanked open the suit like curtains, ripping open the two Velcro sides all the way to Duncan's belly chain.

"There," Duncan said. A smile of afterglow on his face.

Gray stepped back to take in the view.

CHAPTER 15

The green etchings depicted practically every bone of Duncan's torso. Most prominently on display were his clavicle, ribs, and portions of his spine. Similarly, his organs — his stomach, intestines, and lungs — were outlined in red ink. Inside his intestines a snake slithered. In his lungs, scorpions, spiders, and roaches scampered. The bust of a demon surrounded by fire had been depicted inside the stomach walls. Though, one area looked fresh — the skin was swollen and irritated, scabs had formed over much of the space. *This must be what caused the punishment,* Gray guessed. A circle had been drawn around the outline of Duncan's heart tattoo. Then the "artist" had begun darkening the circle with black ink. When he'd stopped — *or had been caught* — only half of Duncan's heart had been colored over, leaving just the right atrium and the veins and arteries visible.

"Buffalo does not like tattooing," Duncan said.

"How many times have you been 'punished?'" Gray asked, stepping away from Duncan.

"Too many to count." Duncan turned his head straight.

That, along with the perspective Garrity shared earlier, told Gray what he needed to know about Duncan and Garrity's relationship. Garrity despised Duncan. Duncan paid Garrity no mind, and he did what he wanted without worry of punishment.

"Detectives," Munro called from outside the cell door. "It's advisable not to touch the prisoner. And please close his shirt."

"I'm sure you've seen enough." Duncan motioned toward his jumpsuit then turned his head to the right again.

"I don't care what he says, Kenneth. Is that all you wanted to show me?"

"Yes."

Nodding, Gray stepped closer and attached the two Velcro sides, covering the gaunt canvas of artwork.

"Thank you," Duncan said.

As Gray returned to his chair, Duncan said, "You asked what I remembered about you. "It's this. You had an air of not caring a stitch about what anyone said or thought. I liked that."

People often liked in others the qualities they thought they didn't possess. Gray wondered if that was true in Duncan's case. Maybe that was one of the reasons he had dressed in costume when he was younger. He couldn't gain acceptance as himself, but he could as comic book and movie characters. Maybe that's why he had marked up his body in prison. To appear scarier — or crazier — than he really was.

"And you still don't," Duncan concluded with a gleeful smile on his face. "I'm glad you haven't lost that."

Gray nodded, though not accepting the feedback as an honor. "That's gotten me in a lot of trouble over the years. Cost me friends and a lot of opportunities." *Might even get me fired,* he thought, thinking back to the ongoing investigation in Lakeland.

Salah struggled against her urge to look at Gray, guessing he was working Duncan, yet unsure he wasn't being partially truthful.

"Tell me about your friends, Becker."

"No."

"What if your attitude hadn't cost you those people? Where do you think your life would be today?"

"I've never thought about it, and I don't care to start."

"My father died when I was young, you know that, right?"

"You know we do."

Duncan grunted acknowledgement. "I sometimes wonder how my life would've been different had he survived."

"What did you come up with?"

Duncan feigned offense. "You won't tell me what I ask, but you expect me to spill to you?"

"You don't have to, Kenneth." *But I know you will.* "You brought it up."

"My father … " He paused and shook his head, the subject matter appearing to be too emotional for Duncan. "Let me put it this way: I've realized that my limited amount of days on this earth have amounted to nothing, and it's time they do."

"Is that why I'm here, Kenneth?"

Thinking of the body parts on her beach, Salah blurted, "I bet your victims' families think your days here amounted to something."

Gray wished Salah hadn't said anything, as he watched a dirty look spread across Duncan's face. He felt like Duncan was just about to open up, and he feared this would stall progress. He realized then just how much he missed Parker and the rhythm of their fine-tuned working relationship.

"So, you blame your father for the way your life turned out?" Salah asked, either not caring or not noticing the tensing of Gray's muscles.

Duncan looked away from Salah and spoke with no sense of apology in his voice. "No. I blame nothing. I blame no one. And I feel nothing for those families. They can hate all they want. I don't care."

"What do you care about?" Gray now tried to right the conversation.

He responded to Gray, gesticulating toward Salah. "Can't you and I *please* speak alone?"

"No," Salah said.

Duncan closed his eyes and exhaled, in an attempt to remain calm. While Duncan's eyes were shut, Gray looked at Salah and pointed his palms toward the ground, telling her to ease up on her approach. She bit her tongue and rolled her eyes in response.

"Kenneth, why did you ask for me to visit you?" Gray asked, once again trying to keep the interview on track.

Duncan opened his eyes. His disdain for Salah now gone. In fact, there didn't seem to be any emotions at all expressed on his face.

"Out of all the police I've spoken to in my life, you stood out as the only one who might believe me. You were the only one wouldn't care what all the others would say."

"Believe you about what?"

"About the murders."

"What about them?"

Duncan spoke with a sudden exuberance in his voice.

"Noah Chritton. Twenty years old. Shy of six feet tall. A Leo. He had three tattoos. One on his left calf. The Iron Man logo. Not because he'd completed one of those races, but because he had set that as a goal. One on his right arm. An eagle. Represented freedom. He said he got that tattoo when he moved out of his parents' home at eighteen. And one on his left shoulder, on his back. It was an electric guitar. A Gibson, I believe. Another goal of his." Duncan shrugged his shoulders. "He was strangled in the back of my car behind a bar in Orlando, Florida.

"Cornell Hughes. Twenty-seven. Thinning black hair. A cook at a restaurant. Came to Comic-Con dressed as Dr. Emmett Brown from the Back to the Future movies. He wanted to cook at a New York restaurant one day.

"Carlos Fernandez. Twenty-three. An orphan. No one missed him.

"Jeremy Little. Twenty-two. Had a birthmark on his cheek. It was an unfortunate gift from his mother. You know what it looked like, now that I think about it? It looked like a skin graft procedure gone terribly wrong. Poor child.

"Jacob Cruise. Dressed as Maverick from Top Gun. Claimed to be a third cousin of Tom Cruise. How could you believe him, though? I mean, Cruise wasn't even the actor's real last name." He shook his head at Jacob's assertion. "He was strangled to an inch of his life. Resuscitated and strangled again. He deserved the repeated choking for his stupidity."

"What are you doing?" Salah asked.

Duncan ignored her and continued.

"Thomas McNamara. Another twenty-three-year-old. Jobless. Lived on his father's generosity. Despite not having attended college and having missed the NHL draft, he was convinced he could play professional hockey. He was a tough one. Almost a whole bottle of vodka before he could be controlled.

"James Watson. A gym rat. I thought he'd be a big, bad motherfucker, but he wasn't. He shit himself when he realized he was going to die. He was beaten pretty bad before he was strangled. It was a beautiful night, too. In the desert outside Elko, Nevada. Population twenty thousand.

"Harvey Miller. Looked after his kidsister because his mother ran off when they were young, and his father was in jail. He got chained to a tree in the woods of a mountain in North Carolina. Left there overnight. He screamed and cried. Then as the sun came up, hands went around his neck.

"Brandon Hardesty. Twenty-five. Suffocated with a plastic bag over his head."

"Enough," Gray declared. "We know all this."

"I've never forgotten them."

"Most killers don't forget their victims." Salah couldn't help herself.

Duncan glared at Salah for the continued interruptions. Then he looked at Gray. His face stilled. No signs to indicate he may be lying. "That's the thing, Becker ... I wasn't the one who killed them."

CHAPTER 16

Salah chuckled at Duncan. "You're kidding?"

"He's not," Gray said.

After what Duncan had said about why he asked for Gray, the detective had to act like he believed Duncan. Yet, it was easy because he did believe Duncan.

"I'm not." Duncan smiled, grateful that Gray believed him.

"He confessed," she reminded Gray.

She had a point, Gray conceded. Plus, Garrity had said Duncan's manipulation would be believable. Was Gray off his game? Was Duncan playing him?

"That's true. I was just as guilty, just as complicit in their murders," Duncan said.

"How so?" Gray asked.

"Because I wanted to be the one who killed them. I wanted their deaths to be mine. I hunted them. I watched them die. I see them in my sleep. I just couldn't actually finish them."

The rush of the change of direction in the interview surged inside Gray. In Salah, too. If they believed Duncan, then it wasn't that the wrong man had been arrested. It was that only one man had been arrested.

"Why couldn't you finish them?" Gray asked, trying to keep the conversation linear.

"I remember on the farm with my father. I didn't like killing the animals. Not even for food. I mean, I liked bacon and ham. Turkey and chicken. Beef, especially. I just couldn't kill and eat any of our own animals."

Interesting that Duncan compared humans to farm animals. Animals that were slaughtered for food, for life sustaining purposes. Were they the same to him?

"What did your father think of that?"

Duncan smiled, thinking the answer was so obvious that even Gray should've known it before asking. "Oh, he beat me with a switch when I told him that." His smiled faded as the memory went by. "He made me bleed pretty bad. Then he made me watch him kill the animals. Made me help my mother prepare the meals. Made me eat every last bit of my dinner."

"Did that make you hate him?"

"No." He looked past Gray as if the memory were being projected against the cinder block wall behind the detectives. "I loved him for it. He taught me the strong eat the weak."

"And that's what happened to your victims? They were weak, and you were strong?"

"Exactly."

"You had a partner then?"

"Indeed."

"He must've been strong, too?"

Usually in partnerships like Duncan was saying he had with an unknown subject there was one alpha male not two. Gray assumed Duncan was the alpha and his partner was the subservient one.

"He was an ox."

"He'd have to be to crush people's necks. That's not the easiest thing to do."

Duncan shrugged his bony shoulder. "Easy enough."

"But you couldn't do it."

He held up a bony index finger, indicating a point of clarification but saying nothing.

"You had to convince someone else to do it?"

Duncan finally spoke, dropping his arm to the table again. "No, he wanted to."

"Whose idea was it the first time?"

"I think it was his."

A lie! It was the only time Duncan had expressed uncertainty in his statements.

"No, it was your idea, wasn't it? You were a hundred times smarter than your partner, weren't you? I think you treated him just like you treated your father."

"What are you talking about?" Duncan's voice contained a tinge of anger.

"Back on the farm, I don't think you gave a shit about the animals. Your protest wasn't about them or even their slaughter. I think you wanted to control your father. And it worked, didn't it? Same as your partner. You controlled him and made him do the choking. In fact, you were so good at this deception that he thinks it was his idea. And that's the thrill for you, isn't it? It's not the killing. It's the manipulation of people, the power over people that gets you off. You convinced the victims to come with you, you outsmarted them and put them in compromising situations, then you overpowered your partner mentally to where he wrapped his fingers around their throats and stole their breath."

Salah liked where Gray was going with this.

Duncan's anger hid poorly behind smugness. "That's an impressive theory, Becker, but you're incorrect."

"Am I?"

"I loved those animals. They were my only friends." Duncan worked his way back to his story of being his father's victim. "I didn't want to kill them."

"But you ate them." Gray wasn't going to allow Duncan to spin that lie without a little more pushback.

"I had to. My father forced me."

"Right. Because ultimately he still had the control."

Salah spoke up, her own mind spinning scenarios. "You killed your father, didn't you? For control?"

Duncan spat venom. "Goddammit, Saleena. Becker and I are having a fucking conversation." He slammed his fists onto the table. His cuffs and the chains clattered again.

Now we're getting somewhere, Gray thought.

Munro's lackeys at the door jumped to attention at the sudden outburst. Gray held up his hand, halting them from entering.

Gray turned toward the prisoner again and asked, "Did you kill your father, Kenneth?"

"That's absurd. I was seven."

"How did he die?"

"It was a tractor accident."

"That's right. I remember now. So, you didn't kill him?"

"No!"

"It was an accident?"

"Of course."

Salah had done well to get the first emotional response from Duncan. Gray liked that she'd tuned in to the questioning and was willing to take a risk and push Duncan's buttons. It's when people feel anger, love, or loss that they think the least; therefore, when a person being interviewed is feeling, they often say something they didn't mean to. Gray bet that Salah's approach worked quite often for her.

"Good, then we can put that to rest."

"Thank you," Duncan replied. "Now, I'd like to only speak with you from here on out."

"We need to know the name of your partner, then maybe," Gray said.

"Phillip Sutter. Twenty-nine. An accountant with a new wife. Tyler Rhodes, a college student. Ely Epstein worked at a coffee shop. Wyatt Nelson had a twin brother."

Gray cut him off. "And Marty Cross was a thirty-eight-year-old technology consultant from Wichita, Kansas. We know, Kenneth. How did the body parts end up in the Gulf of Mexico? Was it your partner who dumped them?"

"I haven't communicated with him in years."

"Then who?"

"That doesn't matter. I won't tell you that now."

"Then tell me what you did with the bodies after the murders."

"Obviously, they were chopped up and stored."

"Where?"

"In a freezer."

"Where was the freezer located?"

"I won't tell you that either."

He was protecting someone. The person who dumped the bodies had a clear and obvious connection to Duncan. The location of the freezer would identify the person.

Gray noted that he needed to check Duncan's visitors and communications log. Duncan had to have contacted someone on the outside. Or, maybe it had been someone who'd recently been released from prison, like an old cellmate. Gray would need to ask the warden about Duncan's cellmates.

Gray grudgingly realized that his focus was narrowing on his handling of the case. He was taking it on his shoulders alone. Even though he and Salah had developed a slight rhythm in this interview, he was taking it over in his own mind. But it was her case, he reminded himself. These were her tasks to complete. He needed to allow her to do so. Then another realization reluctantly took hold in his mind. Maybe if he'd allowed others into his cases, then he wouldn't be the focus of the inquiry in Lakeland. Maybe Parker wouldn't be so mad at him.

"But, under one condition, I'll tell you anything else about these people and their demise. Anything at all. No detail left unspoken. I'll tell you why I buried the two bodies I led the police to. I'll tell you about my partner. I'll tell you about the other bodies. And so much more, Becker."

Duncan let that carrot dangle a moment before telling the detectives the cost of such information.

"Only you, though. Only to you."

CHAPTER 17

Duncan clearly was manipulating the situation, trying to control it, them, and the flow of information. That meant Duncan couldn't be trusted. *Not at all.* On top of that, Gray wondered what was so important to Duncan that he'd been asking for privacy with him since the conversation started? While he didn't have the answer, Gray appreciated Duncan's ability to hold the room hostage. Duncan had the perfect audience to get what he wanted. And the prisoner knew it. Gray wasn't hard to read: all he wanted was the precious information Duncan held, and it didn't matter to Gray how he got it. Whether they spoke alone or in a group of a hundred people. Gray didn't care.

Salah was the wildcard for Duncan. It was her case. Gray was her guest. Duncan figured that she'd be the one who would adamantly demand to be present. The prisoner had to wonder if he'd teased his information correctly, would Salah bite and leave the two men alone?

Gray wondered the same thing. While at the beginning of the day, Salah was amenable to having Gray be the focus of the conversation, she may not be now that Duncan was nearly insisting on talking only to him. Normally, Gray would just do what he wanted, lowering his shoulder and plowing forward. This time, though, he thought about it differently. He needed to protect Salah and her case. He needed to protect the victims' families who deserved to hear the truth from Duncan.

He recalled what he had told Jordan Butler the night before about pushing to become a detective. He had originally wanted to provide hope to the families in these types of crimes; he wanted to protect them from being helpless. And in the years since becoming a detective, he'd forgotten that desire, having lost it to years of drinking and selfishness. He realized in this case that if he plowed forward as he always had, then he wasn't helping the families. This was his chance — *perhaps his last chance* — to work a case for the right reasons.

Salah moved first. She stretched her arm across the table and pressed the Stop button on her phone's recording app.

"If we're to do this, Mr. Duncan," Salah said, "you're going to provide us every detail of what we want to know. Even if we ask you five times to repeat yourself. And if you don't, I'll have the warden rip your world apart. Whatever it is you enjoy here, I'll make sure it goes away and never comes back. Even if it's something as small as tapioca pudding. You'll never taste it again. Understood?"

Duncan sighed and rolled his eyes. "Detective Salah, I don't enjoy anything?"

He enjoys control, Gray thought.

"I don't think we should do it," Gray said.

Salah's willingness to allow the private meeting surprised Gray, but he was rolling with it. He wanted to give Salah the power to make the final decision, and he wanted her to decide in front of Duncan. The prisoner needed to know that Salah was in charge.

"Oh, but you'll be glad you did, Becker," Duncan said.

"This has nothing to do with me, Kenneth. Detective Salah is lead investigator on the case. This is her interview."

Salah knew immediately what Gray was doing.

"No, we'll do it, but we're ordering lunch first."

That will give them time to collect their thoughts and find an angle.

"I'll take a Monte Cristo," Duncan said, smiling victoriously. "It's been years."

CHAPTER 18

There were no Monte Cristo sandwiches served. Just pizza and water. Gray and Salah ate their lunch on the outside of the large cell, while Munro sat inside with Duncan. Munro freed Duncan's non-dominant wrist so the prisoner could eat, and his right hand remained secured. They chatted quietly as Duncan ate.

Gray and Salah, though, used the time to get on the same page.

"Are you sure you're all right with this?" Gray asked. "I don't want to step on your toes."

"Just get the information, so we can get out of here."

Gray nodded and continued eating his slice.

"How are you going to handle it?" she asked.

"He's a narcissist and dying to talk about himself. I guess I'll let him start the conversation. I'll try to figure out his agenda and go from there. What do you think?"

"We keep thinking," Salah said, "that this is all about him, right? What if it's not?"

"Then who's it about?" Gray asked.

"You."

"No. There's nothing there. I don't see it."

She shrugged her shoulders.

"If you think something, spit it out," he told her.

"I don't. I'm just trying to turn it around and see if something's there."

They both thought it through and came up with nothing.

"The narcissist thing ... That's as good an approach as there is," she said. "Change of subject ... Do you believe him? That there's a partner? I know you said in there you did, but I think you may have said that just for him."

"I don't know. Yes, I think. The more he talked, the more I thought he'd need a partner to pull off the killings."

"I don't think he was telling the truth. I'm not sure he knows what the truth is."

"Right. Exactly. Speaking of that ... I made a couple mental notes of things I'd check out, if this were my case. Do you mind if I give them to you?"

"I made some, too. Go ahead."

"They mainly related to the person who dumped the body parts. I think Duncan's visitor and communication logs should be checked, as well as getting a list of Duncan's cellmates or known acquaintances who were recently released. I'd go back to the original case files and examine them again with fresh eyes in search of any fleeting mention of a friend. There's got to be something in there to connect him and whoever dumped the body parts."

"That's good." Salah didn't say if she had or had not already thought of those things. "I wonder, too, if Duncan or his mother own any property in Florida. I don't recall reading about any, but I'm going to check into that."

"Sounds good."

From the cell, Duncan wretched. He bent violently at the stomach, and he growled in pain. Gray and Salah jumped to attention, wondering what was going on, concerned for Munro's safety. They found Munro standing, unharmed, while Duncan twisted and groaned in his chair.

"Is he okay?" Salah called to Munro.

"He'll be fine," Munro assured them. Then he said to the other two correctional officers, "Get a bucket, will ya?"

"What the hell?" Gray asked, wondering if the food was bad and if he and Salah should be worried about food poisoning. Though, Duncan's reaction seemed too fast for that to be the cause.

"I don't know," Salah responded, keeping her eyes on Duncan.

The two officers hustled in their tasks. One rushed down the hall, while the other unlocked the cell door. Soon the officer who'd run off reappeared, and he carried a plastic bucket. The door swung open, and he hurried in. The remaining officer outside the cell with Gray and Salah closed the barred door again and locked it.

Gray moved closer. "What's going on?" he asked the officer.

"This happens practically every time he eats."

Duncan groaned again, vomiting this time. Salah gagged, watching the scene play out. One of the two guards inside with Duncan held the bucket while the other watched. Most of the vomit made it into the bucket, but not all of it. That which missed the bucket splashed on the floor and onto Munro's shoes and pants.

"Goddammit," Munro shouted, tugging on some rubber gloves. He scolded himself for not having been better prepared for Duncan's lunch and his typical reaction to food. He handed a pair of gloves to the officer holding the bucket. "Get us a cleaning crew and some wash cloths. And hurry up."

The officer outside with the detectives said, "I'll be right back. Leave the door locked. Don't go inside." He bolted down the hall.

Salah edged over to Gray.

"You okay?" Gray asked.

"I hate it when people vomit," she said.

"The guy said this happens just about every time Duncan eats."

"Why?"

"I didn't get a chance to ask."

The officer returned from down the hall. "Cleaning crew will be here in a few minutes."

Duncan heaved again. More vomit launched out of his mouth and most of it shot into the bucket. He moaned loudly again.

"Tell 'em to hurry up," Munro shouted, stepping away from the newly spewed vomit.

"We're going to need you two to hang out here until we get all this cleaned up," the officer at the door told the detectives. "Feel free to finish your lunch in the meantime. We'll probably need about 30 minutes."

"Like we can eat now," Salah said.

"What is going on?" Gray asked the officer.

"Stomach cancer."

CHAPTER 19

For more than thirty minutes, Gray had nothing else to think about except Duncan's fate. Death apparently approached at a steady pace. Duncan had been suffering with the disease for almost twelve months, and he likely only had a few months left to live. Did that mean something to Duncan? Gray tried to retrace the conversations that took place before lunch, looking for any clues. The closest he could come up with was Duncan talking about his time on Earth being a waste. But, was Duncan being philosophical or was he simply manipulating Gray and Salah? Could someone like Duncan be philosophical? Could someone like Duncan truly, genuinely wish to make amends for his sins? Gray didn't think so. What was a waste about Duncan's time on Earth? That seemed to be the right question. One that didn't yet have an answer.

More correctional officers had come and escorted Duncan back to his cell, where he was getting cleaned up and changing his clothes. Munro had done the same, only he'd gone to the officers' locker room. The cleaning detail, prisoners armed with buckets and mops, cleaned the large cell quickly, while Munro's two lackeys looked on. The cleaning crew mopped the floor and hand washed the tabletop, the legs of the table, and Duncan's chair. The smell of bleach invaded the large area.

As if Duncan's vomiting wasn't enough to stop Gray and Salah from finishing their lunch, the bleach definitely put a stop to it.

"I'm getting a headache," Salah said, rubbing her temples.

"I don't blame you. I'm sure mine's on the way, too."

"So, his stomach," she said, moving closer to Gray to keep her words from reaching the officers and the prisoner cleaning crew.

"What about it?" Gray kept his voice low as well.

"You remember the tattoos on his torso? The stomach tattoo specifically?"

Gray didn't, having had focused mostly on the heart tattoo.

She said, "Inside the stomach, there was fire and some evil looking demon thing. You think it represented the cancer?"

It was possible, but it didn't matter to Gray. Neither the tattoo nor Duncan's suffering. All that mattered to Gray was extracting as much information about the murders — specifically the murder of Noah Chritton — as possible.

"Makes sense to me," he said.

"Do you think this is some deathbed confession that Duncan's doing?" she asked.

"That's not in his genetic make-up?"

"I guess not," she replied. "Maybe it's something more primal."

"Like revenge or something?"

"Why not?"

"Against who?"

Salah shrugged her shoulders. "No idea. Maybe his old partner? Even though Duncan never identified him, maybe now that he's about to die, he wants to sell him out."

Gray wasn't certain he believed that, but he said, "That makes sense."

Salah chuckled. "And that's the problem, isn't it?"

"What?"

"We're logical human beings. We work off of motives and processes. Explanations. Maybe there is no explanation."

"Maybe we're making this more difficult than it needs to be."

"Right. Like maybe he's bored and we're his entertainment through his dying days. Maybe there's no partner. There are no other secrets to tell. It's just him toying with us?"

Gray laughed at the idea, shaking his head, not believing that to be the case. "Maybe."

"I guess you'll find out when he comes back."

Gray nodded. He leaned close to her. "I wonder why no one told us he has cancer. Like, how did that not come up?"

Shrugging her shoulders, Salah said, "I would think that would have been in his file."

The sounds of rattling chains eerily made their way through the hallway. Soon the rattling coincided with the sound of shuffling feet. Munro had rejoined the party and led the way. His lackeys each held one of Duncan's arms and helped him walk. Duncan appeared weaker and paler than he had in the morning. Seemed hard to believe that was even possible.

The detectives stood and watched the group of men enter the large cell. Duncan didn't make eye contact. The lackeys directed Duncan to his chair and gently set him down into the uncomfortable wooden seat. Leaving his hands cuffed, they disconnected the belly chain and routed it through the steel rod in the table top before reconnecting it to the cuffs. They followed the same type of methodology in securing Duncan's ankles to the legs of the chair. When they finished securing the prisoner, each of the guards filed out of the cell, leaving Duncan inside alone. His posture was hunched.

"He's not feeling well," Munro said, as he passed. "Probably won't be very strong until his stomach feels better."

"Should he be in the infirmary?" Gray asked.

"What he should do and what he will do are typically two different things." Munro held the door, ready to close it when Gray entered. "You going in?"

CHAPTER 20

The cell door grinded to a locked position before Gray had made it to the table where Duncan had been sat and restrained. As the prisoner awaited his chance to be alone with Gray, the detective paused, if only slightly, to take in the man's appearance. Duncan's face looked more drawn than it had that morning, which gave the skull tattoos and scars a graver authenticity. In addition, the sun had moved across the sky, dimming the streams of sunshine coming in through the high, narrow, barred windows above, and that resulted in a darkness cast over Duncan's drawn features.

Gray sat opposite Duncan again. Salah's chair had been removed.

"They told you," Duncan said. It could've been a question, but it didn't sound like one.

Gray nodded.

"Those sons of bitches."

Gray didn't respond, not believing Duncan's affronted attitude. Prisoners didn't have the same HIPAA protections as patients in a doctor's office. Duncan knew that. He likely just wanted to use the sickness for his own gain with Gray. But how and why? What benefit would Duncan gain from surprising Gray with this news?

"It's a bastard of a situation, Becker. They said I probably got it from too much drinking and not enough vegetables." He laughed at his doctors. "They may be right about the vegetables, but I hardly ever drank alcohol."

"How do you think you got it?"

Duncan's smile looked eerie. "You want me to say karma, don't you?"

"No. I just wanted to know what you think."

"I don't fucking know." His tone was lathered with irritation. "Acid reflux. Tripping on shrooms? What's it matter now?"

"You sound bitter."

"Sure, I'm bitter."

"Why?"

Duncan laughed at the question. "Because this fucking disease tastes like aluminum and bile somehow mixed together with lime juice. And all my taste is gone. Sweet, salty, whatever. All I taste is aluminum and bile and lemons. That'd make you bitter, too."

"So why deny treatment?"

"And prolong my stay here? If I was outside, maybe. In here? Life. No parole. Surrounded by these people. Why would I fight it?"

Gray nodded, then moved on. "Does that happen every time you eat?"

Duncan cocked his head. "Do you care? Really?"

"I was just asking."

"Well, don't, but I'm sure my ailment makes you happy."

Gray chose not to acknowledge Duncan's postulation, thinking it better to get right to it. "We have a few things to discuss, don't we?"

"If you're up to it," Duncan said, as he moved his tongue through his mouth, tracing its outer reaches, wetting his lips.

"I was going to say the same thing to you."

Duncan smiled again, tucking his tongue away. No longer eerie, the grin appeared more subdued than it had previously. Gray wondered if Munro had given the killer any pain medicine. If it was kicking in. If it would make Duncan more forthcoming.

"I'm ready," Duncan confirmed.

Gray pressed record on his cell phone's recording app and introduced the scenario for the recording, first detailing the date, followed by the location and time, and then identifying himself and Duncan as the participants in the audio. Finally, he stated the purpose of the recording.

Gray waited for the clearance to proceed. Duncan nodded.

"Kenneth, tell me how all this got started."

Gray wanted Duncan to tell the story, so he could — now or later — pick apart his statement to determine if the man was lying about anything.

"Becker, I'm far too weak for that. It'll serve you better to get right to it."

Damn. His plan was already off course. "Then start with Noah Chritton."

Duncan shook his head, breathing deeply. "I don't want to talk about Noah."

Gray gritted his teeth at Duncan's response. Was he playing games again?

"Then tell me about your partner, and we'll circle back to Noah."

"I don't want to talk about that either."

Gray snapped at him. "We had an agreement, Kenneth."

"I want to talk about you, detective."

"I'm not a topic of discussion."

"Oh, but you are. You're the reason for all this, don't you know? I asked for you specifically."

Reluctantly, Gray went in Duncan's direction. The path of least resistance. He said, "You told me you liked my attitude of not giving a shit."

"I only said that for Detective Salah's benefit. Plus, you asked for a reason. I gave you one that you'd believe."

It worked, but Gray wasn't going to tell him that.

"Then why'd you ask for me?"

"Do you know what it's like cutting the extremities from a lifeless carcass?"

"I thought we were talking about me."

"We are," Duncan assured him. His strength seemed to magically reemerge. Color returned to his face. "That's what I'm doing to you, detective. Cutting the extremities from your lifeless carcass."

"I don't know what you're talking about," Gray said.

"You will."

Duncan's smile returned, leaving Gray with an unnerving sense like he had been set up.

"Let's go ahead and discuss Noah. Would you like that, detective?"

"No," Gray said. "Tell me what you're talking about. Cutting the extremities. What does that mean?"

"Detective, I'm ready to discuss the murder of Noah Chritton. You don't want to?" Duncan's eyes fell to the phone recording their audio conversation.

Gray leaned over the table. "Are you threatening me, Kenneth? What do you mean by a lifeless carcass?"

"Detective, I thought I would be the one refusing to participate, not you. Would you like to discuss Noah Chritton or not?"

Gray seethed. Mostly from confusion and feeling played by Duncan, who firmly believed he had control of the interview.

"Okay," Gray said, acknowledging to himself — and to Duncan — that Duncan indeed had control.

"What do you want to know that I didn't already admit to when I was originally convicted?"

"You met him in a bar in Orlando?"

"Not far from the convention center, yes."

"It was late at night?"

"About midnight."

"How did you meet?"

"Same as most people. It started with a simple greeting."

"You said earlier you had a partner who helped you with the murders, including Noah Chritton."

"I did."

"You did what? You said that? Or, you did have a partner?"

"Both."

"Which of you approached Noah?"

"I did."

"What was the simple greeting you used to meet Noah."

"I just used the word hello."

"Why did you approach Noah and not your partner?"

"I was blessed with the gift of the tongue."

"And your partner wasn't?"

"Not at all."

"He couldn't come up with 'Hello' on his own? You couldn't coach him that? Doesn't seem that hard to me."

"What can I say? He wasn't a talker."

"What happened after you greeted Noah?"

Duncan leaned on his elbows, supported by the table, tilting toward Gray. "What is it you really want to know?"

Gray's irritation was evident. "I thought I was clear in my question, Kenneth. What happened after you greeted Noah?"

"No. You're leading up to something. I'm dying of cancer here, Detective Gray. Why don't you skip the story details and get to the point?"

Gray's eyes held Duncan's with a cold connection.

"Just. Spit. It. Out," Duncan said.

"What. Happened. After. You. Greeted. Noah?"

Duncan threw his body into the back of the chair. "I'm tiring of this, detective."

Gray thought it interesting before this recording that Duncan was calling him Becker, and now he was being called by his job title and last name.

"What do you think I want to know?" Gray asked.

"Did Noah die quickly? Was his death painless? What were his last words?"

"I'll take the answers to those questions, sure."

"No." Duncan continued, "What you're really doing is laying the groundwork for me to tell you who my partner was."

"You seem surprised. This is what you agreed to talk about. I believe you said, 'No detail left unspoken'."

"Maybe I changed my mind."

"Did you change your mind?"

"No. No. And, fuck you."

Gray sat in silence, his eye contact remained unwavering.

Duncan leaned forward again. "Those are your answers, detective."

"What answers?"

"Did he die quickly? Was it painless? And his last words."

"His last words were 'Fuck you'?" Gray asked.

"They were."

"Are you lying?"

"Not a bit."

"Why did you kill Noah?"

Duncan began playing with the metal bolt in the center of the table. "I didn't, remember? My partner did."

"Why did your partner kill Noah?"

"Because he was there."

"That's it?" Gray purposefully projected a skeptical tone.

"If it wasn't him, then it would've been someone else."

The nonchalance of Duncan's delivery grinded coldly on Gray's nerves.

"Why was it him?"

"Because when I said 'Hello', he said it back."

Gray nodded and decided to push the conversation in an old, raw direction. "I noticed all of your victims were the same height ... within an inch. They all had dark hair."

"We had a type. Don't most serial killers?" Duncan asked.

"Well, it's just interesting to me that those are the same physical characteristics of your father."

"Coincidence is a bitch," Duncan said, trying to shut down the conversation about his father.

"Is it?" Gray responded.

Duncan shot Gray a pathetic look. "You think this had something to do with my father?"

"Tell me again about the tractor accident that killed your father."

Duncan shook his head. But only slightly.

He said, "Noah's neck crinkled and popped when he was strangled."

With Duncan steering clear of his father as a topic, Gray felt like he'd finally gained some footing.

"I want to know about your father, Kenneth. What was your relationship like prior to his death?"

"After Noah was killed, it was my job to dispose of the bodies. I had a home. It was a small shack of a place, but it was home. Behind the house, I had a private place."

"Kenneth, did your father beat you?"

Duncan's continued avoidance of the topic amped Gray's confidence and energy.

"I had four chest freezers. I could get two full bodies in each one. I mean, after rigor mortis went away. If I was lucky, I could get the bodies home before rigor set in. Most of the time I wasn't lucky like that."

"Did your father abuse your mother?"

"When I finally had too many bodies, I had to start cutting the limbs and burying the torsos."

"Why did you hate your father?"

Duncan shouted, tired of Gray's insistence on asking questions about his father. "Are you even listening?"

Gray waited a moment before asking, "Did your mother kill your father?" And that finally got him somewhere.

With a dead face, Duncan said, "Maybe. If she did, good for her. If she didn't, then God smiled on us. And if neither happened, eventually I would've."

CHAPTER 21

Gray thought he'd finally broken through Duncan's performance persona.

"How does it feel to get that off your chest?"

"Not as good as killing him would've," Duncan quipped.

"Tell me about him."

"He was an abusive, cruel piece of shit." His demeanor changed and became very casual. Conversational even. "Think about that phrase. 'Piece of shit.' People throw that around so casually it's lost all meaning. But, think about it. Piece. Of. Shit. While it has a physiological purpose, it's really the unwanted, unneeded, and empty components of the food we eat. It's smelly, steamy, the absolute filth — "

"I get it."

"That's the kind of person he was." His conversational tone morphed to one of detachment. "My father, the equivalent of human feces. I hardly even remember him, but I know that much."

Gray believed Duncan's dislike of his father. There was more rage under the surface that could be explored, but with Duncan finally admitting his feelings about his father, that topic had been extinguished. Gray needed to move on.

"You said that once you had too many bodies, you had to start dismembering them."

"You were listening!" The fact elated Duncan, who now seemed bolstered by Gray's attention, leaving him happy to elaborate. "By the end of my run, I had chopped all of them up. Except for two."

"You led the police to these two?"

"I did."

"They were the only two ever recovered?"

Duncan shook his head, denying Gray's assertion. "Until the beach."

Gray nodded, acquiescing to the correction. He pressed forward, staying on track. "Why did you bury these two and none of the others?"

"Well, I buried the others, too."

"You just said — "

"I know what I said, but what do you think I did with the torsos?"

"You buried the torsos and kept the limbs?"

"Yes, exactly." Duncan shifted in his seat, grimacing slightly from the pain in his abdomen. "I buried the two bodies – in whole – because I needed to. It was simple logistics."

"Tell me."

"We attended a convention in Kansas City, Missouri. We had our fun, but we had to be in Cleveland four days later. I wasn't returning home between conventions, so I dumped the bodies."

"Where were you living at the time?"

Duncan shook his head. Again, he was keeping a secret, likely to protect someone. He was protecting the location of his home at that time, which included the location of the freezer. And he wasn't telling who dumped the bodies.

"You and your partner, by my assessment of what you've told me so far, were quite organized. Why kill at the first of the two conventions and not wait until the second? Why add the inconvenience of burying the bodies in the middle of a business trip?"

Duncan shifted in his seat again, moving from a position where most of his weight was supported by his left hip to one where he sat squarely on the chair's surface.

"You can't always control when impulse and opportunity strike."

"Do you miss it?"

Duncan shook his head, a casual and nonchalant movement. "Not at all."

They all miss it, Gray thought. And that solidified Gray's profile of Duncan that he'd been developing during their interview. The beginnings of the profile had germinated once Gray accepted that Duncan had a partner in the killings. Then the theory grew as Duncan spoke more. Gray hypothesized that Duncan was never in it for the kill. Instead, Duncan preferred overpowering people with his intellect and manipulation. If the work had been about the kill ritual, then he would certainly miss that. Yet, for Duncan, it was about the manipulation. That's what got him off. And he didn't miss that because he still was able to manipulate people. *Including Salah. Including me. And this process.*

"Why did you tell the police where those bodies were and not the torsos and body parts?"

"I wanted to keep the rest for myself. But, more importantly, I had to give them proof."

"Were you afraid the police wouldn't believe you?"

Duncan shrugged his shoulders and tried to hide a smile. When he smiled, though, Gray noticed anew the scars and etchings on Duncan's face. It unsettled him how they'd become so ordinary in such a short time.

"Or is it more appropriate to say that you wanted to be caught?"

Duncan looked disappointed in Gray's question. "You think I wanted to be in here?"

"I do."

Duncan let anger enter his tone. "And why would I want that?"

"You tell me?" Gray asked.

"Monsters and dead men are in here."

"And sometimes they're one in the same," Gray said, referring specifically to Duncan.

Duncan pointed to the thin slits of windows above, which showed dark clouds forming in the sky. "Do you think it's any different out there?" His chains rattled again when he moved his arms. "It's not. The only difference between in and out is all of you are waltzing around pretending you're free, but you're hiding from your true selves." He leaned toward Gray. "Every human is an animal. Every. Single. One." His eyes locked on to Gray's eyes. "But you've all been domesticated by the governments and religion and the puritanical rules of society, where every statement and every act is condemnable as some sort of offense, so you bottle up all your natural instincts to keep from losing your freedoms, which are really just addictions to the material things the world offers, slaves to bragging about your so-called happy lives.

"The only good thing about being in here is, most of the people here, they know what it's like to have lived fully. Before they were imprisoned, they embraced their animal, their true self, and none of the rules of society stopped them when the animal came out. Take my partner, for example, he was born to kill, so that's what he did. He lived his true life.

"At least in here you know what you're up against and you know who the people are and what they're capable of. How many sanctimonious politicians out there falsely represent the good of humanity and then turn out to be horrendously greedy and morally corrupt?

"So, no, while I didn't want to be in here, at least the people are real."

Duncan's viewpoint turned Gray's stomach. It was a sickening and warped viewpoint. Maybe Duncan believed what he'd said, but more likely he was trying to prove some point by bending reality, so he could entangle Gray into a winless debate. It went against a police officer's sense of logic to have people in prison espouse its cultural superiority over free society. Duncan had to know that, and he had to know Gray could battle him point by point. He didn't know, though, that Gray figured that was

Duncan's goal. He didn't know that Gray realized jumping into this rabbit hole with Duncan was a waste of time. It was simply more manipulation, more distraction. The thinking was flawed. The logic tainted, twisted, and corrupted by possible insanity. And Gray refused to be drawn into it.

"What about you, detective? You're no different than the rest of them."

Gray spent a few seconds too long thinking about what Duncan had said. It gave Duncan the opportunity to poke at Gray further.

"You have a true version of yourself that you're not setting free. I know what you're capable of. I know what you want to do. I know." Duncan flashed his creepy smile. "I know."

"Kenneth, just answer my questions."

"I'm going to help you, detective. I'm going to get you closer to your goal. It will almost be as if I put the gun in your hand myself and help you ease back on the trigger." The smile was still engraved on Duncan's disfigured face. "And you're going to thank me for it."

CHAPTER 22

Duncan had steered them in a new direction. Far away from what Gray wanted to discuss. Gray resisted the urge to roll his eyes and sigh in frustration at Duncan's games.

"I don't know what you're talking about."

"I think you do."

"When did you lose your trust of society?"

Pleased with what was to come, Duncan knew he was going to play with Gray's words, believing he'd won Gray's curiosity. "I never said I didn't trust society. I just don't like it."

"When did you stop liking it?" Gray fired the question quickly, hoping to cut off any follow-up comments Duncan had planned to go along with his horrific smile. "Was it the incident at the movie theater when you were sixteen?"

That question unsettled Duncan. His smile faded slowly, revealing an underlying anger.

"Your mother told the police about it," Gray said, further hoping to drill into Duncan's sudden change of mood.

"Nice try, Detective Gray. She didn't know anything about it."

"She knew whatever happened turned you into what you are today."

Duncan nodded. "She was smarter than I thought."

"What happened?"

"Do you really care, detective?"

"Not really. I thought your mom might like to know the truth, so she can stop blaming herself, but I'd much rather discuss your partner."

"Let her blame herself."

"Your partner?"

When Duncan didn't respond, Gray let the silence in the room grow. He considered rethinking his approach. *What leverage do I have?* He couldn't offer a letter to the parole board in favor of Duncan's release because the man would never be paroled. He couldn't offer to get Duncan better medical assistance because Duncan didn't even want medical treatment. He wondered about offering less time in solitary confinement following offenses, but Gray figured Duncan didn't mind the solitary time. And that brought him back to the real issue in this interview: how to motivate someone who seemingly cared about nothing?

Could he motivate him negatively? What if Gray threatened to bring Duncan's mother for a visit? Make him confess to her what he'd done? Or, could he fabricate a story about going after Duncan's mother for his father's death? *No, that won't work.* Gray was willing to bet Duncan didn't like his mother.

"We're not getting anywhere," Gray said, stating the obvious.

Duncan agreed. "Because you aren't talking about the right things."

"What are the right things?" Gray asked.

"You. I want to talk about you."

The cryptic comments about Gray being a lifeless corpse and putting a gun in Gray's hand were both troublesome and curious. It was part of Gray's stubbornness that he stayed away from that line of conversation and remained focused on his own agenda with Duncan. But, maybe it was time Gray gave in. Maybe Gray had made a mistake trying to maintain control of the conversation. He'd not garnered much new information.

"Let's be fair. We'll split question for question," Duncan suggested.

"Explain that," Gray said.

"I thought it was self-explanatory," Duncan remarked with a tinge of dominance in his tone. "I'll ask a question, you answer it. Then you ask, and I'll answer it. And that'll last until one of us can't think of another question to ask."

Gray considered playing along. "And you'll be honest in every answer? No more games?"

"No games."

"If I agree to this, I get the first question," Gray asserted.

"If that'll make you feel better, sure, Becker."

CHAPTER 23

Gray went first. "Who was your partner?"

Duncan leaned against the back of his chair. Despite his arms stretched before him, locked to the table by the short chain and steel bolt, he looked relaxed, pain-free even.

"Wesley Murch." Then he moved onto his first question without taking a breath. "How often do you think about your daughter?"

The question sent an electric charge through Gray's body. If this wasn't Salah's case, he'd reach across the table and try to drag Duncan's wrists through the steel bolt's hole. Instead of that, though, he said, trying to maintain his temper, "I'm not — "

"Before you respond," Duncan cautioned, "I answered your question, and now it's your turn. Honestly. Or the whole game ends."

Gray grinded his teeth. "Every day." His jaw stayed locked when he spoke.

"Thank you," Duncan said, enjoyment in his voice.

Gray was sidetracked now. "How did you know about my daughter?"

"The news." Duncan had the answer cocked and loaded like a bullet in a gun, like he knew Gray would veer away from the case. "When is the last time you drank alcohol?"

"About twenty-four months ago."

A cough, originating outside the door, echoed through the cell. Without looking, Gray recognized that the cough had come from Salah. He didn't need to look at her to know she was sending him a message. He needed to stay focused. He planned out the next few questions — *Duncan clearly had* — wanting to gain as much information as possible in as few questions as possible.

"What does Wesley Murch look like?" Gray asked, thankful to Salah for reeling him in.

"The big guy from Game of Thrones. How often do you want a drink?"

"Rarely. Where is Wesley from?"

"Raleigh, North Carolina. Where is your daughter's mother now?"

"Not sure. We aren't close." They agreed to be honest, but there was no way Gray was going to allow his ex-wife's location, name, age, or anything else to filter into Duncan's mind — certainly not with someone on the outside helping him. "Where did you and Wesley meet?"

"Los Angeles. Did you solve the case of your mayor's murder?"

Gray didn't mind lying to protect his ex-wife. There was no way for Duncan to know if he was or wasn't lying. But he needed to be careful with this response. Duncan had clearly seen and studied the news surrounding the Pen Pal and mayor's cases. However, that gave Gray an advantage. Duncan only knew what had been reported through news outlets. And on that front Gray, too, figured that some of the television news coverage Duncan had seen may have included Jordan Butler's reporting. He hated that her image had been beamed into Duncan's mind, where such terrible ideas lived.

"I did, along with my partner. Where is Wesley's last known address?"

"When I knew him, he was living in Oshkosh, Wisconsin. I don't know his actual residential address. How was the mayor killed?"

"Shot in the face. Who dumped the body parts into the Gulf of Mexico?"

This elicited Duncan's first hesitation. "My mother."

"Your mother?"

And the rope of protection had been snapped.

"It's not your turn, Becker." He stayed quiet, making sure Gray understood that he was sticking to the rules.

"It was a clarifying response. Nothing more."

Duncan accepted the reasoning for the rule breakage and said, "Tell me about the other murders."

"That's not a question, Kenneth." He wanted Duncan to know he had to stick to the rules, too. Plus, the statement was too vague to address.

Duncan leaned forward, resting his arms on the table, using them to support his weight. He was enjoying this more than Gray preferred. "How did the gang members die?"

That again proved to Gray that Duncan had followed the news coverage, but Gray didn't know what information Duncan was looking for with his line of questioning. Was he simply getting aroused talking about murder? Or, was it something else? Why were these details important to him? He'd waited all day to talk to Gray, so what did Duncan deem important about these questions?

"Most were shot. One drank quite a bit of bleach. How and why did your mother do this?"

"That may be cheating, Becker. Feels like two questions to me."

"Why?"

"It's simple. Because I asked her to. And I gave her the impression that after I got cancer, I became a reformed man. I found God, Becker. I'd say she liked hearing that."

He used her.

"Beyond the bleach," Duncan took his turn, "were there other forms of torture involved in the killings of the gang members?"

Gray wondered about the properness of telling this information to Duncan and it being recorded, but, ultimately, he would likely be fired after the inquiry in Lakeland was completed, so what did it matter?

"Bones were broken. There was some craftsmanship with nails. Eye gouging. Now, how did your mom dump the body parts?"

"I asked her to use the trolley boat in my barn and take all the body parts to sea. I kind of hoped the gulf water would take her along with the limbs, if I'm being totally honest. A trolley boat isn't exactly seaworthy. Unfortunately, the sea let me down, just like she did. She obviously fucked up because the limbs were never supposed to wash up on the beach. But, divine intervention, if that hadn't happened, then I never would've been able to see you again." His eyes gleamed wildly, as he asked, "What mutilation was performed on the gang members' bodies?"

This information wasn't made available to the public, so the question intrigued Gray. How did he know? Why did he want to know about it?

"A couple of the victims were cut side-to-side." Gray slid his finger from one hip to the other, providing a visual representation of the wounds. "He pulled the insides out of one man. Used the blood to ... " He thought better of giving away too much information. "He splashed it on the walls." He took a moment to think if there was anything else he wanted to tell Duncan about the mutilations. There wasn't, so he moved on. "I want to know where the torsos are buried."

"That's not a question, Becker."

"Where are the torsos buried?"

"Unless I marked each grave with some sort of GPS marker, we'll never find them. I'm talking deep in wooded areas. Dumped in raging rivers. One in The Everglades. One stuffed into an oil drum in Louisiana. I mean, really, they'll never be found." Duncan didn't have the look of satisfaction or regret on his face. Everything coming from his mouth wreaked of fact. Nothing more. Nothing less. "The guy who drank all that bleach. What's the general feeling on how that played out?"

Humoring Duncan left a bad taste in Gray's mouth. He hated this game. Hated being in the same room as Duncan. Hated that Duncan thought he had power over him.

Gray said, "I figure the killer wanted information from the victim. Maybe the victim made him mad. Maybe the killer got the information then decided to be creative in the way he killed the guy. Not really sure."

Gray set up his next question, returning the topic to Wesley Murch. "Despite having pled guilty to multiple murders, you're now claiming Wesley Murch was the killer and you were solely a willing partner in the killings. If that is correct and truthful, then why did you tell the police you had killed them?"

This question took a long time for Duncan to answer. The wait wasn't one of hesitation, uncertainty, or making up a story. It was different. More like one of building the courage to speak the truth. More like saying the truth for the first time in who knows how long. Maybe it was the first time ever.

"Because I was complicit in their murders, Becker. No doubt about that. Wrapping your fingers around someone's throat isn't the only way to kill a man. I did lure them in. I did overpower them mentally. It took both of us to kill the men. My hands weren't dirty, but I was just as guilty."

Gray wished he could ask two or three quick follow-up questions, but he stifled them and hoped the momentum would still be there when it was his turn to ask questions again.

"How was Morgan Beringer murdered?"

Gray felt the same nerve burst in electric spasm as when Duncan had asked the first question about Gray's daughter. What made him so interested in Morgan? Why was she the subject of Duncan's imagination? None of the questions Duncan was asking were senseless. They were leading somewhere. Gray was sure about that. *But why? Where?*

"Morgan Beringer, the mayor's wife, was pregnant. We think she was chased down the stairs and then shot. Afterward, the baby was cut out of her and saved. Parentless, but allowed to breathe and given a chance to grow up."

Maybe Duncan had done this before, but Gray hadn't noticed it until now. He appeared to be quite deeply considering Gray's response. Gray noted it and asked his next question.

"Why didn't you give up Wesley's name when you were arrested?"

"I saw no need," Duncan responded.

There had to be more to Duncan's answer.

"No. You need to elaborate."

"I answered your question."

"No way." Gray's blood flowed hot. He realized this wasn't going to work if Duncan kept answering in short, glib, and vague bursts. "Why didn't you give him up?"

"I told you."

"Did you love him?" Gray asked. "Were you two romantically involved? Was this another way you were overpowering people? By corrupting the justice system? I want to know why, Kenneth."

"Easy, Becker."

"Don't tell me to take it easy. Answer the question, like we agreed. Honestly and completely."

"First of all," Duncan shouted in response to Gray's rant, "I'm no rat, so there was no way I was going to spit out his name. Second, he wasn't going to kill anyone without me. He's harmless alone. I turned him fierce. I showed him his true self. I set him free. So, there was no need to tell the police about him. There was no danger without me."

Gray's theory about Duncan's role in the killers' relationship was spot on.

Duncan asked, still speaking forcefully, charged up from the fervent response Gray had garnered, "Did you have a personal relationship with Morgan Beringer?"

The question stole Gray's breath, his thoughts, and his emotions. The look he gave Duncan, if Duncan weren't a psychopath, would've frightened him. No matter what Gray said, the look on his face said it all. And he could see the recognition in Duncan's eyes. He had to tell the truth, or Duncan would suspect Gray of lying and shut down the back and forth they had built – such that it was. Then the case would be harmed. Duncan would win. Salah and the families would lose. Because of him.

"We had a moment. There was nothing physical. I may have read more into it than was there. No," he thought more about it and said, "I'm sure I did." His teeth grinded again. "I cared about her, yes."

Gray considered taking a break. He wanted to process all that had been said in the interview with Duncan. He suddenly wondered what would happen if the recording found its way to the TEAM inquiry investigators. What would they think of his responses? How would they interpret them? How would they apply them to their agenda? And how could he counter the team's assertions?

But first things first. It was his turn to ask a question.

"Why are you asking about the mayor's case?"

CHAPTER 24

D uncan's eyes gleamed, like he was finally happy with one of Gray's questions. Like he was finally getting to the root of what he wanted to talk about.

"Because I think I can help. The killer is still at large, right?"

Gray pushed back from the table, creating more space between the two of them. He stood, studied Duncan, and began pacing slowly, keeping his eyes trained on Duncan. Skepticism forged a path across his face, as he struggled with Duncan's focus on the Tony Mason case.

"Yes. How do you think you can help?"

"That depends on the collective information you share with me. I have more questions before I can say for sure."

Gray's patience and temper, ever connected in a volatile, codependent marriage, were in the midst of an extramarital affair with frustration and confusion. And the activities of the affair resulted in a clouded thought process. The clarity he needed was being cloaked by his own personality as well as Duncan's well-planned manipulation. After hours of talking, Gray felt a conversational vertigo descending on his mind. He didn't know if or when Duncan was lying. And the constant back and forth made it difficult to keep track of his questions and the information being exchanged. Atop all of that was the Mason case, the questions about Morgan's murder, the faint connection to Jordan Butler, the inquiry in Lakeland, feeling Salah's eyes on him from outside the cell, and the hopes he held to provide Noah Chritton's family some closure — it was a perfect storm inside his head. He should take a break.

Palms down for support, Gray leaned across the table at Duncan. "So, ask."

"Did you see my heart tattoo?"

Gray stood straight. More manipulative redirection from Duncan. Gray was on the cusp of finding out what Duncan thought he knew of the Mason case, and the killer played with him again. Gray wondered if he'd gathered enough information for Salah and her case, for the Chrittons. He could just end the interview. But, he was fooling himself. He'd sit there another hundred hours if it was even remotely going to help him with the Mason case.

The tattoo, Gray recalled, was an outline of the heart muscle. Duncan had been in the midst of painting over it with a black circle when he'd been caught by the correctional officers and sent again to solitary confinement.

"I don't care about your tattoos or your cutting. What do you think you know about the Mason case?"

"I'm trying to tell you yet again!" His voice raised in aggravation. "But you've struggled to listen to me this whole time."

Another moment of acting from Duncan.

"Don't raise your voice at me again," Gray commanded.

"Then listen! We could've had this whole conversation finished hours ago, if you would have just listened and cooperated."

Gray wondered if Duncan was right about that assertion. Wondered if Duncan was telling the truth again.

"I have no heart, Becker, so I didn't need it on my chest any longer."

Gray gave him a skeptical turn of his face.

"You don't believe me?" Duncan nodded, then proved Gray wrong. "I don't care about Wesley, or the men I led to their deaths, not their families, definitely not this prison or the people I share it with. I don't care about you or Detective Salah. I don't even care about my own mother. And

I have absolutely no regard for myself," he raised his hands, jingling the chains as he did, and presented his face as evidence, "as you can tell from my overhaul. I. Simply. Don't. Care. Period. About anything.

"Or so I thought.

"Because during the first visit with Detective Salah, I realized that I do actually care about one thing."

Gray raised his eyebrows, hoping Duncan would get to the point, unsure if they still were playing their question and answer game.

"I know." Duncan misread Gray's facial expression. "I was surprised, too. But, don't get your hopes up. I didn't suddenly realize I cared about puppies and kittens. Or even tapioca pudding, like Saleena thinks. No, there's no turn around happening here. I wasn't saved by mystical religions, as I told my mother. I haven't been reformed by this amazing correctional institution. Nothing like that."

"What is it?" Gray asked.

"Like the circle around my heart, what I care about is black." His eyes burned into Gray's. "I need you to help me obtain it. And I promise you'll want to help me."

CHAPTER 25

Gray pushed back from the table. He wasn't in the business of helping convicted killers. But that didn't mean Duncan didn't have his attention.

Gray asked, "So Detective Salah comes to see you and you suddenly realize you care about something? And you need me for some reason?"

"Exactly." A smile slithered across Duncan's lips.

Gray folded his arms across his chest. "And that reason is connected to the murders of Douglas and Morgan Beringer?"

"Yes." The smile extended further.

Gray dropped his arms and scooted his chair back to the table. "I'm all ears."

"Yes," Duncan agreed again, things going perfectly his way. "There is more I must know first."

With slumped shoulders, Gray said, "My patience is thinning."

Duncan ignored Gray's warning. "I've read everything I could get my hands on related to the case."

"I picked up on that."

"And I've been watching you closely since you sat down to see if my impression of you holds firm."

Gray leaned forward. "You were studying me?"

"Yes."

Duncan leaned on the table again. He scooted as far forward in his chair as the chains would allow. The movement appeared painful.

"I truly believe you should have a black circle over your heart, too." Duncan pointed his bony index finger at Gray's face. "I see it in your eyes, Becker. You're capable of killing."

Gray rolled his eyes, settling into his seat again. "Kenneth — "

"Have you ever killed a man?"

The answer came slowly, unsure if he wanted to play along with Duncan. "No."

"Then no one ever gave you the right reason, I presume." Smugness shrouded Duncan's presence. "Until Tony Mason killed Morgan Beringer."

"Get to the point quick."

"The point, Becker, is that Tony Mason has brought you and I together. Killer to would-be killer."

"Quicker," Gray advised.

"News articles and TV pundits praise you for chasing Tony to Sumterville. Yet, the city is investigating you for not following proper procedure. I want to know what were you going to do when you caught up to Tony?"

No response. Gray's teeth grinded together one more time, his jaw muscles flexing where Duncan could see.

"I know what you wanted to do." Duncan's eyes widened, and his face filled with demented delight. "Vengeance," he uttered.

Gray let off his teeth. "What do you think you know about this case?"

"You're not going to tell me if I'm right?" Duncan's demented delight morphed to faux realization. He pointed to the cell phone. "Oh, is it because we're recording? You don't want everyone to know your sole purpose for hunting Mason was to kill him? Is that it?" Duncan waited a beat before saying, "They know, Becker. Everyone knows."

Gray's stomach turned over and lodged in his chest. Duncan's words burrowed under his skin. Festered. He tried to steel himself against their infection, but he was slowly losing the battle.

"A man like you won't rest until Mason is dead, right? That's the impression I have of you, Becker. Am I correct about that?"

"The case or I walk."

Duncan faked a look of defeat. "Won't you tell me anything of your desire to kill Mason?"

Gray stared stoically.

"Your silence tells me I'm right about you, and that's just perfect." Duncan continued before Gray could object. "You're pretending, if you think you just went there to arrest him. That's you playing by society's rules. That's you hiding your true self. Think. Really think. And at least admit to yourself that I'm right. You wanted to slash that bastard from chin to gooch, and if you'd had the chance, you would've. That's what makes your heart black." A beat. "Just like mine."

"You're wrong." Gray hardly controlled his frustration.

"No, I'm not!" Duncan spoke as if that were one word, *NoImnot.* "Tell me, has the Tony Mason who killed your Morgan been tracked across the globe to places like Laos, Somalia, Senegal, Pakistan, Afghanistan, Turkey, Iraq, and Indonesia? I could go on."

Frozen, Gray swallowed hard. Last he'd heard of this subject, Mason had been tracked to Iraq, Afghanistan, Pakistan and Turkey. He hadn't heard any updates detailing travel to the other countries Duncan had mentioned. What froze Gray was that the information hadn't been released to the media. He even had trouble getting it.

"He has. I can see it in your eyes." Duncan said, reading into Gray's silence. "He was in the military, right?" Duncan's tone was that of a mother trying to spoon-feed her 9-month-old baby.

"Army," Gray mumbled. He didn't mean to respond. The word simply escaped his mouth.

Duncan delivered an expectant nod.

Just as Gray was about to ask a question, he remembered from Duncan's profile that he'd served in the Army as well. Thinking back to the report in greater detail, Gray remembered that the dates of Duncan's service and that of Mason's overlapped slightly.

Then he realized his jaw had dropped. His mouth hung open.

"You know him," Gray said.

Elation splashed across Duncan's face, excited that Gray had finally figured out his secret.

"Yes! Yes. Finally, Becker. Finally. I thought you'd never catch on."

How? was all Gray could think.

"Would you like to sit back down?"

CHAPTER 26

Gray felt like he'd fallen through the floor with the revelation that Duncan and Mason had served together in the Army. Ideas and scenarios careened through his head, but he had to be careful. The cardinal rule of dealing with serial killers — don't let them get in your head — was broken. Duncan was now — and had been — imbedded in Gray's mind. Gray realized that Duncan had been mentally throwing him around the cell, slamming him here and there with convoluted ideas and manipulative responses for hours. Was this more of his manipulation, or was he now suddenly telling the truth?

Despite that uncertainty, a well of hope sprung inside Gray's thoughts. Could Duncan actually help Gray find Mason? His hopefulness raced wildly, so much so that he didn't even hear the cell door open and Salah hurry toward the table.

"Ah, Detective Salah has joined us," Duncan said. He sounded disappointed.

Even with Duncan's announcement, it took Gray a moment to collect his thoughts.

"Let's pause for a few minutes," she suggested.

"No," Gray said, snapping back. "We're fine. We can keep going." Eager to get to the information about Mason.

"Agreed," Duncan said. "I'd love a water though. And perhaps a mint. My mouth still tastes like vomit."

"Gray, now."

Salah tapped Gray's shoulder, prompting him to stand. When he stood, his muscles wobbled. He took a moment to get his balance. Salah saw that he couldn't stop scrutinizing Duncan's facial expressions, searching for his truthfulness or deceit. She grabbed Gray's phone, killing the recording, and nudged Gray's arm.

"See you soon, Becker."

Salah led Gray out of the cell. They paused at the cell door.

"Duncan asked for water." Then she whispered, "I need a quiet place Detective Gray and I can talk."

Munro sent them with one of his lackeys. They made their way through the halls that had led them to Duncan's interview cell. They rushed through two security checkpoints and then were provided an empty office.

"I'll be out here when you're ready to go back," the officer said.

Salah closed the door. Locked it.

"Holy shit, are you okay?" she asked, turning away from the door.

Gray leaned against the desk in the office. His head hung low, and his trunk bent like he was trying to physically recover from being sucker punched in the gut. Coincidentally, that was exactly how he felt.

"You were right to pause the interview." He raised his head and saw there were no chairs in the office. Only an empty desk and two bare bookshelves called the room home. "Did you get what you needed for your case?"

"I think we're good, yes."

"Good." Gray lowered his head again, thinking of the next steps with Duncan.

"It's like talking to an insane seven-year-old who's high on meth, chewing saltwater taffy, is shooting flames from his eyes and speaks a different language," she said.

Gray laughed, amused by her comparison. "That's about right."

The laugh lightened the mood.

"You look exhausted," she said.

Gray let the comment pass. "He knows Mason. That's why he called me here. He wants something from me, and Mason is the leverage."

"Yeah," she said, but it sounded like the opposite.

"You don't believe him?"

"Not in any way whatsoever," Salah answered quickly and confidently.

Gray pushed off the desk, ready to support his belief. "He knew what countries Mason had been to. That information was never released to the news media."

But Salah fought back. "The media reported Mason's military background. Where else would Mason have been except for those countries? He's fucking with you. He's been jerking you around since we walked in the door."

"What if he's not?"

"He is!"

Gray reconsidered his position, his presentation. "He has terminal cancer and probably won't be alive a year from now. Whatever he may or may not know, I need to get it now."

"This is stupid," she said. "There's nothing to get. He's probably in there right now touching himself, completely turned on by weaseling his way into your deepest desires. That's what he does. That's what he did with his victims. Shit, I think you're turning into one of them."

Gray took slight offense, and his posture stiffened. "He won't kill me."

"No, but I bet he makes it into your dreams. Is that what you want?"

Gray lost his temper. "No! I want Tony Mason!"

It was now Salah's turn to reconsider her position and presentation of her argument.

"I don't know you. You're not my partner," she said. "But I'm drawn to you. I think you're a great detective. I think you're a good man. I think that inquiry back home is bullshit, and they should leave you alone. And that makes me want to protect you." She shot him a penetrating look. "You shouldn't go back in there."

She stayed silent while Gray considered her statement.

Then she said, "What could he possibly want from you that you can actually give him?"

"I don't know, but if he tells me where I can find Tony Mason, then I'll give him anything he wants."

Salah moved to Gray's side. She leaned against the desk and settled her arms crisscross in front of her.

"That's what I thought you'd say. And, incidentally, that's what he thought you'd say, too."

Gray propped himself against the desk beside her.

"Was he right?" she asked. "Did you go to Sumterville to kill Mason?"

Gray stared at the floor, keeping his eyes from meeting Salah's. He thought she would see right into his soul when their eyes met. He didn't know how he was going to answer her question, but he didn't want her to see the truth in his eyes, if he chose to lie.

"He killed good people."

He left it at that, which resulted in a heavy silence filling the small, bare office.

~ ~ ~ ~

The break served Gray well. He grabbed a cup of coffee and cleared his head, put the previous interview content aside, along with the worries about manipulation, trying to right his regrets from the first time they spoke, the Chrittons, his emotions about the Mason case, and Duncan's flimsy and desperate comparison between him and Gray. It gave Gray an opportunity to re-center his mental focus and push aside everything that didn't matter. Now there was only one thing on the table to discuss: *Tony Mason*.

Gray entered the cell alone. Salah and the guards remained outside the wall of steel bars, waiting, watching, and listening. Gray sat down in his chair and scooted closer to the table.

"It's just you and me," Gray said.

Duncan's face was filled with arrogance. It was the kind of aura that only a sense of complete control could give a person.

"I knew you'd come back," Duncan said.

"Detective Salah didn't think I should."

"That figures."

"She believes you're manipulating me by drawing obvious conclusions from what's been reported in the news."

"But you don't believe her?"

"I do not," Gray said.

That boosted Duncan's sense of superiority and control.

"But I need to know something first. Something that'll prove you're not making all of this up. This is her interview, remember? Not mine. She can shut it down. So, if we're doing this, she needs to know it's legit."

Duncan's smile spread. The ink and scar markings curved and stretched.

"I see," he said. "How about this: go fuck yourself." His anger fired. "This isn't her interview, it's mine. If you want to know about Tony Mason, then it's not up to me to prove I knew him. It's on you to prove to me that you'll keep your end of the deal."

Gray showed no visible reaction to Duncan's heated words.

"We don't have a deal," Gray said.

"We're going to make one." The pain again was impossible to hide. "Or I'm not talking."

Gray leaned forward. "What is it?"

"Just one thing." Duncan's eyes met Gray's again. The pain in his torso present but evening out. "A promise."

"That's it?"

Duncan nodded. "A simple promise."

Gray doubted it would be simple.

Duncan played with a legal-sized yellow piece of paper in front of him. Writing filled every line on the page. Some of the writing was in paragraph form. Other parts were bullet pointed lists.

"What's that?" Gray asked.

Duncan folded the paper in half and covered it with his cuffed hands.

"It's what you're looking for."

Gray eyed the paper, wondering if he could just snatch it from the prisoner. A last resort perhaps. Gray jutted out his chin, telling Duncan to move forward with the presentation of his conditions.

Duncan smiled, his aura of arrogance widening.

"I'll give you all you need to find Tony Mason. All of it." He smiled again, imagining Gray taking the bait. He whispered, so the guards and Salah wouldn't hear him. "But … if I give that to you, you have to kill him when you find him. Not arrest him. Kill him."

Gray blew out a big breath. How could he possibly even contemplate making a deal with Duncan? He looked over to Salah and the guards, wondering if they could hear the conversation. And he was glad he hadn't recorded this part of the conversation. That was Salah's idea, so Gray would be the only one with the information Duncan provided about Mason; it would ensure Gray remained involved with the task force hunting for Mason. That is, if any of the information was authentic.

Noting Gray's hesitation, Duncan said, "You're thinking that you'll eventually find him on your own, and when you do find him, you're going to kill him anyway, just like you'd planned in Sumterville. So why make a deal with me, right?"

He had considered that. "Okay," Gray played along.

"Beyond that, you're thinking you can just agree to the deal, get the information, then back out of it once you have what you want."

"It's a fair thought process."

Duncan smiled. He had picked Gray apart so easily.

"You'll never find him."

Duncan's demeanor was sincere.

Besides, that's not how this deal's going to work. I'll tell you about Mason, but I won't give you everything you need to find him until later."

"When?"

"Tomorrow."

Gray said, "I won't be here tomorrow."

"It'll be delivered."

"To me?"

Duncan nodded.

"I could just walk out of here and wait for the package," Gray said, shrugging his shoulders, simplifying the agreement.

"You could. But the information won't make sense without this conversation today. You see?"

"I understand," Gray said.

"Then say it."

"Why do you want Mason dead?"

Duncan tilted his head, confused by the question. "What does it matter?"

"It matters."

"It shouldn't."

"It does. Why, Kenneth?"

Duncan grunted, considering his response.

"How's this for the way the universe works. Mason has brought us together, and he's supplied us the same reason to kill him. Revenge. Now, say it."

Gray's eyes shot over to Salah and the guards again.

"Say it," Duncan prodded.

Gray hesitated. Had the murder of Morgan Beringer turned his heart black? He had gone to Sumterville to kill Mason. A premeditated act. An act solely focused on murder. Undeniably, if he were honest with himself. Yes, Duncan was right. Gray had already surrendered to that end. He'd already accepted his fate to kill Mason. He'd already blackened his heart. He just hadn't realized it yet.

Gray leaned across the table and spoke softly, hoping Duncan couldn't hear his heart pounding in his chest frantically working against the blackening.

"I promise you."

"Say it," Duncan said. "All of it."

Gray's breaths were short.

"I'll kill Mason. But not for you."

Duncan's eerie smile pushed his cheeks to the side. It was done. He'd beaten Gray. He'd live with Gray forever.

"I don't care who you do it for, as long as you do it."

CHAPTER 27

*D*irty. It was the only appropriate word for how Gray felt. Not remorseful, not embarrassed, not guilty. *Dirty.* Partially for making a deal with someone like Duncan, but also for giving in to Duncan's condition. He knew Duncan would believe he'd beaten Gray. He had, to an extent, Gray admitted. But Gray didn't like Duncan knowing that. Mostly, he hated seeing the smirk of power on Duncan's face. Because the truth was, all Duncan won today was getting Gray to say out loud that he'd kill Mason. That decision was Gray's alone, and it had been made the second he saw Morgan's dead body.

Dirty or not, Gray now needed to collect his payment.

Duncan slid the paper across the table as far as the chains would allow. "It's a list of information about Mason. When and where we served together in the Army. Names of others who served with us, including one of our commanding officers. I thought you'd want something to confirm the accuracy of what I'm about to tell you."

Gray skimmed the content of the paper. He read the names of the countries that Duncan had previously listed verbally. He'd added Yemen, Sri Lanka, Chad, Japan, Jordan, Ukraine, and Poland to the list. He saw mention of Fort Drum and Fort Hayes. And he noticed a list of names: Smith, Tolson, Chevy, and Billings. The list included one name that sent a charge to his system — Carpenter.

That name, and that name alone, gave Duncan full authenticity in Gray's eyes. The name James Carpenter had not been released to the public, so there was no way for Duncan to include it unless he was telling the truth about his own connection to Mason.

Duncan shifted in his seat, finding a comfortable, pain-free position. Then he spoke, ignoring the subsiding ache. "You would say men like me are rare, yes?"

"Not rare enough unfortunately."

Duncan ignored Gray's comment, preferring to focus on their common goal.

"It's the same thing in the military. Men like Tony Mason were rare, but they were there, they were needed, and they were praised for their abilities. They were gods, to some degree."

Gray noted the comparison Duncan made between himself and Mason.

"The brass treated them as such and so did the enlisted men. Even the enemy began to know them and reacted accordingly. Some tried to kill them, others quaked in their boots."

"How did you treat him?"

If Duncan compared himself to Mason, as if perhaps they were equals in some way, then his response to this question would be telling.

"I treated him better than a god."

That was the response Gray had expected.

"I liked watching him work. He just had this sixth sense when it came to killing. You know, I saw him single-handedly gun down eight enemy soldiers. I saw him kill with his knife. With a two-by-four. I saw him break a light bulb and twist it into a guy's eye socket. The man's a machine."

Clearly the conversation about Mason aroused Duncan. Gray could hear the silk in his voice and see the elation blushing his skin. There was either an infatuation bordering on love, or Duncan had fallen prey to the effects of idolization.

"During one mission in Afghanistan we came under fire from a group of tribal soldiers. Two of our guys were pinned behind a utility truck. The rest of us were either behind trees or large boulders. I mean, we were all relatively pinned in, I guess. I thought we were all going to die. I peeked around the corner of my cover and saw Tony running off ... *away* from the action. I thought he was leaving us to die.

"Turns out, though, he was drawing fire away from us. Three of the enemy chased after him, and he somehow killed each one of them. One with a knife, and two with a handgun. Then he rounded the field of action and came at the remaining tribal soldiers from behind, killing all but one, who ran away and escaped.

"The best part of that battle was," Duncan said with glee in his eyes, "Tony took his knife and went to each of the men and cut their guts wide open. He loved desecrating their Muslim bodies. And I loved watching him do it."

He finally took a breath. With it, some of the elation deflated, overrun by his stomach pain.

"Thing about someone like Tony is, all he knows how to do is kill. He had a wife and kid back home, but I don't think he was much of a husband and father. He talked about the kid mostly. Ryker, I think his name was."

Duncan had the name of Mason's son correct. He'd also nailed a few of Mason's killing characteristics, as far as Gray knew them. Killing multiple people at one time. Using a broken light bulb to either torture or desecrate. Eye gouging. Slicing stomachs from side to side. All methods used in Mason's Lakeland killings.

"He cared about the boy and his wife," Duncan continued talking, "but he was a killer. An animal. And he never should've married. I mean, that's him trying to operate within society's guidelines and expectations of people, not him being who he really is. And who he is, is a killer. Born that way. He will fail at everything else in his life, except that."

"His true self," Gray said, referring to one of Duncan's consistent themes throughout their conversations.

"Exactly." Duncan smiled, having finally gotten through to Gray.

"How were you teamed up with Mason?"

"We served in the Middle East together. I was just an intelligence analyst and communications officer. Officially, we were there to perform recon and security training for allied forces. Off the record, our team performed covert extractions and ordered killings. We hunted terrorists and tracked down opposition tribal leaders."

Gray couldn't say he'd paid much attention to the war in the Middle East. Sure, he knew about it, shook his head at the increasing number of casualties, and had his own opinion about it, but he had cases to work. And at that time in his life he probably had a lot of whiskey to drink, too.

"That doesn't sound like you," Gray said.

"It wasn't, but my mother ... I saw it like this, every day was a costume party. I got to dress up like Sergeant Slaughter every day."

"Bullshit."

"Pretending I was someone else was the only way I got through it. I kept to myself and did my job. I didn't care if I made it back."

"Did you join Mason's team because you had a death wish?" Gray asked.

Duncan shook his head. "I was told I was going to be on his team. And that's that."

"It was fate."

"Maybe so."

"Get back to why you want him dead."

Duncan looked past Gray at the cinder block wall, like Kabul was there.

"Because of Tony's specialized abilities, our duties were strategic. So our team ultimately had a fair amount of down time between missions.

There was always PT to do, but you can only do so much of that. A lot of the guys played board games, and card games, they read, and they did these inane tasks day in and day out. Cleaning the weapons. Packing their gear and unpacking it. I did what I had to, but I preferred to read in my bunk as much as I could. Tony, though, didn't do the stuff the rest of us were doing. He didn't have to. He had a ton of briefings. I think he worked with other teams going into the field, helping them with strategy. Stuff like that.

"But the thing that most intrigued me was he left the base all by himself very often. I kept seeing him leave and come back hours later. I got so curious about it that I couldn't sleep at night wondering what he did alone outside the base perimeter."

Gray knew what was coming next.

"So, I followed him one day."

Of course, you did.

"I don't know how he didn't see me, sense me, or whatever because on the battlefield he would've sniffed out someone following us even if we were upwind."

Gray leaned forward, resting his elbows on the table. He thought the story was finally getting interesting.

"At first, he didn't do anything of note. He hit the market. Got coffee and some food. And I started wondering if risking him seeing me was worth it, but then I saw his demeanor change. He went from browsing at the street merchants' tables to a battlefield rigidness, and then he ducked down an alley. By the time I got there, I saw him rendezvous with a woman. She took him inside a shop. I hid outside in the market. About ten minutes later, he left out the same door. Alone. He seemed to be in a hurry. It took everything I had to keep up with him."

"What city were you in?" Gray asked.

"Kabul."

"Was the woman a prostitute?"

"No!" Duncan snapped sharply at Gray. "He wasn't like that. He was married."

Duncan's response matched what Gray thought it would be. Duncan saw Mason as a god, and a god wouldn't succumb to that type of temptation.

"Were you like that when you were married, Becker?" Duncan lashed out at him in rebuttal.

"It was just a question," Gray said.

"It was dumb."

Gray nodded. Then asked, "Where'd he go after the rendezvous?"

"I don't know." Duncan sounded annoyed. "He paid someone to use their scooter, and I lost him."

"What did you do?"

"I went back to where Tony had met the woman, but she was gone. I couldn't really do anything else, so I bought a coffee and some food, then went back to the base."

If Gray had a notepad, like he usually did in interviews, he would've sketched more evidence of Duncan's idolization of Mason. After Duncan lost Mason in the Kabul market streets, he did the same as he'd seen Mason do at market — coffee and food. Gray would bet that Duncan sat in the same seat and at the same table, too. But that train of thought derailed when Gray saw Duncan tense, when he saw Duncan wrap his hands around the chain before him and began tightening the slack. The arousal Gray had seen before in Duncan seemed to have drained from his face. Something dark had cast a shadow across the skull designs on Duncan's face.

"That night ... " Duncan started, then changed gears. "Remember I told you that I was surprised Tony hadn't seen me?" He waited for Gray to nod before continuing. "He had. Actually. That night he came to my bunk and dragged me into the showers. He slammed me against the ground a few times. He stopped short of beating me to death. And I think he only beat me so much so I'd be relieved when he stopped, so I'd think he was done. It was part of the torture, that mental thought process. Because it got way worse."

Duncan had pulled the chain so hard that no slack remained, and the cuffs were practically cutting into his skin.

"He forced my mouth over the shower head and turned on the hot water. Did that about five times. I thought I was going to die. My gums were burned raw. I couldn't eat the next day. Couldn't drink. I couldn't talk. My esophagus was ate up and welted. My lungs and stomach ... " His voice trailed off.

The events, even in retelling them, shook Duncan. Gray guessed it wasn't the physical beating or the water in his lungs that shook Duncan the most. The damage likely came because it was Mason who was inflicting the torture.

Duncan's eyes refocused on Gray and his mind came back from Kabul. "When I was released from the infirmary, he arranged for me to have the worst jobs on base, be it cleaning the latrines, filling and moving sandbags, or whatever." He shook his head. "Those fucking sandbags. I swear I filled over four thousand bags. And when he'd see I was about finished with my daily count, he'd come over and empty thirty or forty of them, so I'd have to redo them. He made sure I didn't have a single second of free time to follow him ever again.

"He left me off the mission rosters. I was there, but I was dead to the team. No one was allowed to socialize with me, no one was allowed to help with my tasks. I was a ghost."

"Did anyone on the team wonder why you were all of a sudden a ghost?" Gray asked.

"They followed orders. Mason told them to leave me alone, so they did. And even if they asked, I wouldn't have said anything."

"What could you say?"

Duncan's eyes met Gray's. "Exactly. But that wasn't the worst of it," Duncan said.

CHAPTER 28

Duncan's tension hadn't relented. His knuckles were white from pressure and his vise-like hold on the chains.

Normally Gray would have been sympathetic to the victim in a story like this, but Duncan deserved no one's sympathy after the evil acts he'd committed. Gray, nearly lost in thought, struggled to figure out what these interactions with Mason really meant to Duncan. Horrible and torturous, yes. Evil, yes. Enough for a normal, mentally-balanced person to want to kill Mason, yes. But there had to be more for Duncan. He was evil and horrible, and he wasn't balanced mentally. *What is it?*

"After a few months, I couldn't take it anymore, and I requested a transfer. A few nights later, Tony came to me in the middle of the night again. I expected to be dragged into the shower, but this time everything was different. He dragged me from bed and forced me to get dressed. I know, because I saw their eyes, the men in my unit saw this going on, and yet they didn't do anything to stop it."

"Who saw you?" Gray asked. "Chevy? Billings? Tolson?"

Duncan nodded. "Not Billings. But Smith, yeah."

"Do you think they saw you when Mason dragged you into the showers?"

"Of course, they did! Everyone was afraid of Tony. I told you, he could do whatever he wanted. He was a god. They weren't going to go against him."

"What happened next?"

"He dragged me to a company Jeep. He made me drive, and he directed me through the front gates of Camp Eggers."

Duncan finally let go of the chains. His hands were sweating. He stretched them, working out the soreness and stiffness from strain. He wiped his damp palms on the tabletop and then interlaced his fingers as if praying.

"Have you ever been in the desert?" Duncan asked, watching Gray shake his head. "It's darker than the darkest night you've ever seen. I thought Tony was taking me into the darkness and leaving me there. I thought he'd gut me and rip out my eyes. Instead, he made me drive into Kabul. I didn't know what we were doing. It was late, like one in the morning. There were locals everywhere, staring at us. I was afraid any of them could be Taliban lookouts, and Tony was going to get us killed. But, like I said before, even the enemies knew who the military gods were.

"We parked outside a four-story, battered building. A crowd gathered round. He said something to them, and they dispersed. He pulled out a shotgun and tossed it to me. He grabbed an M4 automatic rifle, along with a .45, a serrated knife, and I hoped at the time a lot more ammunition.

"He guided me though the front door of this," he thought about the appropriate word, "apartment building, basically. As we made our way up the stairs, Tony was shouting at people in Dari to go inside their homes. There was a weird energy about the place. Everyone obeyed him. I mean, we were the enemies in Kabul, the occupiers, right? Yet here he and I were … two American men with weapons … charging up the stairs in a place we had no business being, and everyone was afraid of us. It didn't make sense to me, except that I was with Tony."

And you liked the power, Gray thought.

"Then at the top of the stairs, Tony stopped and pushed me forward. He pointed to a door and told me I needed to kick it in and secure the room."

Duncan looked at his hands, thinking of grabbing hold of the chains again.

"I'd seen — I don't know how many times — Taliban soldiers holed up in places just like this, using civilians as shields. Our guys would go in and take the fuckers out. Sometimes they'd get a civilian or two. It was always harsh and ugly, you know? The costs of war and all. But I had never led the way. I was always one of the ten or so guys storming in after the lead. But Tony was making me lead this time."

His face changed, reliving the excitement.

"He said he'd follow me in." Duncan shook his head, as the scene replayed in his head. "I had so little reason to trust him." He looked at Gray again. "After the beatings he'd given me, I really thought he was setting me up. I thought there was someone on the other side of the door waiting to blow me away. I thought he'd heard I requested a transfer, and he was snuffing me out in a late-night mission so covert that none of the others from their unit were present.

He paused.

"I was right. Yet wrong, too."

Duncan finally surrendered to the urge and grabbed hold of the chains. He pulled on them and leaned forward.

"I busted through the door, but there wasn't someone on the other side pointing a gun at me. There was a family of four, sitting in their living room playing a board game. The wife started screaming and shielding her children. The children were frightened and crying. The father stood and was shouting at me. I thought he was going to attack me. I didn't secure the apartment. Everyone, as far as I knew, was in the living room. That was secure enough for me. I mean, I didn't even know what we were doing there.

"Tony finally entered. He showed me what securing the room meant. He made the wife and children lay face-down on the floor. Their arms were stretched over their heads. The father, he made stand and backed him into a corner on the far side of the living room. Then he told me to check the rest of the apartment. I didn't find anyone else there. So, at that point, Tony told me to block the apartment door with the couch. We'd busted the lock and the door frame when we had entered, so we couldn't lock the door behind us. We had to prop something up against it, so no one would sneak up on us.

"He made me stay with the father, and he told me to shoot him if he moved. Meanwhile, Tony took the wife and kids down the hall and closed them in a bedroom. When he returned, he didn't look soldierly. He looked evil. I don't know how else to describe the look on his face. I don't know. I guess I just got the impression when he came back from the bedroom that this was personal and not a military mission. I don't know … but I loved it. I wanted to look like that."

The smile on Duncan's face disgusted Gray, who anticipated the father's death.

"Tony grabbed the father, slammed him against a wall. The serrated knife magically appeared at the man's throat. They talked quietly. I couldn't hear exactly what they were saying. I know it was a combination of English and Dari, but that's it. Tony punched the man in the stomach. The man fell to the ground. Tony walked to me, pointed at the man, and told me to kill him."

Duncan's smile faded, which surprised Gray because after months of isolation, he was on the front line of a man's murder with his mentor, with his god. Yes, Duncan's arousal should've been stirred at this point. *Why did his smile fade?*

"I was ready. I thought I was. I had the shotgun. I had the desire. But … I couldn't pull the trigger. I kept thinking back to the farm with my father, trying to make me slaughter the farm animals. It was so stupid! I couldn't do what I wanted to do with every fiber of my body. It was something I wanted to do since as far back as I can remember."

Duncan leaned his body as far forward as he could. He bent his arms and barely reached his jumpsuit. He yanked his body backward, pulling apart the Velcro keeping the suit together. Most of his chest tattoos were now visible. The circled and blackened heart was partially exposed.

"I've already told you, I don't care about anything or anyone. So why couldn't I kill that man?!"

CHAPTER 29

Gray took a beat, trying to comprehend all that Duncan had told him. But he feared losing the drive of the conversation if he didn't ask another question quickly. "What did Mason do when you couldn't shoot the father?"

"Tony screamed at me, telling me it was an order. But I froze. Tony kicked the back of my knee and knocked me over. I landed face-to-face with the man. He was ugly, and his breath stunk. He kept sobbing the same phrase over and over. Something in Dari. I assume he was pleading with me, I don't know.

"Tony mounted me and held me down. He pushed my head into the ground. So hard I thought the floor was going to give out or my skull would crack apart like a ketchup packet.

"While that was going on, I guess the man thought he could escape, so he jumped up and ran. I had moved the couch in front of the door, right? But I guess I didn't move it all the way across the doorway. I just jammed the corner of the couch against the door, so the man was able to grab the door handle and yank. The door pushed the couch aside.

"Tony was pissed. He yanked me off the floor and pushed me into the hallway to go after him. I chased him through the halls of the building. The guy was screaming his head off, and people were cracking their doors and coming out into the hallway. I didn't even have my shotgun, but, honestly, I was more afraid of Tony at that point than I was of any Taliban that may have been in the building. I'd let Tony down by not killing the guy. I'd let him down by not securing the front door properly. I had to catch him!

"When I caught up to him, I slammed him to the ground. I cocked his arm behind his back and pushed it way up. So high, I thought his shoulder would pop out of the socket.

"I remember looking up and seeing Tony coming down the hall." Duncan looked at Gray again, like he was looking up at Mason coming down the hall. "As he made his way closer, the people in the hall scattered back inside their homes. I remember hearing locks turn and feeling his footsteps."

Duncan looked down at his exposed body and the tattoo of his blackened heart.

"Tony had these intricate dragon tattoos on his arms. His shirt sleeves were pulled up enough that I could see the dragons' mouths. One on each arm. On a man like Mason, the dragons were frightening. But not as frightening as the look on his face. It was pure wickedness, and I was afraid it was all directed at me."

The tattoos were another fact that Duncan got right, although they were part of the description given to the media. Gray, too, wondered if Mason's tattoos had anything to do with the tattoos Duncan had put all over his own body.

He had me take the man back inside his home. He told me we needed to hurry. The commotion in the hall was surely going to receive a Taliban response. He said we didn't want to get stuck in a shootout. And he handed me his gun."

"The .45 or the M4?" Gray asked.

Before he'd been suspended, Gray had heard that ballistics had confirmed the use of a .45 in the Sumterville killings which had been attributed to Mason. This could prove important in finding Mason, if it happened to be the same .45 he used all the way back to his military days. That would mean that he'd kept the weapon in rotation and likely used it in other killings. It also meant it may be used again in the future. That would make him traceable to a degree.

"Yeah. The .45." Then he continued with his story. "He took the man from me and he set him on the ground. On his knees. Facing me. He told me to do it. Told me to hurry. I pointed the gun at the man," Duncan yanked on the chain, "but I couldn't do it." He leaned his body back in his chair, pulling the chain with all that remained of his cancer-stricken strength. "But I couldn't fucking do it."

He let go of the chain, and his body jerked free of the tension. There was nowhere for his body to go. He couldn't fling forward or backward because of the wide distance between the chair and the table, and the short length of the chain. His body just jerked and remained in between the two.

While Duncan caught his breath, Gray saw the puzzle coming together.

"Again," Duncan said, leaning his elbows on the table, "it wasn't the man, his crying, or his family being close by. It had nothing to do with religion, or disappointing my mother, or anything. I just couldn't. What kind of killer can't kill? Even with Tony there, making it acceptable to kill and me wanting desperately to please him ... I couldn't." Duncan shook his head, looking away from Gray in an almost shameful manner. "I wanted to. So bad."

The last puzzle pieces secured against one another for Gray. No matter how this story ended, this was the night Duncan reenacted over and over in his killings. In Kabul, Mason directed the killing, as Duncan did with Wesley Murch in the United States. Mason was the setup man, as Duncan became in his killings. Mason used force, strength, and intelligence to overpower people. Duncan used intelligence. Duncan's whole killing career was nothing more than a worship of Tony Mason, with a dash of his father sprinkled in.

Therefore, in Gray's rationale, Noah Chritton and Duncan's other victims were just as much Mason's murders as they were Duncan and Murch's.

"Did Mason kill the father in your story?" Gray asked.

Duncan slowly nodded.

Duncan had twisted the mentorship to fit his own needs. He latched on to the characteristics of Mason that he identified with, but he still couldn't kill. He needed Wesley for the fantasy to be complete, to be intelligently manipulated, and to do the killing.

Gray rubbed his face, hoping for a pause in Duncan's long story. He yawned and leaned forward.

"I'm confused, Kenneth."

Duncan looked exhausted, like the story had taken a difficult toll on him.

"Was the revenge you want against Mason because he beat you in the showers or because he stole this kill from you? What is it?"

"No," Duncan replied, copying Gray's posture and leaning forward as well. "He opened up that world to me that night. He changed the trajectory of my whole life. That night was exhilarating."

"But you didn't kill the man."

"No, but I came close." His eerie smile returned. "Really close."

Gray asked, "Why revenge?"

Duncan slammed his fists onto the tabletop. The cuffs echoed against the walls. The chains clanked against the wood.

"Because no matter how much I begged him, he wouldn't take me out again. He wouldn't give me another chance. He could've showed me so much!

"I wanted to learn more from him. He had all the knowledge I needed. And his conscious was clear about all of it. With his training, I could've learned how to truly kill. With my own hands! I just wanted him to teach me." Duncan slammed his fists and the cuffs on the tabletop again. "But the fucker refused.

"He showed me the way, then left me there alone." Duncan looked as if he was going to cry. "I can't explain the relentless noise in my head after that night. I went to him and begged him to help me, but he pulled me from my bunk and took me back into the shower and jammed my mouth over the showerhead and blasted hot water straight into my lungs."

Then he did cry.

CHAPTER 30

A low rumble of thunder skirted across the clouds outside the prison. A thin rain began to fall, tapping against the barred windows. Gray ignored the thunder and the tapping, keeping his concentration on Duncan's story about Tony Mason.

"Do you need a tissue?" Gray asked.

The darkened areas around Duncan's eyes were wet with tears, which inched down the etched cheek bones and scarred tooth outlines.

"No."

The rain picked up, and the tapping on the windows sounded more like a million moths colliding repeatedly against the windows trying relentlessly to reach the light in the room.

"I want to go back to the names on this paper," Gray said.

Duncan lifted his right shoulder and bent his neck in that direction, wiping his tears on the jumpsuit. He did the same on his left side.

"They were just points of reference."

He ignored Duncan's comment. "Were they all picked by Mason to be on the team?"

"No. Just Carpenter. And Billings was Tony's commander. The rest of us were just picked for our specialties based on the needs of the whole."

"What was Billings' first name? And rank?"

"Crawford. Captain. Third Infantry Division."

"And Carpenter?" Gray knew the answer, but he asked anyway not to give away any hint that he believed Carpenter may be dead.

"First name is James. He's the one you should find, if you want to know more about Tony."

"Why's that?"

"Jimmy was second in command in all of Tony's units, far as I know. Tony handpicked him every time. And, yeah, of the two, he was the chatter box, but that wasn't saying much."

"What else about Carpenter?"

"Jimmy wasn't as intense as Tony. The general belief was that he evened out Tony's severity. No one could imagine Tony functioning without someone like Jimmy in his life."

"What did you think of Jimmy?"

Duncan chuckled. "I think he held Tony back from greatness."

"Were you jealous of their relationship."

"Jealous, no. I didn't understand it, but that never mattered."

"What do you recall about Jimmy's life outside the Army?"

"His mom left him a farm in South Carolina that, I think, after he and Tony left the Army he returned to."

"Where in South Carolina?"

Duncan thought about it. "It was a long time ago. Spartanburg maybe."

"You remember his mom's name?"

"Not at all."

"Anything else about Jimmy that stands out?"

Duncan shook his head. "I don't know. He was competent in the field, but toward the end, he started losing his marbles a bit. PTSD started taking its toll on him. Tony protected him from the brass, but he was becoming a liability. And around that same time, I heard he was visiting prostitutes. That wasn't a big deal in and of itself, in my opinion. I mean, Tony and I were the only ones who didn't visit them. It was a practice that was relatively acceptable, but Jimmy took it a little too far. He beat up a few, and he liked them really young."

"How young did he like them?"

Duncan shrugged his shoulders. "As young as he could get, I guess."

"Take a guess."

"I don't know. Fifteen, maybe."

Gray shuddered at the thought of someone in Carpenter's alleged mental state and with such violent training preying on young girls.

"Did Carpenter have any tattoos like Mason?"

"Nothing like Mason. He had an Army tattoo, I think. On his arm. Nothing really too impressive."

"If I got a picture of Carpenter, do you think you would recognize him?"

"Sure. You have one with you now?"

"No."

"That's a shame," Duncan said, dismissing the idea.

"Tell me about Billings."

"Ain't much to tell. He was one of the commanders who treated Tony like a god. Tony made the man's career. That's about all I know. I never really interacted with him."

"What about Tolson?" Gray asked.

"I'm tired, Becker."

"I know."

The weariness was starker on Duncan's face than the tattoos and scarring.

"I don't have much time left."

"Hang in there. Please. A little more," Gray pleaded.

Duncan sighed, building strength with a big breath of oxygen. "I think Tony was from West Virginia because I heard him and Benji Tolson talking about Spruce Knob. I've never been there, but they were saying it was beautiful and a great place for hunting."

"That's great information," Gray said, hoping to build Duncan's strength with positive reinforcement. "What else did they talk about?"

"I think they talked about Tony's family. His father died before he enlisted. His mother was still alive, I think. I don't know. They weren't talking to me. I just overheard."

"I understand."

Once Mason's identity had been discovered, the information about his birthplace and parents had been easily discovered. The mention of Spruce Knob could mean something.

"You going to ask Tolson about Tony?" Duncan asked.

"Was planning on it," Gray said.

"I think he died in the war at some point."

Gray nodded, disappointed at how quickly the hope of a new lead could turn to the despair of a dead end.

"Becker, let me go. I'm hurting bad, man."

Gray considered Duncan's request, as he calculated how much information about Mason had been provided. The list of "facts" jumbled in his mind. They'd been talking since morning, and for a long time the conversation amounted to nothing more than a confusing pissing match between the two men. It was only the last couple of hours that the conversation seemed to flow in any linear fashion. Considering the exchange of information, he looked at the yellow piece of paper. Gray had names he didn't have before. He had insight into Mason's psyche — at least during wartime. He had ways the man had killed. He had locations. He had weapons. He knew about Mason's tattoos. He had confirmed Mason's torture methods.

"Becker?" Duncan asked.

His body was now slumped in the chair, weak from pain and sitting up all day.

"Let this be the end," Duncan pleaded.

Gray sighed, giving up, having mercy on the man who may have helped catch Tony Mason. "All right, Kenneth. Just tell me about the delivery tomorrow. How does all of what you told me tie together?"

Duncan's energy was low. His skin pale. His strength sapped.

"Did you know he won't kill kids?" Duncan asked.

"No." But that may explain why he saved Morgan's baby, Gray thought.

"There was a massacre in Chad. A school. It was one of the only stories Carpenter would tell of Mason from before the formation of our unit. I mean, the only war story. I heard about bar fights and that kind of thing."

"I thought you were tired," Gray nudged him.

Duncan nodded. "Their unit went in expecting a meeting of high-level terrorist leaders, but it was bad intelligence. They had orders to kill everyone there. Unit commander didn't care that the building was full of kids and not terrorists. Orders were orders. The way Jimmy told it, he and Mason were the only ones who tried to stop the killing."

"Holy shit," Gray said.

"The incident got blamed on Boko Haram."

Gray sat up. "That's an extreme Islamist group, right? They've kidnapped school age girls from all over West Africa, right?"

Duncan nodded with his weak neck. "Mason sends money to the village. You'll find out how."

Gray nodded, excitement raging through his veins.

"Anything else?"

Gray's mind spinning, he said, "I can't think of anything else right now."

"Thank you." Duncan smiled, the skull-like features of his face standing out again. He'd really made a mess of his face and body. "Then it's time."

CHAPTER 31

At hearing from Gray that the interview was completed, Duncan's strength seemed to return. He slid his body into an upright sitting position.

"Becker, how do you feel?"

The question caught Gray off guard.

"What do you mean?"

Duncan's face still hung haggard with exhaustion, despite his body's erect posture. "Your heart. How does it feel?"

"I think your tiredness is getting the better of your mind, Kenneth."

"It's not," Duncan said. "When you arrived this morning, you were lifeless."

Gray held out his arms in a look-at-me pose. "Totally healthy." And the information about Mason had given him strength he hadn't had in two weeks. His mind was clear, his limbs strong, and his rib pain nonexistent.

"I told you I was going to cut the extremities from your lifeless carcass. You'd been suspended from duty, removed from anything related to Tony Mason. And that bothered you. That's why I saw so much excitement in your eyes when I mentioned his name. I cut away the lifelessness from you. I brought you back to life."

Gray shook his head. It never ceased to amaze him how narcistic men like Duncan were.

Duncan stood as much as he possibly could, the chains keeping him hunched over. "I gave Mason to you," he said, his voice grave and intense. "Just keep your promise. When you find Mason, you let your true self take over. Don't let society's consequences get in the way of what you want to do. And when you pull the trigger, think of me."

Gray stared at Duncan, unsure how to respond, yet realizing that Duncan was trying one last time to manipulate a person into committing murder on his behalf. This was how he worked. This was what thrilled him. But Gray didn't need anyone's help in wanting to kill Tony Mason.

Gray stood, keeping as straight a face as he could, and motioned to Salah, Munro, and the other two correctional officers, indicating they were finished talking.

The doors to the cell opened. Advancing footsteps could be heard echoing. Salah, Munro, and one of the correctional officers made their way toward Gray and Duncan. The sound combined with the steady rain spitting on the above windows, making an ill-timed rhythm.

Salah followed the guards and stood in the background. Gray watched from his side of the table as the guards reached Duncan.

"Promise me, Becker."

Duncan's eyes pierced Gray's soul, sending a spark of chilling energy through his body.

Munro unlocked Duncan's right wrist from the cuff. The chain was removed and then slid through the steel bolt in the middle of the table. As one guard moved to attach the chain to Duncan's belly chain and as Munro raised his hands to reattach the shackle to Duncan's right wrist, Duncan mustered strength that his cancer-ridden body shouldn't have been able to produce. He kicked at the correctional officer and then laid his shoulder into Munro's chest. The guard at Duncan's waist lost his footing, and he stumbled backward. Munro held on tighter, though he almost tripped over the table behind him. He yanked on the handcuffs, which thrust his left arm toward the floor and halfway twirled Duncan in a circle. Yet, Duncan's right hand was free.

Duncan slipped his right hand under the lip of the table and produced a shiv.

"Kenneth, no!"

Gray jumped forward and leaped atop the interview table, as Duncan plunged the shiv into his own neck. Gray used the sole of his shoe to push himself forward. Yet, by then Duncan had stabbed himself three times and broken off the shiv's blade inside his throat.

Gray tackled Duncan at the same time Munro and the other guard reached him. With their momentum, Duncan flew backward and hit the ground hard. Under the weight of the three men, bones cracked beneath them. Blood quickly gushed in all directions.

"Help! Get help!" Salah screamed at the correctional officer at the door to the cell. "Hurry!"

"Shit," Munro shouted, pushing the other guard and Gray off of him and Duncan. He tore off his shirt and used it to apply pressure to the wounds in Duncan's neck.

Gray got to his feet, bent at the waist, out of breath, hands on his knees. He saw the broken shiv in Duncan's hand.

"Stop," Gray said. "He broke off the tip. There's too much blood."

"No. No. No. No. No." Munro continued his efforts, but he quickly knew they were futile.

"Come on, man," Gray said, patting Munro's shoulder.

Munro stood, leaving the bloody shirt next to Duncan. "How the shit did that get inside the cell?"

Gray watched the wine-red blood pumping feverishly from Duncan's neck find its way down his chest where his jumpsuit was still open from when the killer had last ripped it apart to show Gray his tattoos. The dark syrup streamed down Duncan's sternum and then curved left and flowed over his blackened heart, covering it. It slipped gently down the side of his torso and pooled beneath him through the jumpsuit.

The pulsing of blood weakened quickly before stopping altogether. And soon all that was left inside the room was the stench of confusion and panic. The rhythm of the rain pelting against the windows above replaced the rhythm of Kenneth Lamont Duncan's heartbeat.

CHAPTER 32

Sticking around to answer as many questions as were asked, Gray and Salah found it was easier to regurgitate the facts of what had happened with Duncan rather than experiencing it firsthand. Warden Garrity was furious. He threw blame around like it was free. Salah received quite a bit. Gray more. He reserved most of it for Munro, despite both Gray and Salah vouching on the officer's behalf. What irked Garrity most was the attention. He hated this type of negative attention. It was bad press for him, for the correctional institutions of Florida, and it was defeating to all the families of Duncan's victims who still wanted to know where their sons' bodies were buried.

However, Garrity, in Gray's view, only cared about one of those three things.

He and Salah were asked — *ordered* — to stay in town until the investigation had been completed. They were told it would likely just be overnight. Then, if there were no additional questions, they'd be free to return home.

The rain had stopped by the time they reached Salah's car. It left the air moist and smelling earthy, of dirt and mildew. On the way to their hotel, Salah had convinced Gray to stop at a department store, so she could buy a change of clothes and toiletries. Gray looked down and saw Duncan's blood on his clothes. She had suggested he get some, too.

Tucked away behind an intricate, artful partition in the hotel lobby, Salah pointed out the bar and a restaurant.

"I'm starving," she said, realizing food was long overdue.

Although Gray only wanted to lock himself inside his hotel room, take a hot shower, and spread out in bed, he said, pointing at his clothes, "I'd like to get cleaned up first."

After showering and changing into his new clothes, which gave off the scent of cardboard, Gray considered canceling his dinner plans with Salah but didn't. The shower relaxed him, and he felt he could've gone right to sleep. Yet he realized he also wasn't ready to be alone. Arriving first in the bar, he declined an alcoholic drink, asking the bartender for a ginger ale instead.

At the department store he had purchased a couple T-shirts, a pair of jeans, and several pairs of underwear and socks. The shirts fit fine, the jeans were looser than he liked, and he wore his work shoes. It didn't look like a complete, planned outfit, but he didn't care. He had never been one for making fashion statements. He realized that Salah was a different story when she came down a few minutes later. She'd found a linen outfit and a pair of sandals. It all matched perfectly. Her face was make-up free, and her wet hair had been bunched together in a thick bun at the back of her head.

"I didn't know what you wanted to drink, or I would've ordered it for you," Gray said.

"Are you sure you don't mind if I have one?" She had heard the dialogue between Gray and Duncan about Gray's alcoholism.

"Not at all." He hadn't wanted a drink for a long time.

She turned to the bartender and ordered a double Jack and Coke on ice. They sat in silence until the drink was delivered. Salah held up her glass for cheers. After the day they had, Gray didn't think they had anything to salute.

"Here's to never knowing what the fuck is gonna happen," she said with a wry smile on her face.

It was just about the only appropriate thing they could salute, Gray thought. "I can cheers to that."

They clinked glasses. Salah took a long draw of her drink. Gray sipped his ginger ale and studied her. It may have been the first time all day that he'd actually looked at her, had actually seen her. Without makeup, he could see the finest of lines tracing a lifetime of laughs and experiences across her face. Before he could wonder about what made her laugh and what experiences she'd lived, the lines made him think of Duncan's face.

Duncan. He instantly wished she had worn makeup.

He set the glass down on the coaster and ran his fingers around the rim, hoping to expel the images of Kenneth Duncan and wondering if Salah was right about Duncan finding his way into Gray's mind forever.

"I can't stop thinking about it," she said, looking at the bubbles rising from beneath the ice cube in her drink.

"The whole thing was planned," Gray said.

"I know."

Gray folded his arms in front of him and leaned on the bar. "He played us."

"You're right." She took a mouthful of her drink. "I got a call when I was upstairs. You remember, after Duncan threw up, the cleaning crew that came in? One of the guys hid the shiv in the bucket of water."

Gray shook his head, wondering how the guards didn't pay better attention.

"They came in, mopped up, armed a killer, and then left."

"Easy as that," Gray said. "I guess, Duncan could get people to do what he wanted."

Salah was glad Gray said that. She'd revisit it soon. "Garrity warned us."

"Just to cover his own ass, but, yes, he was right."

Silence fell between them. Instead of talking, they watched two business women at the end of the bar flirt with the bartender. One had her laptop open, seemingly working while nursing her second pinot noir since

Gray had arrived. The other woman had pushed aside her stack of folders and papers before Gray had even arrived.

Gray finally spoke up. "I need to apologize to you."

The statement took Salah by surprise. "What for?"

"I was there today to help your investigation, and I wasn't at my best. Duncan got the best of me a couple times. I mean, I was lost in there with him. I should've been more prepared. I should've pushed harder for you to stay with me."

"How could you be more prepared? We sprang this on you."

Gray appreciated what she'd said. "You're making excuses for me. Thank you."

"He didn't want to talk to me, you know that. Besides, you didn't look as lost as you think you were."

Gray smiled. "Well, whatever. I wasn't my best today, and I didn't like it."

"Every now and then a foul ball hits us right in the head."

She held up her drink again to cheers. Gray begrudgingly obliged, hiding an appreciative smile.

The bartender broke away from the flirty women, who were more than ten years his senior, and approached asking about food and refills. Salah told him they'd get something later, which freed him to make a hurried return to the attentive twins who were giggling and talking under their breath to one another.

"Thinking about what you said, that Duncan played us. Do you believe anything he said about Wesley Murch or Tony Mason?"

Gray pondered her question. "Some of it."

She expected him to explain himself. When he didn't, she asked, "What part?"

"I believed the part about Murch. I think Duncan overpowered him." He played with his glass. "Murch did Duncan's bidding. I think that's true."

"And Mason?"

He waited a long time to respond.

Salah wondered if he'd waited so long to see if she'd let him off the hook and carry on. But that's not her style.

Plus, that wasn't what he was doing.

Duncan's whole Mason story didn't land properly in Gray's mind. There was part of him that believed every word. Mason was definitely a monster. He was capable of depths of human evil that Gray had never considered possible. He'd killed men, women, and children. Mutilated. Tortured. Desecrated. Yet, Mason had worked to save his family; had cut the Beringer's baby from Morgan's womb, and he'd let Gray and Parker live.

For Gray, those two ends of the Mason spectrum were too far apart to meet in the middle. So how could Duncan's story be true?

"How could it be untrue?"

She accepted his response and motioned to the bartender to bring her one more Jack and Coke.

"Assuming it's all true," Gray said, "Duncan wanted to kill with his own hands, right? But he never could. That's what he said."

"Right." Salah waited for Gray's point.

"He finally did. The only person Duncan killed with his own hands was himself."

Salah nodded. "If Mason had shown him how to kill … "

Then the number of victims would've been prolific, Gray thought.

Neither finished the statement aloud.

"You remember that lame-ass excuse you used today in your chief's office earlier today?"

Gray nodded at the bartender for another ginger ale. "No. What do you mean?"

"They were beating you up over not going to your appointments with the … I don't remember who it is. The people running the inquiry."

"Oh. TEAM, I think they're called."

"You told them you had stomach issues."

"Oh, yeah." Gray remembered having been pleased that he'd put a stick in the McKee's spoke. "What about it?"

"I knew right then that I'd like you, but then the car ride was dreadful. You had your nose in that report the whole time. You must've read it five times."

"Nine," Gray fired back.

"Nine," she repeated. "Well, the point is, this is nice. Just talking."

Gray, ever one to kill a good mood, said, "Are you not fucked up over today at all?"

Salah took her drink from the bartender, who also set a new ginger ale in front of Gray. She waited until the bartender went back to the two women, who were now too drunk to be subtle in their flirtatiousness.

"I'm trying to forget the day, Becker." She raised her freshened drink to her lips.

Gray scolded himself for what he had said to her.

"Sorry," he said. "I'm not always on point with my interpersonal relationships."

She shrugged her shoulder. "So you owe me."

"How's that?" His stomach was beginning to rumble, hunger rearing its head.

"You were rude just then, so now you owe me something."

Trying to copy her playfulness, he fired back, "You're assuming I think I was rude and that that would compel me to make amends."

"You apologized." She looked at him like he was stupid. "It wreaks of guilt and sorrow."

Caught, Gray said, "Fair enough."

"It won't be difficult, I promise," she said.

No more promises, he thought.

"What is it?"

"What was the promise Duncan made you make?"

Gray sighed immediately. This was more difficult than she realized.

"For legal reasons it may be better if we change subjects."

She chuckled. "Legal reasons."

He liked seeing her smile, even if it was at his expense.

"Becker … " Her eyes were those of a close friend. Warm and trustworthy.

He exhaled heavily then said, "He made me promise to kill Mason when I caught him."

She nodded, looked away from Gray. She thought about that, while Gray stayed quiet, taking her nonresponse as judgment of some sort.

"If you didn't agree," she said, "he wouldn't have told you what he knew, right?"

Gray hesitated again. It wasn't the smartest move to share this information. "Right."

She nodded and thought how to phrase her next question.

"If you were to have agreed with his demand," she said, presenting a hypothetical situation – *you know, for legal reasons,* she thought, "what would he have told you?"

"How to find Mason."

"Wow."

She took an ice cube in her mouth and sucked off any lingering whiskey from the cold rock.

"You two talked a long time," she said, spitting the cube back into the empty tumbler.

"We did."

"Why do you think he killed himself?"

Gray shrugged his shoulders.

"Damn, it almost makes me wish your phone's voice recorder wasn't malfunctioning." She has the smile of a partner.

Salah nodded again and drank from her empty glass, looked at Gray, and smiled. "Are you hungry? You want to eat?" Her tone indicated that the subject had changed. That she'd keep his secret.

"I am, yes. And you're buying."

CHAPTER 33

After a rough night trying to sleep, Gray grumpily stomped his way to the breakfast bar. If he had driven, then at 2 a.m. when he couldn't sleep, he would've just gone down to the car. However, Salah had the keys, so he had to muscle his way through the churning of thoughts about what Duncan had told him, of how bad of an interview he felt he'd performed, and of all that surrounded Tony Mason at home – all in the discomfort of the hotel bed. Images whirled of Duncan's face and the blood from his neck wounds. The absurdity of Duncan's act playing out in front of him ran like a river over a cliff, falling down into a deep lagoon of unsettled mental disorder that slowly, ripple after ripple left Gray with a calmness that gently lapped against the fate of James Carpenter.

It always bothered Gray that Mason had rescued his family and then left them behind to chase down Marcos Cervantes, the head of the Mexican drug cartel SL-4 and the man responsible for their kidnapping. It didn't make sense to Gray. Mason had killed over twenty men to find his family. Why didn't he find a way to get out of the country with them at his side?

Yet, alternately, if he felt he had to kill Cervantes, then his family would need to stay safe. Who would Mason leave them with? The answer had to be Carpenter. His best friend going all the way back to his early military days. The man who kept Mason's secrets.

And where would he leave them? The loft. The name on the property was one of Mason's aliases. One he rarely used. One that kept him hidden, protected.

Yet Cervantes' men somehow gained access to the loft.

Carpenter. And the loft. The two ideas oscillated in Gray's mind. Then more ideas came together.

The loft. Carpenter. Safety. Murders. SL-4.

Gray wondered if the revelations Duncan provided about Carpenter's PTSD and his treatment of very young prostitutes had played a hand in his demise and that of Mason's family. They had to have, right?

Three blood stains, three people murdered. Three people murdered, two bodies recovered. Two bodies found in Crestwood, so where was the third? Whose body was it?

Carpenter.

Where is Carpenter's body?

At nearly three a.m., he thought he'd figured it out. Gray figured one of two things happened. One, Mason figured out that Carpenter had been compromised by SL-4. Or, two, he'd been followed to the loft. Each had the same result: Mason's ire.

Remembering the trash shoot in the loft building, Gray had used the phone in the hotel room to dial in an anonymous tip to the Mason hotline. He had given the hotline staff Mason's loft address and told them he thought he'd seen a body in that dumpster. He answered a few qualifying questions, then hung up. He knew the staff would vet the specifics of the call, then seeing that the specifics check out, they'd rally the troops from the task force's different agencies and search the appropriate landfill.

After the call, his mind wound down. The clock read 3:43. He fluffed his pillow and bent it in half under his head. And he fell asleep. Gray slept solidly until his alarm went off at six-thirty. He showered quickly and dressed in a fresh T-shirt and pairs of underwear and socks. He wore the same new jeans he'd purchased the night before and his work shoes. All of his other gear was thrown into the plastic laundry bag the hotel provided.

Salah wasn't downstairs when Gray arrived just after seven. He took a glance out the front door. Her car was there, but she wasn't inside it. He guessed she was still in her room. Gray grabbed a plate and a bowl. He loaded the bowl with oatmeal. On the plate, he stacked numerous slices of bacon and a mound of sugary fruit. He skipped the muffins and biscuits, as well as the egg-like substances the hotel was passing off as real eggs. Finally, he grabbed two cups of coffee.

Gray was nearly finished with his breakfast when Salah finally approached the table. He greeted her. She apologized for being late.

"I'll tell you why in a minute. I need coffee."

She hurried over to the coffee machine and filled a cup. She splashed in some creamer and then quickly scanned the food. She grabbed a banana and a bran muffin before returning to the table.

"Good news," she said. "We're cleared. We don't have to go back to the prison."

"Great. We can just head home then."

~ ~ ~ ~

The car ride was quiet. Salah drove. Gray looked out the window, thinking more about his interview with Duncan, about Mason, and the inquiry he was returning to face.

"Oh shit."

"What?" Salah asked, slowing the car's speed, thinking something was wrong.

"I never turned on my phone after the prison."

When Gray and Salah arrived at the Florida State Prison, the prison staff took all their belongings. Gray turned his cell off to conserve the battery. But, after Duncan's suicide, he forgot all about his phone being powered down. He wasn't an avid phone user, and since he'd been suspended, it had only rang because Julian Weech from TEAM had called him to arrange his interview. He had really only used the phone to text Jordan Butler.

Salah grunted a response and accelerated the vehicle, getting it back up to the speed limit.

Gray pulled the phone from his front pocket. It was more difficult to retrieve it from jeans than from business casual slacks, like he usually wore for work. He powered it up. The process took about 20 seconds. Then his messages and system notifications began making all sorts of raucous noise. When that finished, he saw he had three texts. Two from Jordan Butler and one from Ambrose.

The text from Ambrose had a higher likelihood to contain bad news. Then he would want Butler's texts to cheer him up. Ambrose just inquired when Gray would be returning, so they can set up another interview date and time with TEAM.

Gray flipped over to Butler's texts. One read:

Hope your interview this morning went well.

That text likely came in some time yesterday afternoon. He hadn't told her he skipped the interview and darted up to Raiford to talk to Duncan.

The next one read:

Just finished the 11 pm news. Congrats. You have made it zero days without being in a news report. Hope you're well.

Gray fired a text back to her:

Yesterday was a rough day. Heading back to Lkld now. Will call later.

He hit send.

"Everything okay?" Salah asked.

"All good. Thanks."

He turned the phone to vibrate and tucked it under his leg. He'd feel the vibration if Butler responded or if a call came in.

The texts brought him out of his own mental funk. Gray asked, "Will you go after Duncan's mother first or go straight for Wesley Murch?"

"The mother, I think," Salah responded. "We know where she is. I've already asked Cord and Dallas to start working on finding Wesley."

"You told me Cord was a nickname. Is Dallas one, too?"

"Yeah, he grew up there, so that's what he's called."

Gray nodded then reversed the conversation. "Have they found anything yet?'

She checked her phone for messages. "Nothing yet, I guess. They would've messaged me."

He thought about offering his assistance with a profile on Murch or to assist with the interview, but he thought that may be insulting. Salah was good at what she did. Plus, with the ramshackle of an interview he had just conducted on Duncan, the offer most likely wouldn't be an appealing one. So instead, he said, "I don't know what it would be, but if there's anything I can do, please let me know. I'll drop everything and help out."

"Thanks. I'm sure it'll work out. And you said yourself last night that you have a lot on your plate."

He sighed, looked out the window again. "I do."

"I don't like telling people what they should do, but maybe you should just get through all that first."

Hearing that hurt a little, but his ego would survive. "Well, whatever I can do."

"Thanks. You've already done so much."

He felt his phone vibrate under his leg. He waited a minute to make sure the conversation with Salah wasn't going forward. When she didn't say anything else, he grabbed the phone and swiped across the screen.

A new text message from Butler awaited him. He opened it, sending his eyes across the words. Then he read it again. And a third time. Just to be sure.

"What is it?" Salah asked, sensing the tension suddenly inside the car.

He didn't know why he was so shocked. It was inevitable with the inquiry into the police department, but he still wasn't expecting it.

"My chief of police just resigned."

"What?"

"He resigned, and the inquiry's been halted for a few days."

"Holy shit."

"Yeah," he said. "Could you drive faster?"

CHAPTER 34

Salah dropped Gray in the parking lot of the Lakeland Police Department, off Massachusetts Avenue. She thanked him for his willingness to help, said they'd be in touch, and then drove off.

He found his car quickly. He kept a go bag, which contained a change of clothes for days that ran too long, in his trunk. He winced at the reignited rib pain from lifting the bag and slamming the trunk closed, but he tried quickly to forget about it. As he headed into the building to change, find out what happened with Boudreaux, and check his mail, his phone vibrated in his pocket. The information displayed on the screen surprised him. The vibration resulted from a text from Jeffrey Parker.

We need to talk. You back in town?

It was nearly lunch time and Gray was growing hungry, so he factored that in to his response.

Lunch. 20 minutes. And he gave Parker a location.

Hurrying back to his car, Gray was stopped by a patrol car blasting a horn at him. The cruiser pulled alongside Gray.

"Thanks a fucking lot."

Gray did a double-take into the car cabin.

"Hey, did you hear me?"

The sunshine combined with the hostile greeting left him unsure of who was speaking.

"What's the problem, Bonnin?"

Gray hadn't seen AJ Bonnin since the patrolman had been sent to collect him by the TEAM consulting firm.

"You promised me you'd be at the department at seven that next morning, and you weren't. I got called in by TEAM Consulting. They threatened to swear me in if they thought I was lying. I had to tell them I saw you that night, and I let you go. I knew that shit would burn me."

"I showed up. The donut store took longer than I expected. But I kept my promise. I was only fifteen minutes late. Why didn't you wait for me?"

"Who fucking cares? This isn't my fault. Don't turn this around on me, pal. I got docked two days' pay. Two days! Thanks, asshole. Don't ever ask me for anything again."

Then with the roar of the engine, Bonnin and his patrol car were gone.

~ ~ ~ ~

Gray arrived at the meeting place prior to Parker. He hurried into the restaurant and changed his clothes in the bathroom. He felt more comfortable in his regular clothes than in the clothes he had purchased with Salah. When he came out of the bathroom, Parker was waiting by the restaurant's front door.

The restaurant's walls were exposed brick. The floor was concrete with a dark stain pushed across it. It gave the restaurant an industrial feel. A bar ran through the center and tables were arranged on both sides of the bar. The industrial feel continued with the wrought iron accents on the tables, chairs, bar, and stools. The plates were metal and there were motorcycles and car parts hanging all over the walls, along with license plates and other transportation art. Sports programming played on all the televisions in the place.

Gray and Parker met in the middle of the restaurant and sat at the table nearest them.

"How's Karen feeling" Gray asked. The chair's wrought iron features weren't enjoyable against his ribs.

"She's well. The baby, too."

A hostess came over and told them they weren't allowed to seat themselves. Parker snapped at her and she scurried away. His mood was a taste of what was to come from the conversation, Gray decided.

"Kenneth Duncan, huh?" Parker asked.

Gray nodded. "Just got back to town."

"You hear about Boudreaux?"

"I did. What happened?"

"I don't know. I was in the middle of my interview with McKee when he was pulled out. Next thing I know I'm told to go home. And then this morning ... Boudreaux's gone. They've halted the inquiry. Not permanently, but they're taking a few days to settle in after this announcement."

"Have you heard any rumors from anyone? Anything about how it went down? Or, why now?"

"Only thing I know for sure is what was said at the press conference. Other than that, there's just all kinds of stories floating around. None of them really connect with each other, so I can't make heads or tails out of any of them. Anyone who knows anything for sure ain't talking."

"So, you haven't talked to Boudreaux?" Gray asked.

"No."

"Marshanda?"

Marshanda was the chief's wife.

"I didn't call her. I think they're still staying with family out of town. Besides, I'm not going to invade their privacy. They've all been through enough."

Gray agreed, then he said, "Boudreaux figured he was going to be fired. He told me as much, so I don't know why I'm so shocked."

An annoyed and reluctant waitress came and asked for their orders. Gray ordered food. Parker did not. That also told Gray his time with Parker was going to be limited and this wasn't a "let's be friends again" meeting. But that wasn't going to stop Gray from trying to mend fences.

"I wasn't going to let them come after you."

Parker slammed his fist on the table. "You couldn't have stopped them."

"I was going to try."

Gray waited a moment for the emotion to die down and for the people in the restaurant to return their attention to their own conversations.

"I was going to take the blame for the whole thing. I was going to tell them I manipulated you into coming with me. I was — "

"You didn't manipulate me into going. I went freely and on my own. What pissed me off was that I knew better than to move in without backup. I told you we should wait, but you didn't listen to me. I should've stopped you. But, ultimately, I went in anyway."

Gray figured out the problem. "I know. You covered my ass. You weren't going to let me go in alone."

"Exactly."

"It was against your better judgment, and you did it anyway."

Parker let silence be the answer.

"Shit," Gray said.

Parker remained quiet.

"You're right," Gray said. "One hundred percent. And it'll never happen again."

"I know it won't," Parker finally spoke up. "If we don't get put on the street, then I'm requesting a new partner. I'm not playing your games anymore. I've been a good friend to you, and this inquiry is what I get in return. I think we're done. Altogether."

"Jeff, come on. Don't do this." Gray's voice rang earnest and humbled. "I know what I did wrong. I'm different than before. I got past my daughter's death. I mean, as much as a person can. I'm really trying to do the right things. I get it now. I mean, we're going to lose our jobs. We don't have to give up our friendship."

"No." His voice pitched sorrow and pain.

Parker stood. Sadness filled his eyes. He did care about Gray, but with the baby coming, he needed to care about that more.

Gray stood, following Parker's lead, and held out his hand. He wanted to protest further. Maybe tell Parker that they should talk again in a week and see if he felt the same way. Although, there just didn't seem to be anything Gray could think of that he thought would change Parker's mind. Gray instead said the only thing that made sense, even though it crushed him.

"Thanks for telling me face to face."

Parker shook his hand.

CHAPTER 35

Seeing how Boudreaux had resigned and no one contacted him to reinstate his suspension, Gray thought it ill-advised to go roaming the halls of the police department. But, like so many things he did that were considered ill-advised, he did it anyway. And he'd do it by going in the front door.

The glass doors opened into an immense entryway. To his left, the stairs ascended in plain view to the top floor of the department. The ceilings were open in this area, so anyone walking the stairs could be seen from most viewpoints in the lobby. Directly in front of him, eight people gathered in front of the reception area trying to work through some disagreement. Gray hoped they'd block the view of the public safety aide and anyone else positioned behind the bulletproof glass. That left the elevators. With their close proximity to the reception area and the typical wait for the doors to open, Gray knew he'd be seen for sure. So, the stairs were his best option.

As he mounted the stairs, the elevator doors parted and Walters, Collanger, and McKee stepped off. They were three of the people Gray definitely wanted to avoid. It was a huge relief that he took the stairs instead of the elevator. He quickened his pace and took the steps two at a time. He kept a watch of them out of his periphery. Luckily, they were so involved in their own world — now free of Boudreaux — that they didn't notice anyone else in the lobby. Or on the staircase.

Gray turned his gaze and attention back to the steps, and he found two uniformed officers walking up the stairs in the opposite direction. One of them grunted at Gray and moved to ram his shoulder into Gray's body. But Gray quickly maneuvered around the officer and avoided the attack to protect his still-healing ribs. The officer then called Gray an asshole and kept walking. Gray snapped around to verbally object to the officer's actions, but he stopped himself, thinking better of that action since he wanted to keep a low profile. *Another time.* Plus, it wasn't like name calling hurt his feelings. He'd been called an asshole a thousand times.

At the top of the stairs, he considered going to Boudreaux's office to see if he was still there, maybe packing up his belongings, but Gray figured Walters and Collanger rushed Boudreaux out of here as soon as the press conference was over. His personal effects were probably already boxed up before the announcement. Gray turned and headed toward the Major Crimes office, where his desk was located. As he pressed his palm against the door, he noticed movement down the hall to his right. He saw Julian Weech from TEAM Consulting exit a small conference room with someone in tow.

I thought the inquiry was halted, he told himself.

Weech thanked the woman, shook her hand, and then sent her on her way. Weech then returned to the small office. Gray had ducked around the corner to spy on Weech, but when he recognized the woman meeting with Weech, he stepped into the walkway, and he charged straight for her.

Frances Vandenhill hesitated briefly when she saw Gray marching toward her with heavy steps. He flashed her a scowl. Prior to coming face-to-face with her, Gray checked a small office on his right to see if it was empty. It was. He pushed the door open and steered her into it. He closed and locked the door.

"What is this, Becker?" she asked, humoring him for now.

"You were in with them?"

"Them? You mean the firm hired by the city who employs me to keep the police officers mentally stable. Yes, I was. They asked me in, and I came."

"I thought we had an understanding."

Gray and Vandenhill had a long history. The department had — numerous times — assigned Gray to counseling. After those ended, Gray even voluntarily sought her out. However, they had a falling out when Vandenhill leaked information to him about one of her patients who'd been raped, which set up an investigation where Gray had to work with tainted evidence to find the rapist. However, he felt she'd manipulated him, and that was a bigger crime against him than having to work the tainted case. He used her ethics breach against her as a sort of blackmail. For his silence, she agreed that Gray would never have to attend counseling again, and she'd sign off positively on any requests sent about him.

"We did. We do. I didn't tell them anything we didn't agree to."

"What did you tell them?"

"That you were fit for duty. May I go now?"

"Tell me what they asked you first?"

She sighed and dropped her purse onto the desktop. "They asked me a lot of questions about a lot of officers."

"I don't care about that. What did they ask you about me and Parker?"

"I'm not telling you what I said about Parker."

Gray's agitation showed. "I just want to know what they asked."

"Look. They're using this inquiry to weed out people they deem unfit. Or, how did they put it? 'Out of line with the police and community standards.' They're going after anyone they think is weak. Or, in my opinion, too strong. They want strong police on the street, just not within the department."

"They want a bunch of 'yes' men?'"

"That's how I interpreted it."

"And what did you tell them?"

"I'm not going to share anymore confidential information with you about patients. But, I will tell you this: I told them they were wrong and if they got rid of the strong cops, then they were ruining what actually is a good police force. I told them they should focus on ridding the department of the good old boy network, but I think those are the people they actually want."

"Because they're just like Walters and Collanger."

She nodded. "I'm figuring I'm going to have to beef up my private practice since I'll likely lose this contract."

Gray agreed. He unlocked the door and cracked it open.

"Thanks. Sorry if I came on a little strong."

Vandenhill picked up her purse and hooked it on her shoulder.

"You did."

She moved past him and turned.

"How are you?" she asked.

"I'm fine," he responded, dismissing her. "No need for concern."

"You can call if you need to talk."

"Unlikely."

She nodded and left.

Gray watched her walk down the hall to the elevator before he moved toward the Major Crimes office again. Once inside the office, he heard the sounds of detectives working — typing, phones ringing, emails binging, text messages arriving, and the low din of various types of conversations. Normal stuff. None of the detectives lifted their heads from what they were doing in order to see who entered the room. The Major Crimes office was no library. If detectives picked up their head every time the door opened, they'd never finish any work.

He made his way to his desk and saw a stack of messages and mail. He snatched them up, hoping to find the delivery from Duncan. He stuffed them into his back pocket and headed for the door again before someone saw him.

Still needing to get out of the building before Walters, Collanger, and McKee returned, Gray set his sights on the descending stairs. Yet, he hesitated on the top step. He hadn't found out anything about Boudreaux, and curiosity still ate at him. Then a thought struck him. Although it was Saturday, administrative staff wouldn't be at the department. But with Boudreaux's resignation and the high level of city management involvement, he bet Mary Tillman would be at her desk outside the chief's office door.

Tillman was a tall, thin woman, who'd been at the department almost as long as Lt. Ambrose, having worked directly with the last three chiefs of police. Gray saw her take a break from typing on her computer and wipe a tear with a tissue. Boudreaux was her favorite of all those chiefs.

She didn't have an office. Her work area was more of an alcove. Along the wall, opposite her desk, were four chairs used by the next folks who were scheduled to meet with the chief. Ordinarily, at least one of those chairs was always occupied. Today, they were empty. Today, also out of the ordinary, the chief's office door was open.

Gray knocked on the wall at the corner of Tillman's alcove, as if it were a door to her office. She stuffed the tissue away and pulled herself together, wishing to allow no one to see her upset.

"Hi, Mary."

"Detective." She sounded surprised to see him and looked past him to see if he was alone. "What are you doing here?"

"There's no one with me. It's just me."

She eased her posture a bit. They'd known each other a long time. She was one of the few people who didn't have a chip on her shoulder when it came to Gray.

She noticed his badge. "Are you here to return that?"

"You know they gave me active status, so I could go interview Duncan."

She shot a grimace at him. "I saw the news," she said, referencing Duncan's suicide. "But you were only active for that one thing, right?"

He didn't like lying to her, so he didn't. Mary Tillman wasn't someone you ran a play on. She was almost as powerful and all-knowing as the chief.

"Well, with Chief Boudreaux retiring, I think my status fell through the cracks."

She nodded. "So, you're not giving me your badge?"

He smiled, knowing she knew that wasn't why he was there. "Not yet. I was hoping to talk to you to find out what's going on."

She stood quickly and came around her desk. She gripped Gray's arms — something she'd never done before — and directed him into the alcove. She didn't want anyone to see the two of them talking. He didn't know if it was for his safety or her own. She moved her hands to his face and cupped his head in her hands.

"You're a good man, Becker. I've always known that about you."

As he nodded, she let her hands fall to her side. She leaned against the wall with her left arm, almost keeping Gray in place, like a protective boundary from what was being said in the halls and conference rooms of the department.

"All I can tell you right now is, you and Parker and Boudreaux, you're all tainted to this city management. Chief Boudreaux did what a good chief should do. He protected everyone he could."

"What does that mean, Mary?"

"You should go now." She lowered her arm, unlocking the protective boundary. "If you really want to know, ask the chief. He's home today, packing. He leaves late tonight to go meet his family. I think they're vacationing for a couple weeks before returning."

He decided not to push the issue, figuring Boudreaux took the blame as chief of police and saved his men's jobs. That was good enough for him for now.

"Thanks, Mary."

He moved from behind the cover of the alcove wall.

"Becker, if you want to keep that badge a little longer, I'd recommend you stay away from HQ for a few days."

He smiled, grateful for her counsel.

CHAPTER 36

In total he'd been at the department just shy of an hour. If he was tainted, as Mary Tillman had stated, and everyone in the department knew it, then he'd stick out like a sore thumb if anyone saw him. He worried most about Walters, Collanger, and McKee coming back into the building and finding him. So, he left immediately after talking to Tillman.

When he settled into his car's driver seat, the heat attacked him in a full-frontal assault. He cranked the engine, then did the same with the cooling system. While the car's internal temperature decreased, he pulled the phone from his front pocket and connected it to the power cord resting at home in the cigarette lighter plug. Then he pulled from his back pocket all the mail and messages he had snatched off his desk.

He went through the phone messages first. It was the usual fair. Call backs from conversations he initiated. Families calling to inquire about the status of their cases. Some victims calling to find out who was working their related cases during Gray's suspension. There were many messages from reporters asking for comments after the news broke about Duncan's suicide and Gray's involvement. Nothing about Mason.

The message that attracted his full attention was one from Chuck and Claudia Chritton, the parents of Duncan and Murch's victim, Noah Chritton. Apparently, they'd seen the news too, and were wondering why Gray was talking to Duncan, and what it had to do with Noah's case, and what Duncan's death meant for them. He stuffed that one in his pants pocket. That would be the first call back he'd make.

He moved on to the other items he'd picked up from his desk. Gray took hold of a parenting magazine. Somebody out in the world thought it was funny to subscribe him to a parenting magazine once the news story about his daughters' death — caused by car accident — hit the newspapers and television news. And whoever had done it had been paying for the subscription for two years now. Rather than wasting his time hunting down who was paying for the subscription, it was easier to just throw away the magazine. He shook his head at people's warped sense of being, and he tossed the magazine onto the passenger floorboard.

Sifting through the rest of the mail, he stopped on one with a postmark of Lincoln, Nebraska.

He tore at the seal and pulled the handwritten letter from inside. He unfolded it and read it:

Dear Detective Gray,

My son, Kenneth Lamont Duncan, has asked very much of me of late, and I have only obliged him because of the cancer. I know my son and I know his faults, but I make no excuses for his actions or the person Wesley Murch turned him into. However, I could not deny him his dying wish, no matter how appalled I was and continue to be in completing the request.

I am writing this, per his request, two days prior to your meeting with my son. This is after I moved his "inventory" to the Gulf of Mexico. He asked me to dispose of it in the gulf. I did not expect that any of it would find its way to land. He has quite vocally admonished me for my mistake.

My last task is this letter, and I hope it will salve his anger for my mistakes.

I have arranged for Wesley Murch to be at my husband's plot of land in Fish Creek, Florida, on Saturday of this week. The man believes we will be there to destroy the rest of Kenneth's "inventory."

Gray checked his watch. It told him the day of the week and the date. *Today is Saturday.*

He is expecting me to arrive around 9 p.m., but I will not be there. Kenneth asked me to arrange this meeting as a gift to you for agreeing to his terms, whatever they are.

Then she listed the address.

I am sure someone will come looking for me for my hand in helping Kenneth. I will be home when they do. My affairs are in order. While I am not happy with the actions I took on his behalf, I am happy to have provided some assistance to Kenneth that he so desperately needed.

P.S. Kenneth asked me to include this word: Fada

Gray committed FADA to memory. That was Duncan's delivery. Fada. *What the hell does Fada mean?* He carefully folded the paper and returned it to the envelope. His first thought was to throw the car in reverse and drive directly via GPS to Fish Creek, but he had learned his lesson with the Mason case about needing backup — for now, at least.

He couldn't call anyone in LPD because he was supposed to be suspended. Parker had just written off their friendship and partnership. So he had no one. Except ...

He dialed Salah.

After three rings, she picked up.

"Turn around," he said.

"What?"

"Wesley Murch is in Florida. Turn around and pick me up. I'll tell you on the way."

"What about backup?" she asked.

"We'll call them. We'll have plenty of time in the car."

CHAPTER 37

The plot of land that Duncan had inherited from his father was on a dirt road off State Road 484. The dirt road cut through severe marshland running along the creek and led to a small country house and a barn about twice the size of the house. Satellite imagines showed that the two buildings appeared to be about 30 yards from one another. The images showed that law enforcement had few options for setting up positions around the house. The dirt road was the safest, most effective way in; however, it offered the least cover and stealth.

The agencies — Gray, Salah, the Dixie County Sheriff, Cross City Police, Perry Police, and Taylor County Sheriff — agreed to have a boat ready in the creek. It would be loaded with officers to enter from a small dock located approximately 50 yards from the country house. Additionally, a helicopter would be close by, if needed for emergency transport or spotlight capabilities.

Gray and Salah would accompany a SWAT unit on foot along the dirt road. Once inside the inner property line, they'd split up, fanning out across the perimeter. After they were in position, a vehicle would enter the grounds at 9 p.m., via the same dirt road. The car would appear to have only one person in the car, allegedly carrying Duncan's mother. Inside the car, however, three SWAT staff from the Taylor Sheriff's Office would be hiding. The person acting as Duncan's mother — a female officer from the Perry Police Department — would honk the horn three times. Along with notifying Wesley Murch of her arrival, it would signal the boat to begin its approach from the creek. Law enforcement hoped Murch would come outside to greet her. When he did, the perimeter would close in and he would be captured.

They waited until after sunset at 7:51 p.m. to move in. Gray and Salah followed their SWAT team leaders down the dirt road. Mosquitos buzzed about, crickets chirped incessantly, and frogs groaned all around them. Even after the sun went down, the humidity remained high, and the temperature hovered near 90. The only salvation to wearing their protective gear was the steady breeze from the nearby gulf. Not only did it cool their skin, an occasional gust would push away the annoying and hungry mosquitos.

As the SWAT teams neared the clearing and the barn, Salah and her team moved right, and Gray and his team went left. The most unfortunate part of their whole plan was they didn't know if Murch was there, if he was in the barn, or if he was in the house. One vehicle had been parked on the property, so the assumption was that it belonged to Murch. The way it was parked, in proximity to the country house, gave the impression he had parked and then gone inside.

All the lights in the house appeared to be powered on. Only one light glowed from inside the barn. The front door of the barn was slightly ajar, and light thinly shined out of it from the inside.

It was easy for the teams to see inside the house because of the lights and the lack of curtains. The house consisted of only one room, which acted as the bedroom, kitchen, and the dining and living rooms. The bathroom was an outhouse — not presented on the satellite images — about 10 yards from the house. No one appeared to be inside the house.

Neither Gray nor Salah had an earpiece to listen to the radio communication. Local team members had them in the helmets they were wearing but had none available for visitors. For communication, the collective teams relied on hand signals. Since Gray was next to the team leader of his SWAT unit, he could hear most of what was going on from the communications escaping the man's earpiece.

Word came in to the team leads that all parties were in position. The boat was four minutes away and the car supposedly carrying Duncan's mother just turned on the dirt road. The signal of a thumbs up came at Gray and Salah from their respective SWAT commanders.

Soon headlights bounced along the dirt drive and its surrounding marshland. Then they heard the rumbling of the car's engine, as it groaned down the road. The vehicle had been pulled from the Taylor County repo lot. It ran in such a state of disrepair, it was no wonder the owner never picked it up. It would likely cost more to pull it from the lot than it was even worth.

Soon the car stopped, per the plan, evenly dividing the space between the house and the barn. The engine clunked and rattled to a stop; exhaust blasted out of the broken muffler as it died down. Then there was silence.

Gray wondered if anyone had tested the horn. Could the whole plan blow up in their faces because the horn didn't work? Then finally — delivering a sense of relief — the horn blasted three times. The frogs and crickets fell silent. The officer acting as the mother climbed from the car. And everyone waited for Wesley Murch to appear.

CHAPTER 38

O nly he didn't come outside.

The officer acting as Duncan's mother stumbled forward slowly, unsure what to do and where to go.

Gray felt a wave of heat come over him. This was his mission. He set the wheels in motion. Even though he was likely to be fired in the next day or two, he didn't want his last outing and attempt at closure to be a colossal, visible failure. He thought he could feel everyone's eyes on him, the brains behind them wondering if they'd all wasted a ton of time and resources. He was beginning to wonder the same thing.

The mother moved back to the car and honked the horn again. While she waited, the officer radioed the license plate information on the car. "Nebraska. Echo. Charlie. Zebra. Four. Three. Seven. Please advise on next action." Radio calls flew back and forth. Finally, the SWAT commander — with a raised, closed fist — informed everyone that they needed to hold their positions while two SWAT officers moved closer to ascertain the target's location.

Then a gunshot blasted, cracking across the night sky. Everyone froze as they all attempted to determine the shot's origin. It didn't go off inside the house or barn. That they all knew. Based on the satellite images, there were no other homes nearby. However, in these parts of Florida, Gray guessed it wasn't uncommon to hear a gunshot. It was a rural area where just about everyone carried guns in some form or fashion, and you never knew when you'd have to kill a poisonous snake, a wild boar, or a bear. Gray wondered what season of hunting it was.

Another shot rang out, echoing toward the property. It was followed by some sort of male scream.

The boat — never having unloaded its men — turned away from the dock and moved upstream, shining a bright light into the marshland. The helicopter was called in to do the same but from the air. The rotor chops grew closer. Meanwhile the ground team holding the perimeter split up. One team, Salah's team, entered the barn to ensure no one was inside. Gray's team did the same for the house.

Gray hung back though.

The outhouse bothered him. He hadn't noticed it on the satellite images. The top of it was covered in brush, tree clippings, moss, and dirt, which created the perfect setting for weeds to grow. From the satellite, maybe it just didn't show as a building. The construction must have been solid because Hurricane Matthew came through the area a couple years before and battered the area relentlessly. Duncan had been locked up, and Gray doubted the mother paid for someone to rebuild the outhouse if no one was using it. That told Gray that the outhouse had been there for a while. And he wondered who would build an outhouse so sturdy it would have withstood the wind and water of a hurricane?

Gray moved quietly toward the outhouse door. He retrieved his flashlight and pointed the beam of light at the door. The handle had a lock on it. A lock that needed a key to open. The lock struck him oddly. Why would an outhouse have that type of lock on it? Gray grabbed the handle with the same hand he used for holding the flashlight. The handle turned, and the door clicked open.

"Gray," Salah called from behind him, startling him.

He turned and found her hurrying over to him.

"What are you doing?" she asked.

The door slammed open, cracking Gray against his skull and sending him fumbling backwards. He held onto his weapon, but he lost hold of the flashlight.

Then he heard Salah growl, "Runner."

She snatched up his flashlight and sprinted after the person who had exploded through the outhouse door.

He steadied his legs in time to see Salah's shadow flash through a stretch of thick bushes.

"Saleena," he called after her, but she didn't call back to him, nor did she stop running.

CHAPTER 39

Salah was ten yards in front of Gray, at least. He could hear her footsteps, but he couldn't see her. She had his flashlight, so he was working rather blindly. The only light came from the waning gibbous moon and most of that was stamped out by the copious Florida botany residing within the marshland. Every now and then he'd see a blast of light from the Maglite. That helped him keep track of her, but it didn't help him keep pace.

He tripped and bumped into things in the darkness. His shoes splashed hard into wetland. Suction held onto him. Water soaked through to his socks. But he yanked his leg from the mud's hold and picked up speed again. Rounding a shallow curve, his shin connected against something. He stumbled, as pain shot all the way through his body. His stride faltered while he coped with the pain. When he raised his eyes, he saw he'd lost track of Salah.

Panic set in.

He didn't have a radio to call for backup, and neither did she. Only the team leaders and the SWAT team had them. The helicopter sounded like it was now heading away from their location. And the boat had taken off in the other direction. He and Salah were on their own. With whomever had exploded out of the outhouse. In fact, Gray guessed that the rest of the team hadn't even realized Gray and Salah were gone yet.

As he tried to control his emotions, he listened, hoping to hear her running, but all he heard were the crickets beginning to chirp again and the frogs beginning to groan.

He whispered to himself, "Who took off without backup this time."

Gray thought about Sumterville, when he and Parker had flanked the cabin Mason was inside. They both had ended up injured and in the hospital by the end of that day. He feared this day may be worse. If Murch was the runner — he had to assume he was — and Salah confronted him alone, she would have to shoot him. Based on Duncan's description of Wesley Murch, the man was a monster of a human being. Just massive. She wouldn't be able to handle him in a one-on-one, hand-to-hand fight. He didn't think he'd be able to either. All he knew for sure now was that he had lost her, and she hadn't yet fired her weapon.

Gray broke from his thoughts and realized the sounds of the crickets and frogs stopped. Then he heard shuffling footsteps.

"Where is he?" The female voice was steeped in panic and despair.

He turned his pistol in the direction of the voice. When he aimed true, he found a woman at the end of his barrel. She had a gun, too, and it pointed directly at Gray. The hairs on his neck rose to attention.

She didn't lower her weapon. "I just want Wesley. I thought I shot him, but he got away."

As Gray watched the gun shake in the woman's hand, he realized who she was. "You weren't supposed to be here." The Nebraska license plate finally made sense.

"Are you Detective Gray?"

"Yes, Mrs. Duncan, I am. You have to put down the gun."

"I came when I heard the news about my Kenny." She almost lost control of her emotions. "Wesley made my boy do those things. Wesley made my son kill himself. You were there. You saw it." Then she did lose her control. She began crying, lowering the gun. "I had to kill him for Kenny."

Gray yanked the .22 revolver away from her. She wasn't a threat. She was just a desperate mother in mourning. But a threat was out in the darkness. Murch. And so was Salah.

"Saleena!"

Then from a distance, he heard, "Gray." It was a faint call. Then her gun split the night's silence. The crickets and frogs ceased their noisemaking, frightened by the report.

"No," Gray said to himself. He ran from Duncan's mother in search of Salah.

He didn't know where he was running or if it was in the direction of Salah's shout and gunfire, but he wasn't going to stop looking for her until he was with her or he had Murch.

"Saleena," he called again. Partially for her and partially hoping someone from the SWAT team would hear. There was no callback this time.

His heart raced. His legs hurt. His shin throbbed. He couldn't breathe fast enough to keep his muscles oxygenated, but he refused to stop. Bushes and branches slapped at his body, scratched at his face, and tried to hold him back. Then he hit a tree. The trunk of a tree. A massive tree.

Gray bounced in the air. He went one way. The weapons — his and Duncan's mother's — went the other. He landed hard against the ground, and his ribs immediately set fire to his insides. His injury from only two weeks ago sounded his internal emergency siren. Electric shockwaves pulsed through him, as the pain filtered across his body.

Then the tree moved before him.

Fuck. It wasn't a tree he hit.

Gray ignored the agony as he got to his feet, ready to defend himself. Or try to.

"Wesley, I'm police. Stand down."

Murch chuckled at that notion, showing large gaps between his two front teeth.

Moonlight showed the wound in his shoulder. Blood had soaked the right side of his shirt.

"Where is Detective Salah?"

"No more," Murch said.

No. Gray only had one chance, unless the SWAT team came to his rescue, but he wasn't counting on that. He had to move fast. A monster the size of Wesley couldn't be as agile as Gray. Even with his aching ribs, Gray should be able to move easier than the mammoth before him. And he wouldn't think about Salah being dead yet. He needed to stay alive first, then he'd think about her health. But he did need to get to her because wherever she was and in whatever condition, her gun and his flashlight, he hoped, were close.

Gray held his breath to hold in the pain, and he threw his body to his left, then cut back quickly to his right, shooting past Murch, who tried to grab Gray when he'd cut left. The muscle memory of the standard move from Gray's high school basketball days was still sharp. His body moved fluidly, despite the throbbing in his chest. Figuring Salah had to be close, Gray rounded a thicket of overgrown shrubs. His shoes hit wetland again and the suction from the mud pulled off one of his shoes. As he recovered from a stumble and rounded the large bushes, he saw a dark mound in an even darker shadow. *Salah!*

Then he spotted the flashlight. It had rolled against a fallen tree's trunk. Gray lunged for it, landing on the ground like he was sliding into home plate. He felt as if all his fingers were thumbs; he just couldn't grab hold of the Maglite. He didn't know if it was panic, too much adrenaline, or if the pain in his chest was causing his coordination to falter. He turned to look for Murch, who should be approaching by now, but he didn't see him. *Why?* No matter, Gray turned back to the flashlight and finally successfully grabbed hold of it.

A short roar — maybe a guttural grunt — along with the sounds of leaves rustling, and roots unearthing came from Gray's right. He turned and shined the light in time to see Murch force his body through the thicket of brush Gray had just rounded. The scent of freshly churned mud and dirt hit Gray in the nostrils. He backed away from Murch's slow advance, which gave him an extra moment to see that Murch was dragging something large. A body.

Oh, shit.

Duncan's mother.

Gray immediately shined the light on Murch's other hand, but luckily Murch wasn't carrying a weapon. Gray still had a chance against the goliath. He stood, ignoring his pain.

Murch saw Gray in front of him, challenging him. He flashed his gappy grin. Their eyes rested on one another, as they measured how to attack. Murch's only offense was smashing Gray, which gave Gray more countermeasures. As long as he stayed out of Murch's grip, he had a shot at surviving.

Murch stepped closer, gaining speed in three steps, and attacked Gray like a rhinoceros. Gray sidestepped him, and gave him a shove in the back, hoping to increase Murch's velocity to where his feet gave out. His feet, though, remained under him, but he did collide with a large tree. The man groaned.

It appeared as though Murch led into the tree with his wounded shoulder, and the pain was slowing his turn back toward the detective. Gray took advantage of Murch's back being toward him, held his breath against the pain again, and raged forward. He flipped the flashlight and held the Maglite by the reflector head. He hiked it over his head and plunged forward.

As Murch turned to face his attacker, Gray brought the flashlight down on Murch's head, striking the man's temple with the barrel and tail cap. A thud like Gray had never heard before attacked his ears. Gray went to the ground on Murch's right. Murch stumbled to the earth to his left.

The pain was excruciating for Gray. He didn't know if he could summon the strength to evade Murch again, if attacked. But he would do all he could. He turned the flashlight again and used it to see Murch getting to his feet. The man held his head where Gray had clocked him. Gray moved into a crawling position. He was going to push himself off the ground and ready himself for Murch, but the path of light shined onto Salah's body. Her eyes were closed, and she didn't appear to be breathing. The sight of her sent an anger through Gray, which helped him get to his feet.

Murch straightened his back and shook the dizziness from his head. His eyes landed on Gray again, who was ready for another go. Murch charged. As Murch closed in, Gray dropped to his knees and swung the flashlight like a bat at Murch's right knee. Time slowed, and Gray could see everything passing before him. The flashlight hit bone. The sound of a breaking crack lifted into the darkness. Gray's wrist bent backward to a point of pain. The flashlight fell from his grip. As it dropped, Gray saw the tail cap fly to the right, followed by the batteries launching outward from inside the barrel tube. Murch's knee caved in, but his body's momentum carried him into a collision with Gray. Gray's face felt like it had been crushed by the force of Murch's hip connected with it. Then time seemed to fast forward. The collision flung Gray hard against the ground. One leg caught under him, and he struggled to kick it out, avoiding an ACL or MCL injury. The earth shook under Gray when Murch bounced off the ground. Movement finally stopped, and Gray found himself under the giant's heavy, broken leg.

"Here!" he shouted, struggling against the weight of the man's leg. "Help," he shouted, realizing he needed help quickly.

The leg on top of him moved slightly. Fear rose again in Gray. He pushed harder against it, continuing to ignore the pain emanating from his ribs. Murch's arm rose and whacked down atop Gray. Murch's huge hand gripped Gray's shoulder. The grip held tight, but it grew more like a vise the longer it clung to Gray, who shouted to relieve the pain. Gray grabbed at Murch's fingers, trying to pry them open. When that didn't work, he struck them, hoping to break the grip. But that didn't return his desired results either. Now Murch was yanking Gray toward him, no doubt stretching for Gray's neck. If he got Gray's neck, that would be it.

"Help," Gray yelled again.

Trying to outthink the flow of pain and his impending strangling, Gray leaned into Murch's grip and brought his body forward, almost into a sitting position. He jammed his fist between Murch's legs and clawed at the man's testicles. He squeezed as if his own hand was a vise. Murch screamed at him and somehow extended his arm further, grabbing Gray's neck. He returned the force of the hold. Gray tried to keep his grip tight, but he was quickly losing strength. There wasn't enough oxygen getting in to keep his muscles active.

"Freeze."

"Police."

"Let go."

"Stand down."

Shouts came from every direction. Gray could hardly hear them. He just held onto Murch's testicles as hard as he could for as long as he could. He'd crush them before his dying breath, he told himself. Shadows moved all around him, as black and white spots began filling his eye sight. The weight of Murch's leg lifted off of him. Gray tried to hold onto Murch, but his grip was broken. *No!*

Then the pressure on his neck lessened. Air entered his lungs again. His sight returned quickly. He saw ten members of the Taylor County SWAT securing the area. Murch was on his back. Semi-automatic rifles aimed at his head. His wrists being zip-tied together. Quadruple tied. Men were tending to Mrs. Duncan and to Salah. One man helped Gray to his feet.

"You all right? You should stay down."

"I'm fine," Gray said, surprised at the strength in his voice. Luckily, Murch's angle of attack and the absolute massiveness of Murch's hand only allowed the monster's fingertips to squeeze against the muscles at the back of Gray's neck, not on his larynx.

Gray stumbled and the man helping him kept him on his feet.

"I'm fine," Gray reassured him. "Salah?" he asked the SWAT leader, who was bent over the men working on Salah.

"She's gone."

Gray jerked is neck toward the voice, which came from behind, and saw Duncan's mother. Her eyes were open. Her throat had been crushed and mangled.

"She's breathing, at least. Shallow," the team leader said of Salah, "but breathing."

Gray returned his attention to the leader. "We need to get her to a hospital," he said.

"The helicopter's on its way back," the team leader said. He turned to the men with Salah. "Can you move her?"

"We've secured her neck." They'd placed an inflatable neck traction collar around Salah's neck. "Let's go."

CHAPTER 40

Gray spent the night at Doctors' Memorial Hospital in Perry, Florida. It was the closest hospital to Fish Creek. There was little the doctors could do for his ribs except provide him relief from pain. The scratches from the branches he ran through in the marshland were minor abrasions and easily treated with ointment. And the bruising on his shoulder and neck from Murch's powerful fingers morphed from red to dark purple. There was soreness, but the same pain medicine for his ribs helped with this, too. While the medicine being pumped into him via IV made him sleepy, he was up most of the night worrying about Salah. Other than being told she'd regained consciousness, he hadn't heard anything since they'd arrived.

A vibration announced a text's delivery, but he couldn't reach his phone. He paged a nurse and asked for his phone.

"Do you think I could see Detective Salah?"

"Can you handle the wheelchair ride?" The nurse asked, as she handed the phone to Gray.

"If I can see her, I'll handle it."

She nodded. "Let me see what I can do." And she left the room.

He swiped his finger across the screen and saw Jordan Butler had sent the text. He opened it.

It's now been another zero days AGAIN since you were named in the news. How are you?

He smiled, liking the way she playfully jabbed at him.

Thanks for asking. Ribs broken again.

The nurse returned, and she brought an aide along with her. They both helped Gray transfer from the bed to the wheelchair. Even with the medicine, his body lashed out at him complaining about the movement. As he caught his breath, another text arrived.

"Thanks," he said to the nurses as they attached his IV rack to the chair.

Once they were on their way to Salah's room, Gray's pain subsided to the point of only mild aggravation. Then he checked his phone.

Have you considered NOT breaking your ribs?

He typed back:

Noted for future reference.

He changed apps and launched his Internet app. He typed in FADA. The returns showed that FADA meant *the goddess of fate* in Latin. *And it would be fate,* he thought, *that would eventually bring he and Mason together.* He found the First Amendment Defense Act and the Florida Automobile Dealers Association. He also found Fada, Chad. Africa. He searched FADA and combined it with BOKO HARAM. The results included hundreds of pages of news stories about the terrorist group and their dealings in Fada, Chad. Gray thought he'd verified another part of Duncan's story about Mason.

"We're here," the nurse said.

Gray closed the apps on his phone and turned off the screen.

The nurse turned Gray's chair around and backed him into Salah's room. When the nurse situated him, he saw Salah in her hospital bed, sleeping. A sheet and blanket covered her up to her chest. Her arms were exposed and had been set on top of the covers. IVs, like his, were in one of her arms. Monitors were clothes-pinned to her fingers, and other monitoring wires came from behind her gown at her chest. The monitoring systems next to her bed chimed and dinged. Gray could read her heart rate and blood pressure on the machine's display.

"Is she okay?" he asked.

The nurse grabbed her chart and reviewed it quickly. She shrugged her shoulders. "I think so, yes."

"She's my friend. Please tell me."

"You're the one who saved her?"

Gray nodded, hearing the replay of the crack of the Maglite against Murch's skull. He didn't know if that was fact — that he saved her — but for now he'd go along with it if it earned him information about Salah's condition.

"She may have a laryngeal fracture. They'll do a CT scan in the morning to find out for sure."

Salah's breathing was labored. It sounded grating and resulted in a harsh vibration.

"Is her breathing all right?"

"It's stridor. It's common in these cases. They're watching her for respiratory issues."

"Jesus," Gray said.

The nurse nodded. "Prayers wouldn't hurt."

Another text arrived on Gray's phone. It vibrated in his lap.

"May I stay a few minutes?"

"Ten minutes," the nurse told him. "I'll come back for you."

"Thanks."

Seeing Salah in this condition was depressing. And maddening. He hated knowing she was in pain and having breathing problems. Yet, she'd lectured him on needing backup, then she ran off without him. What was she thinking? She could've been killed. They both could've been killed. Her actions were something Gray should've understood, but instead he was seeing it for the first time from the other side.

Her eyes blinked.

Gray wheeled himself closer to her bed. "Hey, cowboy," he said, referring to her running off without him.

"Murch?" she asked. Her voice was muffled and raw. He thought he could hear the scraping of it against her throat as it left her mouth.

"In here somewhere. Has a cracked skull, a bullet wound, and a busted up knee."

She nodded. And her eyes closed again.

Gray reached out and touched her arm. Squeezed it, so she'd know he was there.

"Thank you," she coughed up the words.

"Go back to sleep."

She did.

Gray stayed there with her and watched her sleep, listened to her breathe, and he let the happiness and relief that she was alive envelop him.

The nurse returned — too soon in his opinion — and grabbed hold of his chair.

"Ready?" she asked.

Gray nodded. "Sure."

As the nurse wheeled him to his room, he checked his phone. It was another text from Butler.

Need a ride home?

Having backup isn't so bad, he guessed.

He responded:

Yes, please. ASAP!

CHAPTER 41

With the IV out of his arm, the pain was more acute, but he stayed in his wheelchair in Salah's room the next morning until she came back from her CT scan. Gray wheeled himself out of the way, so they could get her situated again. They closed the curtain to give her privacy. When the nurses pulled the curtain back, Salah was sitting up in bed and smiling.

He begged her not to talk, but she did anyway.

"No fracture." Her voice sounded like she'd been a smoker for a thousand years.

"That's amazing. I read up on the fracture, and it seemed like there could've been a lot of complications associated with it. I'm so glad you're clear of that."

She smiled, thinking it sweet that Gray read up on her injury. Then she said, "He snuck up on me."

"He got me, too." He pointed to his body. "Ribs." He considered not telling her what else he knew about the raid, but she'd find out eventually. "Kenneth's mother is dead."

Salah gasped at the news.

"Murch admitted to all the killings. He doesn't seem to understand that Duncan manipulated him. I wheeled down to his room this morning while he was being questioned by the FBI, and I think he's intellectually disabled in some sort of profound way."

She shook her head, as a response and in judgment of Duncan. Then she asked, "Duncan's mom ... why?"

"When she saw the news of Kenneth's suicide, she grabbed her gun, and decided to kill Wesley. Maternal blindness, instinct, or something. She blamed him for Duncan's violence, but Wesley got the best of her."

Salah shook her head again, thinking that the best response given the pain associated with speaking.

Gray's cell vibrated. It was Butler.

Here, the text read.

He set the phone down in his lap.

"My ride's here."

Salah nodded. "They're keeping me for another day."

"Do you have a ride home?"

"My L-T." She tried to keep her sentences short and to the point.

"Good," Gray said. "I'll text you and see how you're doing."

She nodded.

Gray wheeled closer and extended his hand. They shook.

"Thank you," she said.

"Just be well."

CHAPTER 42

E very bump in the road shook Gray's insides and sent electric jolts of discomfort through his body. But the good company helped ease the throbbing pain. *As did the pain meds,* he thought. Butler drove the backroads rather than the interstate. The speed limits were slower, but the roads were better maintained, which meant the ride was smoother in most parts. Plus, the stop-and-go traffic was due to red lights and not other drivers' stupidity or accidents. The trip back to Lakeland took more than four hours, but it seemed to fly by because Butler kept Gray's interest with her stories and humorous observations.

The three flights of stairs leading to Gray's apartment nearly killed him. And maybe Butler, too.

"You need to stop breaking your ribs because we are not doing that again," she said, stepping off the top step.

Gray said, out of breath, "Or maybe I'll just get a first-floor apartment."

She laughed, and he liked the sound of it.

She unlocked the door with his keys and then led him to his bed. The room was messy, and he was embarrassed about it, but she didn't seem to mind. She propped him up in bed with his pillows and made sure he was comfortable. Then she took extra steps to care for him. She turned on his ceiling fan. She asked if he had a television to move into the bedroom. When he said he didn't, she offered to go purchase one for him. He declined. She asked about books. He wanted none.

"I can't thank you enough for this. I mean, eight hours in the car, and now getting me settled. I really appreciate it. Thank you."

She smiled, like the words "thank you" meant everything to her. "Happy to help."

"Now, can you leave so I can sleep?" He smiled when he spoke, so she knew the bluntness of the words was a joke.

She acted like she was going to punch him, and he clinched, hurting himself.

"That's what you get," she joked back. Then she said, "Are you okay?"

"I'm good," he said through measured breaths meant to calm the pain.

"All right. If you're going to sleep, I have a couple errands to run. I'll be back in a few hours to check on you."

"You don't have to do that."

"You get one pass on my being your nurse, then after that you're on your own or you stop getting hurt."

She spoke like she'd be around for a while.

"Thank you," he said.

She retrieved a glass of water for him and put it and his pain medicine on the nightstand next to the picture of Gracie, his daughter. She hesitated, having never before seen a photograph of her. She tried to hide her hesitation, but she didn't need to. Gray was already dozing off. Butler stuck two fingers into Gray's pocket and inched his phone free. She plugged it into the charging cable coming from behind the nightstand.

Butler touched Gray's shoulder, bringing him out of his light sleep. "I'm leaving now. Your pills are here with some water. Your phone's charging. When you wake up, text me what you want to eat for dinner, and I'll bring it."

He agreed, though she wasn't sure he really understood her. He fell back to sleep immediately. She decided she'd text him the message, so he'd see it when he woke.

Before she left, she took advantage of Gray's medicated sleep, and she picked up the framed photograph of Gracie. She studied the girl's face.

There were features she recognized from Gray, like her eyes and lips. Butler smiled, combining sweet and sad sentiments.

CHAPTER 43

Sunlight from beyond the thin blinds in Gray's apartment bedroom woke him. His mouth was dry, and he had a slight headache. He found a glass of water on the nightstand next to his bed. He moved slowly reaching for it, not wanting to revive the pain in his ribs. However, he couldn't drink the water in a lying position, so he pushed himself up. The pain woke now, too. He clinched his teeth and exhaled gradually to control it.

"Good God," he whispered to himself, cursing the hurt.

In a sitting position, he hung his legs over the side of the bed and braced his body by stretching his arms out like stabilizers used on heavy construction equipment. Soon he had the pain under control, and he drank from the glass. The water had lost its chill, but it went down easy anyway. He finished the whole glass in a gulping frenzy. Gray hadn't realized he was so dehydrated.

After returning the glass to the nightstand, Gray grabbed his phone, unplugging it from the charging cable. He wanted to check the time but saw a text from Butler instead.

Let me know what you want for dinner, and I'll pick it up.

Then he noticed the time. Dinner had passed almost 15 hours ago.

He set the phone down, deciding to send her a thank you text later. But soon.

Gingerly, Gray pressed his feet against the floor and made his way to the bathroom. He used the toilet, washed his hands and face, then brushed his teeth. Gray unbuttoned his dress shirt, having slept in the same clothes he wore coming home from the hospital, and let it slip down his arms onto the bathroom floor. The mirror reflected a banged-up body. His ribs were wrapped tightly with a compression brace, his shoulder and neck sported purple bruises. Murch had done a number on him.

"You'll heal," he said to himself before shuffling out of the bathroom and down the hallway to the kitchen.

There, he found Butler, wide-eyed and smiling, holding a cup of coffee. He was surprised to see her there so early in the day.

"Good morning," she said. "I was wondering if you were ever going to wake up."

"Hi. I think the pain meds gave me the best night's sleep I've had in years."

"Good. You needed it."

He nodded and caught her checking out his bruises.

"Those aren't from broken ribs?"

He grunted affirmatively as a response. He shuffled past her to the coffee pot and poured himself a cup, while she kept studying the bruising.

"Those on your neck look like the tips of someone's fingers."

Gray turned toward her and sipped the hot drink.

"That's because they are."

"Jesus. Becker, I've not asked you much about your police work."

"I know. Thank you."

"But I'm going to now. What happened with Duncan and Murch?"

Gray nodded, surrendering to the knowledge that at some point she'd ask and he'd tell her. He pointed to the living room, asking if they could sit. She took his coffee and followed him to the couch.

Noticing her large suitcase by the front door, he asked, "Are you moving in?"

Butler chuckled, and then pointed at the couch where a folded blanket sat atop a pillow. She'd slept there, watching over Gray.

"No, I'm on my way out of town. Got a call late yesterday that the FBI is searching a landfill in Birmingham for the body of James Carpenter."

Gray nodded, inching his body into the couch cushion.

"You know who that is?" she asked.

"An associate of Tony Mason's."

She studied his reaction. "I thought you'd be happier. Or, at least, surprised."

"I knew he was out there somewhere."

She flashed a knowing smile. "The tip came in anonymously, from what I understand."

Gray nodded again and took his coffee cup from her.

Her smile remained. "Do you know anything about that?"

He shrugged his shoulder, hiding his face behind the coffee mug while taking a draw of the drink. Then he changed the subject and answered her previous question. He explained to her how he was brought into the Duncan interview, how the interview went, what Duncan shared about Murch as well as Mason, and how it concluded with the inmate's suicide.

"He knew Anthony Mason? Your Mason?" The connection bewildered her. "Do you think he was telling the truth?"

"I haven't had a chance to check it out, but some of what he told me wasn't public knowledge."

"Holy crap."

Gray smiled at her response. He found it a humorous alchemy of childhood and adulthood.

"What?" she asked.

"Nothing."

He went on and told her about receiving the letter from Duncan's mother and that it pointed him to Murch's location. He told her about the property breach and the chase for Murch in the marshland. He watched her face cringe as he told her about his confrontation with Murch.

"I'm glad you're okay," Butler finally said. "It's worrisome a bit."

"Before Mason, stuff like this didn't happen, and I don't suspect it'll happen again."

She countered him. "Until you find Mason."

Gray didn't respond, but his face told her his response. *Until then.*

She stood. Gray took the timing as a displeased response from her.

"I have to go. Need to get to the airport."

Gray set down his mug and pushed off the couch, handling the accompanying discomfort.

"You don't have to get up," she said.

"I want to," he grunted.

He shuffled her to the apartment door.

"I'd offer to carry your suitcase down … "

She laughed. "I'd like to see you try."

He touched her arm, above her elbow. Held it until she turned. "Jordan, you picked me up in Perry." He motioned toward the couch. "You stayed here last night. You made me coffee this morning. Like," he didn't know how to say what he wanted to say.

"And I brought you dinner last night, but you never woke up. There's a meatloaf in the fridge." She wasn't keeping score, but she playfully wanted Gray to know the score.

"And you brought me meatloaf."

It felt like ten minutes before he could mutter the words. He didn't know why they was so hard to say. He didn't know why he felt so vulnerable.

"Thank you," he finally said. "I think I have hope again. Because of you."

She smiled again, touched by his tenderness.

"You're welcome."

"No, I mean it. I'm not great at articulating these things. Those words don't really encompass how appreciative I am."

She touched his face. "You said it well."

She pushed on her toes to lift her up and then pressed her lips gently against his for a brief connection.

"But," she then said, "I wasn't kidding. I'll be your nurse one time. That's it."

CHAPTER 44

After a lengthy, hot shower, Gray dressed and ate a quick breakfast of leftovers. Butler had brought him meatloaf, mashed potatoes, and green beans. Gray ate half of the meal along with two pain pills. After he cleaned his dishes, he risked his safety and made his way down the three flights of stairs from his apartment to the parking lot where the blazing sunshine awaited him. He stood in the shade of a large palm tree until an Uber driver arrived. He climbed into the back of the Prius, hating his body's brokenness. The driver confirmed the destination before pulling away from the curb.

The Chrittons lived on a quiet, dead end street named Kings Point Court in the southeast corner of Lakeland's city limits. Most of the houses were L-shaped single-family homes covered in stucco, as was the standard house construction in Lakeland, Florida, in the late 1970s when the house was built. A few upgrades had been made to the exterior of the house throughout the years, but nothing that deviated far from the original design. There, the Chrittons had raised their son, Noah, and their daughter, Evelyn, who was two years younger than Noah. Their boy had moved out of this house five months prior to his murder by Murch and Duncan.

The mother, Claudia, opened the front door, answering Gray's knock. She looked like Sigourney Weaver in the 1993 movie *Dave* but with more of a graduated bob hairstyle. She froze when she saw Gray.

"Hello, Mrs. Chritton."

"Detective." She held onto the front door for both support and shield. "Chuck and I wondered if we'd see you soon."

"Is he home?" Gray asked.

"He's eating lunch."

"I'm here."

Claudia moved with the door, opening the entryway wider. Chuck Chritton approached from behind her. He was taller than his wife, and he'd lost weight since the last time Gray had seen him. Gray wondered if the weight loss resulted from diet changes, stress, or illness. It wasn't his place to inquire.

"Good. I was hoping to meet with both of you."

Gray felt his cell vibrate in his pocket.

"We saw on the news that Kenneth Duncan killed himself," Chuck said. "And you were there with him."

Gray nodded. He dreaded the questions from the Chrittons. *That's not true.* He dreaded the answers and their reactions to them. Gray longed to have Parker back as a partner. Parker was better at this part of their jobs, no doubt.

"Did he tell you anything about Noah?"

Claudia maintained the power position nearly blocking her husband's access to Gray. She was just as Gray remembered. Strong. Forceful. To the point. Mr. Chritton was the more subdued of the two. He was the one who'd allow Gray to ask all his questions before he'd ask his own. Not Mrs. Chritton. She was going to get what she wanted from the situation whether or not you liked it, and she was going to get it before you got what you wanted.

"That's what I was hoping to talk to you and Mr. Chritton about. May I come inside?"

"Did he tell you anything?" she repeated her question.

Gray sighed, wishing he had actual information to provide them about their son. All he really could do was confirm what they'd been afraid of since Noah's murder. Plus, he didn't want to have this conversation on their front porch, but he didn't have a choice.

"I was asked to consult on a case being worked by the Manatee County Sheriff's Department. Maybe you heard about the incidents in Anna Maria, Holmes and Bradenton beaches?"

He paused for acknowledgement. Chuck waited for Gray to continue. Claudia didn't.

"Get to the point."

"Body parts, like arms, legs, hands, and feet, washed ashore last week." He gathered his strength and pushed forward with the news. "There were pieces recovered that genetically matched your son, Noah."

Claudia gasped. The shock overwhelmed her. Then anger set in. She stepped toward Gray.

"What do you mean *pieces*?"

Chuck set his hand on his wife's shoulder.

Gray regretted the use of the word *pieces*. He moved along though. "I went along with a representative from Manatee County to interview Kenneth Duncan. While I had an official agenda while I was there to assist in the sheriff's investigation, I also had a personal agenda, which was to gather more information about Noah."

"Say it."

He said, "Kenneth Duncan didn't remember where he'd buried many of his victims. Unfortunately, including Noah."

Noah's mother grinded her teeth. Gray could see years of fury and agony rising to the surface.

"I'm sorry."

"No!" she screamed.

Chuck pulled on Claudia's shoulder, which she yanked from his grasp.

"No!" she shouted again. This time at her husband. "No. No."

Claudia bent over to collect her breath. Her left arm reached out to the side of the doorframe for support. It seemed clear to Gray that Mr.

Chritton had already come to terms with the death of their son, and he never expected to retrieve the body. However, since Noah's death Mrs. Chritton had been moving through her life fueled by hope.

Gray thought back to a conversation he'd had with Jordan Butler. The night he told her he was going to turn in his shield. She reminded him why he wanted to become a detective, to give hope to people who found themselves in these helpless situations. He knew what that helplessness felt like.

He realized that for Claudia he was just that — her hope. Her hope that she'd be able to bury her son. Her hope that she'd eventually get closure. Her hope that one day he'd somehow make sense of what had happened to her little boy. And now that hope was gone. Gray fought his natural inclination to blame himself.

"Why did he kill himself, detective," Chuck asked.

"Why does that matter?" Claudia protested, jolting her body erect and facing her husband.

"It matters to me," Chuck barked at her, which Gray suspected was a rare event.

Gray waited until Chuck's temper settled. "He had end stage cancer. I guess he was ready to die."

Claudia turned quickly, directing more vitriol at Gray. "And he stabbed himself in the neck? That's what the news said. Why didn't you check him for weapons?! How could this happen in prison?"

Gray wanted to tell them that the weapon had been snuck into the room, but no explanation would satisfy her anger.

"End stage? Did he suffer with the cancer?" Chuck asked.

"What do you care?" Claudia pleaded to know.

Chuck didn't acknowledge her question. "Did he?" he asked Gray again.

Gray didn't know the answer for certain or to what degree, but he assumed Duncan had suffered since he refused treatment for over a year. He knew, though, what Mr. Chritton wanted — needed — to hear.

"Severely. For a long time."

Chuck nodded. "Good."

That seemed to give the man relief. Gray was glad he could offer that to, at least, one of the parents.

"Manatee County should be able to release the recovered remains of Noah soon." He pulled a business card from his front pocket. "If you'd like to keep in contact with me, I can — "

Claudia nearly spat at Gray. "Is that supposed to be some kind of solace, detective? Is that supposed to make me feel better?"

He expected the response. Steeled his heart for the attack.

"I don't want his arms and legs. I want his mind. I want his heart. I want to put those in the ground, where I can visit them every day. He had a brilliant, funny mind and a good heart, a pure heart. And they both deserve to be here. With me. So, don't stand there and offer me his limbs, like it's the same thing. Do you understand me?"

"I understand."

Tears rose in her eyes, but they hadn't yet fallen. "Now get off my porch."

She marched inside the house, shoving past her husband, and slammed the door.

Gray exhaled audibly, relieved that the situation was over and crushed that he had not been able to offer them more. He stood there for a long time, frozen, unable to move, trying to think of another way he could help the Chrittons with their pain. Finally, he concluded he could do nothing to help them, and he turned and stepped off the front step. The front door opened, and it stopped his retreat to the waiting Uber car. Mr. Chritton stepped from the house, closing the door behind him.

"I'm sorry about that," he said.

"Don't be," Gray said.

"I'd like your business card please."

Gray handed it over. Chuck took it and slipped it into his pocket.

"My daughter, Evelyn ... She had a baby last year. She named him after Noah."

Gray smiled. "That's a nice tribute. I remember you said she and Noah were close as kids."

"They were."

"I'm sorry I couldn't do more you and your family."

"You know, I used to picture what may have happened to Noah," the elder man said, ignoring the apology. "I imagined how he may have been killed. I always thought I wanted to know."

Chuck sat down on the front step. He rested his elbows on his legs. Normally Gray would've joined him, but he was worried about the pain he'd feel in his ribs by doing so.

"Do you know how he was killed, detective?"

Gray stepped off the front step, so he could face Noah's father.

"It seems as though Duncan had a consistent method of killing, but I don't know without doubt if it was applied to Noah."

Chuck nodded his head, lost in thought.

"I worried about his suffering," Chuck finally said.

Gray should say something. He wondered what Parker would say in the same situation. But, nothing profound or comforting came to mind.

"I can't shut off the noise in my head. It's always there. Screaming at me. Invading my sleep. Isolating me. Even from my grandson. I don't know how many times I've kind of blacked out, and when I've come to, I'm in my driveway with the water hose. Just spraying the concrete. What is that?"

Gray understood exactly what the man was talking about, but he had no wisdom to share.

"It's coping, Mr. Chritton," he said. "Just do whatever gets you through the day."

Chuck nodded and sighed at the banality of the response. Then he stood abruptly. The conversation was over. Gray didn't know what the man hoped the results would be and he offered no insight into whether or not the results were achieved. They shook hands, and Chuck returned to the house.

Gray lumbered somberly back to the Uber. As Gray pulled open the car's door, he retrieved his phone from his pocket.

The vibration he'd felt when he began the conversation with the Chrittons had been an incoming text.

From Ambrose: *McKee wants to meet you ASAP. Today. Get your ass down here.*

CHAPTER 45

Although Gray had his badge and service weapon because of the special circumstances surrounding Kenneth Duncan, he didn't believe his magnetic access card would work at the staff entrance. Rather than try it and have to walk around the whole building if it didn't work, he chose to conserve his steps and go in through the front doors again. As usual the lobby was busy. Two people were at the reception desk — a man and a woman. The woman was holding a baby who was wearing only a diaper. Four other children — likely belonging to the couple at the desk — seemingly between the ages of eight and two ran around the lobby. The eight-year-old was trying her best to control her siblings. Another couple sat on a bench awaiting their turn and trying to stay away from the rambunctious children.

Again, choosing to save his steps, Gray walked in a straight line for the elevator. He hung his head low to avoid eye contact with the families in the lobby as well as the safety aide at the front window. His pain medicine was weakening, and he could feel his ribs with every movement of his body. He pushed his hand into his pocket where he had another pain pill on standby. With it, he felt a piece of paper in his pocket. He removed both. Two uniformed officers joined him at the elevator doors, and he slipped the pill back into his pocket, preferring to not be seen popping pills. He unfolded the piece of paper and found Alton Campbell's name and number written on it in Boudreaux's quick script. He returned the contact information for the Tony Mason task force leader to his pocket for safe keeping.

The doors parted, and the two uniformed officers cut off Gray's advance into the car. Then, inside the car, both men stood in the entrance, leaving Gray no path to enter.

"You can take the next one," one of the guys said, as the other officer pressed the close button repeatedly.

Gray thought about jamming his hand in the door's path to stop it from closing and lashing out in a rebuke of both of them, but the doors closed before he could act.

He popped the pain pill and swallowed it.

~ ~ ~ ~

Gray opened the conference room door, expecting to see Ambrose in the room. He was wrong. Only Peter McKee from the external company performing the inquiry into the misconduct and mismanagement of the Lakeland Police Department was in the room. Mr. Sporty Suit sat on the opposite side of the table.

Craning his neck to look around the room, Gray confirmed McKee was alone. And that was the last thing he wanted. He thought the man was unethical in how he was conducting this inquiry, and Gray didn't put it past him to lie about what they discussed in private.

Sitting before McKee on the conference table, there were five folders spread evenly in front of him. Each folder had a badge and a service weapon on top of it except for one. *That one's mine,* Gray thought.

"You're going to do this alone, McGoo?" Gray asked.

"You're a funny man, Detective Gray. I know you know my name."

"I don't care what your name is." Gray stepped into the room but left the door open. "I thought Lt. Ambrose would be here."

McKee moved his right hand and placed it on the folder next to Gray's folder. "He's been relieved of his duties." McKee picked up Ambrose's badge and ran his thumb across the shield.

"He just texted me to come in for a meeting?"

"That was me. I used his phone."

Gray grunted, letting his disdain for McKee settle in his gut. "Why get rid of Ambrose?"

McKee returned the badge to the table. "Clearing the way at the top. LPD's getting some new blood."

"You mean, soldiers for Walters and Collanger."

"I mean, people who follow the rules and regulations."

Gray looked at the other three badges and weapons. "I assume one of those is Boudreaux's. Whose else you got there?"

"Doesn't really concern you, detective." McKee waited for Gray to protest. When he didn't, he said, "Are you wondering if one of these is your partner's?"

"No."

McKee flashed an egotistical smile. "I figured you for a loner and a selfish bastard, and I was right."

"That's likely quite true, but I know Parker's good police, through and through. There's no reason to take his badge. You do, and you're hurting the city."

"That's what Boudreaux said, too."

"Did you listen to him?" Gray asked.

McKee nodded. "Parker's safe."

The relief Gray felt eased the tension in his gut, lessened the worry on his mind, and made his firing more tolerable.

"Come in. Have a seat," McKee said.

Gray did so, moving delicately into the conference chair.

"I spoke with your mental counselor, detective."

Gray knew that was a lie. Weech was the one who spoke with her. It showed Gray that the investigation was about McKee and not the truth.

McKee judged Gray's reaction to that news as unsurprised. "She had a lot to say about you."

"I imagine she didn't, McGoo. Confidentiality laws being what they are."

"What do you have on her, detective?"

"What do you mean?"

"She didn't seem as forthcoming as I had hoped she would. With a guy like you in the mix, it makes me wonder if you have something on her? Did you help with a DUI? Maybe you two dated?"

Gray said, "If you're going to fire me, get on with it."

McKee moved forward, leaning on the tabletop with his elbows. "I want the truth from you, detective."

"The real truth or the truth Collanger and Walters hired you to fabricate?"

McKee leaned back into his chair. "I won't even pretend to know what that means."

"Pretend is the right word. For your bravado and this whole inquiry," Gray fired back.

That made McKee angry. The emotion was clearly defined on his face.

"What were you doing in Crestwood, Kentucky?"

Fuck. "I was on suspension under no order not to leave town. I took a drive. Ended up there."

"Sergeant Roy Axelrod seems to think you had other motives for being there."

"I told you, I just ended up there."

"You presented yourself in an official position to the Oldham County Police Department."

"I did no such thing."

"Then how did Sergeant Axelrod get the impression you were there to officially search the remains of the Mason family home?"

"If I had to guess, I'd say he assumed it."

"An assumption?"

"I never flashed him my badge. I didn't have it. That and my service weapon had been confiscated because of my suspension. I didn't call ahead under the pretense of letting the department know I was coming. I drove my personal car. In my opinion, if Sergeant Axelrod thought I was there on official business, which I was not, and he showed me confidential police reports, you should be in Crestwood talking to his supervisor and leaving me the fuck alone."

Gray hated throwing Axelrod under the bus, but he had to save his own hide. Besides, McKee wasn't going to Crestwood for Axelrod.

"You want me to fire you, don't you?"

"The longer I look at you, McKee, the less and less I care."

"Well, you can thank Kenneth Duncan and Wesley Murch for saving your job." McKee put his hand on Gray's folder. "This one is yours. And the recommendation I made is to fire you. However, with what went down with Duncan and Murch, the city management is afraid to fire you right now. The public perception compounded by the current positive media attention the department is receiving ... It wouldn't be good to fire a perceived hero cop."

Gray pushed off the table. He stood, swallowing the pain associated with the movement. "Then we're done here."

"Not yet." McKee stood, too. "You can report to duty tomorrow. You'll be assigned desk duty until your injuries heal and you can be reinstated fully."

"Fine."

"Parker is being reassigned."

Gray nodded, not wanting to acknowledge that he knew Parker had asked for a new partner. He didn't want McKee to know they'd spoken. He didn't want to give anything away to McKee.

"And so have you."

"What are you talking about?" Gray asked.

"You'll be on nights. Ten on. Four off."

It was a brutal schedule, but Gray wasn't going to let McKee know he hated it.

"Great. See you tomorrow." Gray turned to leave.

"One more thing," McKee called to him. "I've personally made sure that everyone in the department knows you ratted out Ambrose for fixing his hours in the computer."

"What?"

"That you also sold out Boudreaux in your testimony during this inquiry. That you didn't even defend Parker. And that you did all of that solely to save your own ass."

Boudreaux, Parker, and Ambrose were the most beloved officers on the force. If McKee did spread those lies around the department, then Gray would be hated. He recalled the incident on the elevator when the two uniformed officers wouldn't allow him inside. He remembered the officer who almost shoulder-checked him down the staircase. Word had already spread. He was a marked man.

"I'm sure it'll be fine," Gray said.

McKee nodded, speculating that Gray was now faking his own bravado.

"So, you get to keep your job for now, but no one will work with you. The staff will dislike you more than they already do. And the misery will drive you out of here."

Gray smiled. This time he showed a smug grin. "Misery? You think misery will bother me?" He chuckled. "You don't know me so well, McGoo."

Gray stepped through the doorway, never looking back at McKee.

ABOUT THE AUTHOR

CHRIS WENDEL is the author of two separate suspense/thriller series: the Becker Gray series and the Tony Mason series. Two of his Becker Gray novels have placed well in national contests. His novel HUMAN AFTER ALL was the "Solo Medalist Winner" in the Suspense/Thriller category of the New Apple 2017 Summer eBooks Awards. THE WALLS was an "Official Selection" in the 2018 New Apple Book Awards for Excellence in Independent Publishing and beat out over 1,100 other entrants to reach the semifinalist stage in the 2018 Screencraft Cinematic Book Awards. Chris has a degree in English and Information Technology. He is a Florida native, an entrepreneur, and a soccer fan, who has been writing since the third grade. He lives on Florida with his family.

ACKNOWLEDGMENTS

Since 2013 I've published over 330,000 words – three novels, two short stories, and books in the genres of both poetry and business. I've created two characters (Becker Gray and Tony Mason) I love and who challenge me. To my surprise, they've not only been consumed by readers from all over the world, but they've been embraced wholeheartedly by so many of those readers. One email I received recently thanked me for writing the Becker Gray series. While I am appreciative and grateful for comments like that when people feel so connected to the characters, I'm the person who should be thankful. Thankful for the human connections made because of the books, for the ability to travel with the books, for new experiences, for every email readers have sent, every nice word, every constructive comment, for all the people who attend the release parties, every dollar spent on my books, and for the time it takes to read them. THANK YOU. THANK YOU. THANK YOU.

Mostly I'm eternally grateful for the amazing individual support people have provided me. David and Joyce Wendel, John and Peggy Wendel, Mary Wendel, Bryan Wendel and family, and my extended family of cousins Erika, Johnny, Anne Marie, Bobby, Greg, and Carli. Specifically during the writing of this book: Michi Bonnin for the medical advice, providing me freedom to write, allowing me your partnership in love and friendship; Holden Wendel for helping with the name of this book; Bill Wendel for the military information; Amy and Bill Turpin for your friendship and being great salespeople at events and beyond; Karen Hudson and Michael Johnson for all your help with the launch parties; Brian Hall for the web site; the whole Bonnin family for accepting Holden and me; Holly Lopez for taking my books with you on adventures and attempting to take photos with them, Hannah Greer for lending your reading abilities and announcer voice at the launch party for THE WALLS, Lana Swartzwelder for thinking of ways to help promote my writing; Nikki Barnes for your encouragement and advice; Dylan Macklin for your song based on Heart Half Black and for the live performance at the release party; Stuart and Kara Simms for allowing me again to host a release party at Federal Bar; Fred Koehler for your sage advice on kicking off and maintaining a writing career; and Gary White for the really nice feature in *The Ledger.*

Extra special thanks to Pat Berry, who has been the most excellent advance reader. Thanks to Jean Gonzalez who helps mold the stories and characters into what they finally become on the page. You both are gracious with your expertise, time, care, and encouragement.

The knowledge provided by the people in the above list was accurate when they gave it to me. If there are any mistakes, they are mine and were done purposely for what I believed to be the sake of the story.

Last year at the book release party for THE WALLS AJ Bonnin and Chuck and Claudia Chritton donated money to the Crohn's and Colitis Foundation and earned in this book the prize of having characters named after them. I thank them for their donation and their bravery in allowing me to craft their characters however I wanted. For more information about Crohn's and colitis, please visit www.crohnscolitisfoundation.org.

Until next time, thank you and enjoy.

Chris

FOR MORE INFORMAITON

For more information, visit: cwendel.com

Get personalized book selections and up to date news about this author.

SIGN UP NOW at CWENDEL.COM

www.ingramcontent.com/pod-product-compliance
Lightning Source LLC
Chambersburg PA
CBHW020740250626
47155CB00003B/842